# The Trickster

## Dorothy A. Winsor

Published by Inspired Quill: March 2021

First Edition





Chief Editor: Sara-Jayne Slack
Cover Image: Marco Pennaccietti
Cover Design: Venetia Jackson
Typeset in Minion Pro



Paperback ISBN: 978-1-913117-03-0
eBook ISBN: 978-1-913117-04-7
Print Edition

Printed in the United Kingdom
1 2 3 4 5 6 7 8 9 10

**Inspired Quill Publishing, UK**
**Business Reg. No. 7592847**
www.inspired-quill.com

# Praise for Dorothy Winsor

The Wysman *is a delightful coming-of-age story about finding out who you are when everything about your life is changing; when you can't go back but aren't sure you see a path forward; and when the gifts you've counted on most may turn out to be not to be the ones you need to save the people counting on you.*

> – Rachel Neumeier,
> author of Winter of Ice and Iron

*A gripping Young Adult fantasy story, brimming with danger, magic and intrigue, set in a richly imagined world, with a superb cast of characters.*

> – Mary Simms,
> *BookCraic*

*Dorothy Winsor's novel presents an intriguing and well-drawn world, with a very likeable lead. An exciting, adventurous, and thoughtful YA fantasy novel.*

> – Dr. Una McCormack,
> *New York Times Bestselling Author*

*Dorothy A. Winsor is a meticulous writer who expertly balances intelligence and delight.*

> – Saladin Ahmed,
> *Hugo, Nebula, and Gemmell Awards finalist*

*Journeys: A Ghost Story*, is a very good tale that, without any real surprises, still manages to surprise. There's a well-wrought aura of melancholy that permeates the story, even in the funny moments. Another author I'll keep an eye out for in the future.

– Fletcher Vredenburgh,
*Black Gate Magazine*

*[In Finders Keepers], the action is brisk, emotions are deep, and the moral message is subtle but strong, providing excellent depth for all readers, young and not so young. Great story – I loved it as an adult and think it is a wonderful book for older kids and young adults. Five Stars.*

– Melinda Hills,
*Readers' Favorite*

For Krystal

# Chapter 1

## Dilly

IN LAC'S HOLDING, we love the small gods. Unlike the Divine Powers, they aren't all-wise or all-good. They're enough like us to understand our feelings. The stories say that, at Midwinter Festival, they sometimes even walk among us. Of course, despite (or maybe because of) that, they can be jokesters and, let's admit it, pains in the rear. Especially the Trickster, the god Mama always said must look after me. I would pray to be looked after a little less, but frankly, that's the fastest way to make the Trickster sit up and take notice.

So, Trickster in mind, I slipped a thumb under the strap holding the left wing of my butterfly costume and settled it firmly in the hollow of my shoulder before climbing the three steps to the platform. Costume intact, I trotted up next to Jessa, Tira, and Nemay to take my place in the line of Lady Elenia's attendants. I didn't want to look undignified in front of the people jamming Lac's Square, so I smothered a grin. I still couldn't believe I belonged in that line. Against all my life experience, I felt as if one of the more benevolent gods had opened a window and rained honey drops down on me. Then, showing the Trickster is, well, tricky, Tuc bounded after me, sniffed the hem of Jessa's will-o-wisp costume, and teetered as if he meant to lift his leg and pee on her.

Jessa yanked her skirt aside. "Honestly, Dilly. The opening of Festival is a sacred ceremony. That dog does not belong here."

I can't say I wasn't tempted to let him carry out his threat, but it would have ended badly. "Sit, Tuc," I said, and as if to demonstrate that he really was a good dog, he sank to his haunches next to me. Ignoring Jessa's sour face, I folded my hands in front of me and looked attentively at Lady Elenia, the way a good owner of a good dog would.

Unlike my wobbly wings, Lady Elenia's costume fit as if she was born to wear it, which as the lord's daughter, she was. Silk shimmered with all the colors of fire in the Festival Queen's traditional costume, one I'd seen every midwinter of my life until Mama lost her mind over a man and took me to Rin City. I blinked away the sting of tears. The hole that opened inside me when Mama died would never be filled, but at least now, I was off the streets and had a place to call home.

Most of the people in the square had their backs to us because, like Elenia, they were watching the sun's orange disk slide slowly lower, becoming a half circle and then a thin sliver before finally vanishing. The crowd released a muted cheer. Lady Elenia turned to the barrels of Winter Fire piled behind us. "Small gods," Elenia said, "we beg your blessing on us and on the drink we use to celebrate the longest night of the old year and the turn of the world to the new one."

For the first time in my life, I was close enough to hear the stuff in the barrels burst into a fizz and then fall silent.

The man in charge of the platform held a mug under the first barrel's tap, filled it, and offered it to Elenia. His helpers drew tiny cups for all four of us attendants, though like everyone else, we had to wait for Elenia's approval of the Fire to drink it. Elenia sipped, then broke into a smile and lifted her mug. "It's excellent! Go and enjoy yourselves!"

There was nothing muted about the crowd's cheer this time. It bounced off the surrounding three-storey buildings. Eager to find out what this year's batch of Winter Fire tasted like, I drained my skimpy share. Fire was only potent for the twenty-four hours at midwinter, from one sundown to the next, exactly one year after it was put in the barrel. This stuff tasted wonderfully of something like pears and threatened to spin my head if I drank much.

The helpers began rolling the barrels down a ramp

behind the platform to be distributed to all the alehouses and cafes in town, but the crowd jostled one another to be away. The Festival Queen's ceremonial blessing was a politeness for the gods, but the timing was what triggered the Winter Fire, even if it wasn't on the platform. Other barrels would already be waiting, ready for drinkers to flood in. Sadly, I couldn't join them, because Lady Elenia had to go to the small gods shrine before she, and so we were free to enjoy ourselves. Three months ago, I wouldn't have believed there were disadvantages to living in Elenia's household, but it turns out a girl can be wrong.

Elenia led us down from the platform. As two Royal Fortress guards plowed us a slow path through the crowd, I lifted my face to the soft night. Even on a winter evening, it wasn't cold in Lac's Holding, which was a good thing given how much arm and chest my costume showed. Shops and cafes hemmed us in on either side, below floors of apartments with fancy, iron-railed balconies draped with flowers and strings of Festival beads. I tugged on my shoulder strap again. Drat the thing.

"Fair night, Lady Elenia," called a man cooking sausages over a brazier. "Get the best sausage in Lac's Holding right here." He poked a fork at a spicy smelling sausage, sending fat spattering onto the coals. Tuc darted forward and sat at his feet. The vendor laughed and tossed a scrap that Tuc snatched from mid-air. "What's a mutt like you doing with this lot, doggie?"

My eye caught on a man in a huge sea monster

headdress slipping close to our party. I stiffened. In Rin City, I'd been working as a messenger when a man slipped up on me like that and trapped me in an alley. I swallowed bile. Then Tira called a greeting and, at Elenia's nod of permission, slid her arm into the man's and drifted away to our left.

"Tira's fool scared you?" Jessa snorted.

Among Jessa's other annoying qualities, she was perceptive. She should spend a few months living on the streets and see what that did to her nerve. Not that I could tell her that. The last thing I needed was Jessa knowing I'd been homeless.

"Small gods know what time she'll come home," Jessa snipped, watching Tira disappear. "She knows Elenia won't scold, whatever the hour. Elenia's too easy a touch for a romantic story."

In the café to our right, a man stumbled against the table closest to us, spilling a bowl of fish chowder to the ground. "Look out," I said, bumping my hip against Jessa's so her thin slippers slid into the chunky mess. She gave a wordless cry. "Oh, how terrible," I said. "I told you to look out."

Jessa was so shocked she stood rooted to the spot – or maybe glued by the thick chowder. Her mouth still worked though. "Curse you, Dilly."

"Walk with me, Dilly," Nemay called over her shoulder.

I hustled away from Tire. "Come, Tuc." Enchanted by

the presence of sausage, Tuc did his best imitation of a deaf dog.

"Dilly!" Nemay called more loudly. "Tuc will come after you."

I dodged a juggler about to toss a knife through one of my wings and caught up with her. "What if he gets lost?"

"From what I've seen, he knows his way around the city better than I do." She brushed a dark curl threaded with grey off her temple. "Did you shove Jessa?"

I widened my eyes. "Me?"

She laughed. "Try not to annoy her any more than you already do by existing. You have to go back to the Fortress and live with her."

I liked Nemay. She was in charge of Elenia's attendants, but she was fair. "Jessa was nasty about Tira. And you know she's trying to push me out."

Nemay shrugged. "She wanted your place for a friend."

*Too bad for Jessa*, I thought, not very sadly. I had been chosen for Elenia's household, and of course I was happy there. Who could doubt it? I'd admired Elenia from afar since I was seven years old and she was sixteen.

At last, we turned down Sailmaker Street and stopped outside the small gods shrine. It lay three steps down in a cave that had been there when Lac's Holding was a landscape full of twisting creeks, tall grass, and sea birds. Shops crowded close on either side of the crude stone entry.

"You and the sergeant wait outside, Captain Jaf," Lady Elenia said.

"Beg pardon, lady," the guard captain said, "but I can't let you go in by yourself."

"The shrine is small," Elenia said. "There won't be room."

"The sergeant can wait outside," Captain Jaf said, "but I'm coming in."

Elenia raised one eyebrow. "I won't be alone. My attendants will be with me."

"Good company, I'm sure," Jaf said, "but not much protection."

Elenia tossed her head and stomped down the steps, the tap of her high heels announcing exactly how she felt about Jaf ignoring her orders. Jessa, Nemay, and I crowded after her, leaving a harassed-looking Captain Jaf to follow as best he could while the sergeant took up a place outside the entrance. A headache threatened to throb to life behind my eyes. I hated it when Elenia was angry.

Elenia was right about the space. The shrine was even tighter than I remembered. Statues of the small gods lined the cave's walls and even its ceiling. I searched for the Guardian Dog down near the floor, muzzle hovering over a bowl. Tuc looked like him, right down to the torn ear, but that was the end of the resemblance. Like most Lac's Holding mothers, Mama had told me I had an invisible Guardian Dog who'd stop me when I was about to be bad.

Tuc had been with me when I lived on the streets of Rin City, so I knew he wasn't big on stopping bad behavior.

Captain Jaf pushed past me to stand next to Elenia on one side of the stone altar in the shrine's center. Across from them stood the Hedge Mage, waiting to perform the ceremonial healing of its Festival Queen. At least, I guessed he was the Hedge Mage. Mages were always here and there around the city. People used them when they couldn't afford the doctors who came from the university. This one seemed young to be serving in the shrine though. I couldn't see his face behind his Festival mask, but his chin below it was beardless and his body was lean inside his open-fronted Mage coat. Dark hair curled untidily over his collar. His ears were gently pointed, the way you sometimes saw in folks from the islands outside the harbor. The old stories said they descended from the elves who once lived there, which was a charming if unlikely thought.

"You're new," Elenia said, by which I assumed she meant "Where's your nursemaid?"

"A new Mage for a new year," he said smoothly. He swept long fingers through the smoke from the glass, globe-shaped lamp on the altar then extended his hands, palms up. An invitation for Elenia to lay hers in them. "Look into the fire, and we'll ask the small gods to ease all the city's hurts and bring happiness to everyone in the new year." The scented smoke pinched the inside of my nose.

Elenia hesitated but then seemed to come to a

decision. She glanced at Nemay, who turned to Captain Jaf. Whatever she said to him made him swivel to frown at the entryway. That was odd. In a flash of the insight I'd gradually gained from living with these women for three months, it occurred to me that Elenia had asked Nemay to distract the guard captain. I snapped my attention back to Elenia just in time to see her pull what looked like paper folded small from her sash and hold it out to the Mage, who blinked, then reached for it.

In a blur, Captain Jaf swooped between him and Elenia and plucked the paper from her hand. "Forgive me, lady," he said. "I must ask for that."

The Mage looked from Elenia to Captain Jaf and edged away.

"Ask?" Elenia cried. "That wasn't asking. That was taking. This is an outrage. My father shall hear of this."

"Forgive me again, lady, but it was your lord father who ordered me to confiscate any message you might send or receive." He tucked the note into his pocket.

Lady Elenia held herself so tensely that I saw a tiny quiver in the hand no longer gripping a note, a quiver that made me think she might grab for it. Captain Jaf must have seen trouble too because he took a step back, the heels of his boots scraping the toes of my slippers. Elenia popped her lips scornfully, then strode up the steps, towing Jessa and Nemay in her wake. Apparently, we were dispensing with the ceremony.

Caught behind the captain, I hesitated. Elenia had

asked for Nemay's help, not mine, but if I dared, I was the one who could get Elenia what she wanted. The only barrier was I'd have to do what I swore I'd never do again once I was off the streets. Was I the respectable girl living with Elenia or the somewhat more… hm, let's say flexible girl with the skillful fingers?

"Stay with them, sergeant," Captain Jaf called up the steps before taking a moment to loom over the Mage. "The lady was right. You're new. What's your name?"

"Magus," the Mage said evenly, "the name we all bear."

"Right." The captain snorted. "From what island?"

So Captain Jaf had noted the pointy ears too.

"None," the Mage said. "I'm a stranger."

"If I had time, I'd make you choke on that lie," Captain Jaf said. "Don't accept messages from the lady again."

"Fine by me." He opened his arms, spreading his multi-colored Mage coat like bright wings.

"We'll be watching." Captain Jaf spun to go after Elenia.

I managed to stumble in front of him. "Sorry," I said at the same time he did. I dipped my fingers in his pocket, pinched the note, and ducked away. I had to do it in order to serve Elenia, I reasoned, and even if I thought of the excuse after I acted, not before, it was still a good one. Captain Jaf took the steps in one leap and hurried after Elenia. I turned back to the Mage.

His gaze locked on the note in my hand. "Shall I take that?" He reached for it.

I'd run into street hustlers who used that casually careful tone. I saw again the surprised blink he'd given when Elenia held out the note, heard again her puzzled voice to see this boy here. I curled my fingers around the paper. "I don't think so."

"You saw how eager your lady was for me to have it," he said.

"She's eager for someone to have it. I'm just not sure it's you."

His laugh sounded relaxed and unoffended. "Have it your way, but I really am a Mage, and I really was hired to perform a healing tonight, ceremonial though it might be. How about I truly earn my coin with you?" He extended his hands again.

I glanced up the stairs Elenia had taken and saw only the skirts and trouser legs of passers-by. I rubbed my throbbing eyes. *Don't be stupid.* I could walk back to the Royal Fortress on the hill by the river and be let in. Besides, they'd wait for me as soon as they missed me.

"You have a headache?" the Mage asked, making me snap my thoughts back to him. "You're frowning like an old lady. Shall I ease it for you?"

"Thanks so much for the compliment. It truly makes me want to listen to you."

He grinned. "At least you know I'm not trying to flatter you. Come on. Let me earn my pay. Otherwise, as an honest man, I'll have to give it back."

I rocked from foot to foot. I'd had this headache on and off for days. It would be nice to be rid of it. Elenia and the others were gone anyway. I tried to stow Elenia's note in a pocket before remembering that my butterfly costume had none. So I tucked it down my front where I'd also put my purse, lovely and plump with coins Elenia had given me. "I don't need charity. I can pay for my own spell." I wriggled my fingers into my purse. "How much?"

"I told you I've already been paid."

"I insist." I slapped two gulls onto the pedestal next to the lamp.

"Give me your hands," he said, holding out his own again.

I laid the backs of my hands in his and felt calluses that never came from healing. *An island boy*, I thought again. They all spent half their lives handling boats, and the other half, rumor said, smuggling goods past the customs officers. He gripped my fingers lightly, turned them toward the globe lamp, and held them an inch or so away from the glass, far enough that the warmth felt pleasant rather than painful.

"Look into the fire. Let it fill your vision."

I did as he said. The flame inside the globe flickered red and yellow. I felt the push of energy I'd felt every time a Mage spelled me, so at least this boy hadn't lied about being one. I was having trouble letting him work, though. I hadn't been near a Mage in three years, and I was no longer used to letting one help my body right itself.

"Look at the fire, not what's in your head." The Mage shook my hands. "Let go."

I shrugged the tension out of my shoulders and concentrated on the fire. After a moment, it expanded to fill the globe. The shrine and the Mage faded away. My mind drifted. As it did every night when I tried to sleep, my heart contracted with grief and guilt over Mama's death, but the feelings didn't sharpen the way they sometimes did. In the fire, I saw Elenia, who looked much like Mama did when I was small and she was Elenia's age. I wished so hard I could please her. If I did, I'd be safe. I'd never again go hungry or be so filthy people edged away from me. But also, Elenia would be happy. I wanted to make her happy. I should give her note to the Mage.

The street kid in me leaped to life. I jerked my hands out of the Mage's. "What are you doing?"

He lifted his mask a finger-width away from his face as if it had become uncomfortable, then settled it back in place. "What do you mean? All I did was cure your headache. Would you rather have it back?"

I didn't know whether to believe him or not. My headache did seem to be gone. Like doctors, Mages healed. The difference was they did it by using their energy to steer *yours* on the right path again. Nothing about that should have let this boy fiddle with what I wanted. But that urge to give him the note felt way too much like what he'd been asking for.

Claws clicked behind me, and Tuc bounced down the stairs into the shrine. He growled at the boy, who sensibly backed up a half step. "I'm not going to hand over Lady Elenia's note," I said. "I'd never betray her like that. All us attendants are like her family."

With a short laugh, he dropped his hands to his sides. "And that makes you happy?"

"Is there something wrong with being like family?"

"It looks to me like your *family* just left without you. That hurts. And I personally find kin make as many problems as they solve."

I snatched the two gulls off the table and shoved them in the breast pocket of the shirt he wore under his open coat. "Dishing out that kind of wisdom must leave you with mighty few patients. You'll need those."

When I spun to leave, my left wing caught the lamp, making it teeter. The Mage spat something that sounded distinctly like a curse. I glanced back to see him steady the globe and then twitch his fingers off and shake them. Good. Burned fingers were the right punishment for him. With Tuc at my heels, I skipped up the steps, then headed toward where Elenia and the others would have missed me and surely be waiting.

The crowd was thick and rapidly growing drunk. My heart pattered a warning. I'd seen crowds like this in Rin City, and I'd stayed out of them when I could. I kept an eye out for side streets I could duck down if things got out of hand. I needed to find Lady Elenia and get home.

Making progress wasn't easy, though, because when I tried to ease between slow-moving Festival goers, my wings kept getting in the way. I was considering whether to take them off and carry the awkward bundle they made when two men stumbled in front of me, forcing me to halt. One of them lurched toward me, reeking of Winter Fire. He gave a stupid grin. "Well, look at you! Fresh and ripe as a peach. Never been kissed, I'll bet."

"Do it," his companion urged with a snort.

My heart stopped pattering and jumped into my throat, but I knew better than to show fear. "Get out of my way," I said, voice as firm as I could make it. The fur rose on the back of Tuc's neck.

When the man reached for me, I managed to twist out of his grasp, but his drunken momentum carried him forward, and he grabbed my left wing to steady himself. I stumbled as he fell to his knees, pulling me off balance. Then, bless the tricky shoulder strap, it slipped off. With a shake, I shed the whole harness. He sprawled on the cobbles, tangled in the torn contraption. His friend braced his hands on his thighs, howling with laughter. I barely caught Tuc's collar when he tried to lunge.

"It's just a game," the sprawled man said. "A Festival game."

"It's not game," I shouted. "Forcing a kiss on someone isn't a game." The friend's laughs sputtered to guffaws. "Come, Tuc." I whirled and pushed on. When we got free of the crowd, an almost empty street opened ahead of me.

No one had waited. My shoulders drooped.

I looked toward the Royal Fortress on the rise near the river. I could see the multi-colored dome of the Glass Chamber topping Elenia's quarters, glowing from the light inside. When I was little, I'd been dazzled by the sight of it. Now I lived there, and I was about to deliver Elenia's note, which would please her, so that next time, she'd wait for me. My past was past. I drew a deep breath, and with Tuc trotting ahead, I headed through the dark toward the Fortress.

No.

Toward *home*.

# Chapter 2

## Fitch

FITCH BLEW OUT the flame, then sucked on his burned fingers. That hadn't gone well, curse the Trickster. He lifted his mask away from his sweaty face, but let it snap back into place when an elderly man teetered down the steps into the shrine. It took Fitch only an instant to recognize the man's Mage coat. *Small gods. Gavun promised to get rid of the Mage who was supposed to be here.*

"Are you the Festival Mage?" the old man's voice quavered.

That wasn't a question the Festival-hired Mage would have asked. Fitch's confidence flooded back. "I am."

The other Mage baby-stepped closer, and Fitch caught an old-man smell of mint candy and dust before the man's hand snake-tongued out and grabbed Fitch's wrist. Fitch tried to tug free but stopped when the old man tilted.

"Do you need Mage healing?" Fitch asked as politely as he could with his wrist clamped in the old man's claw.

"Don't be impudent." The grandpa squeezed the bones of Fitch's wrist with surprising strength. "You have a gift, and you abuse it. You're seventeen, old enough to know better, and you've had a sharp lesson. Let's see if you're capable of learning anything." He squeezed harder.

"Let go of me." Fitch gritted his teeth. Small gods preserve him from dotty old geezers.

"Pah." The man flung Fitch's arm aside. "Now we'll see what we see."

Fitch rubbed his wrist. "Can't argue with that."

The man toddled up the steps.

Fitch eyed the statue of the Trickster. "A little joke?" he asked and flipped a finger the god's way. Before anything else could happen, he stripped off his mask and Mage coat and stuffed them in his carry bag. He added the now cool globe and ran up the steps to Sailmaker Street where the crowd was considerably drunker than they'd been when he slipped into the shrine. Full dark had come on, and torches flickered in brackets on every building. The pungent reek of their oil blended with the crowd's sweat.

Too bad he hadn't been able to coax Lady Elenia into viewing the flame, he thought as he ambled along between Festival goers. And what was the note about? Gavun would grouse about Fitch not getting hold of it. Fitch himself was half glad the butterfly girl had been too wary. Before he started nudging her, he'd had time to sense her desperate longing to be part of a family again. That, Fitch understood.

He had time to kill before meeting his cousin, so he strolled along Caravan Street, conscious of a swirl of feelings in his chest. Fooling with the butterfly girl's wishes had left him fuzzy on where his emotions separated from hers. That crack about kin making problems had come straight from him. Along with the knowledge of the pain when someone left. The press of bodies forced him to stop where a woman was singing along to the lute her partner was playing. Next to Fitch, a man leaned down and kissed the woman clinging to his arm. Fitch's whole body seemed to twist along with his heart. Last year, he'd gone to Festival with Nera. By the end of the night, she'd been dead, leaving Fitch half out of his mind and fully on the run from Lac's Holding and every memory it held.

He staggered across the street to the Blue Whale, where a couple was rising from one of the tables outside. He collapsed at it and ordered a mug of Winter Fire from a waiter trying to deal with too many customers. The waiter thudded the drink onto the scarred table just as a pair of city Watchmen halted next to Fitch. The waiter ducked his head and scurried away. Suppressing a groan, Fitch struggled to pull himself out of the black place in his head. How could he have missed spotting these two before? The passing people flowed out in an arc to avoid whatever trouble Fitch was in.

"What do we have here?" one of them said. "I didn't know Gavun's boy was back. Did you?"

"I wonder what he's up to," the other said. "If Gavun is king of the smugglers, his boy must be prince."

"Could be." His partner nudged Fitch's chair with the toe of his boot. "What do you think, Gavun's boy?"

Fitch reached for his normal swagger. "I think I'm just having a drink." Which, thank the small gods, was true at the moment. These two couldn't possibly know he'd taken the Festival Mage's place in the shrine.

"Not delivering smuggled goods?"

"Nope."

"Open your bag," the first one said.

Fitch untied the bag's flap and held it up. "Help yourself."

The Watchman pawed through it. "Just Mage gear," he told his partner, sounding disappointed. "You've gone back to doing that?"

Fitch shrugged. "A man has to earn an honest living."

The Watchman scoffed and dropped the bag. Mindful of the glass globe, Fitch snatched it before it hit the cobblestones and set it down gently. "It'd be the first time one of you Rhale Islanders did," the Watchman said. The two of them moved away toward where a fight had started over a woman he'd seen arrive with one man who was now leaving with another.

Fitch mentally kicked himself. After a year away, he

was out of practice at dealing with the Watch. He'd better get back into the swing of it quickly, or he'd end up in jail.

He raised the mug to his mouth then stopped, his lips brushing the brim. Something about the smell made his stomach flip. With careful control, he put the mug down and stared at the amber liquid. He wasn't imagining it, was he? He wasn't finding something because he *wanted* it to be there? No. He was sure. The drink smelled like the Winter Fire he'd shared with Nera last year. Fire spiked with Mage flower. He grabbed the mug and flung its contents out into the night.

"Hey!" One of the men at the next table brushed drops off his sleeve.

Fitch shoved his chair back so hard that it tipped over. He charged inside the jammed alehouse where he recognized Evia working at top speed behind the counter, filling mugs for the waiters to carry to the packed tables. He shouldered his way toward her, ignoring the emotions he seemed to be picking up from everyone he touched. An aftereffect of nudging the girl? He shook his head, trying to clear it.

Without pausing, Evia glanced at him. "Good to see you, Fitch," she called over the hubbub. "Your cousin said you were back. What can I get you?"

"Who'd you buy your Fire from?" He clutched the edge of the counter hard enough to feel splinters under his short nails. As far as he knew, the Blue Whale was still a Rhale Island customer. The thought made all the breath whoosh out of him. What would he do if his own kinship supplied the herb that killed Nera?

As Evia shoved a fistful of mugs at a waiter, she flinched, her eyes darting left and right where other people crowded around. "The Eastway kinship, of course."

"Not us?"

She pressed her lips into a thin line, a sign she thought he was talking too much. Which he was. Only he didn't care. "We bought from Eastway," she said. "The customs agents have doubled the inspections. Anyone dodging them—"

"Smugglers," Fitch supplied impatiently. "Us."

She frowned at him. "Anyone else is too risky."

Fitch wanted to believe her, but by the time he was three, he'd learned that trust was a fool's game. And last year, Fitch had delivered smuggled Fire to her for his father. Still, she probably bought from anyone who sold cheap. The crowd at the bar jostled him onto his back foot. He flinched away from the contact. Should he ask her again? No. He'd learn nothing useful from Evia now. He'd come back early tomorrow when there'd be fewer ears flapping. He had to find the poisoner before the end of Festival, though, because after that, Winter Fire would be gone. A drinker would notice the odd smell in regular ale, whereas the smell of Fire changed every year. Fitch left the way he'd entered, shouldered his bag which thankfully was still there, and strode away.

He loped along Corsair Street, stopping to poke

around anywhere serving Winter Fire, mostly because he hoped to find spiked stuff at a place that always bought from someone other than his kinship. A rogue smuggler would be best so he wouldn't have to accuse another kinship of poisoning people. There'd been no open war between kinships in his lifetime, and he swallowed at the idea of starting one. He found three more alehouses where the Fire had the same flowery smell. When he tried to find out where they bought their drink, two pretended not to hear him in the chaos and the other gave him the same frustrating answer Evia had. For all Fitch knew, it was true. The Eastway kinship brought in most Winter Fire because they had the legal contract. He couldn't picture them spiking the stuff though. They were the legitimate supplier for a reason. But maybe one of their people had gone bad?

Finally, he realized it was almost time to meet Loni. He branched off onto a street, then a lane, then a path through waving grass. To his left, an owl hooted. Something splashed into a pond. The water running down to the sea here didn't all flow in the Winding River. It split off in streams and creeks that Fitch had learned to navigate from the time he could toddle. Even blindfolded, he could have made his way back to the hidden dock, one of several his father used to stay one step ahead of the Watch.

He dropped onto the dock, dangling his feet off the side. Away from the Festival's torches, moonlight silvered the sleek dinghy he'd tied up here. Fitch found the *Sea*

*Wind* as beautiful now as he had on the day shortly after his twelfth birthday, when he nudged his father to buy it for him. It had been the first time he realized that if he could touch someone, he could often nudge them into doing what he wanted, not just use his focused energy to ease their ills.

When he'd cautiously asked his Mage teacher about nudging, thinking it might be related to healing, his teacher had spoken sharply and called it a perversion of the Healer god's gift. Fitch had quickly backpedaled and swore he'd never done it, never would do it, never wanted to do it. But the power of it had been hard to resist.

He managed to hide that talent from Gavun for a good two years, during which he'd collected a number of coveted objects before his father caught on and set him to prodding people for the kinship's profit. In the years since, he'd never wanted anything as much as he wanted the *Sea Wind*. The moment he saw it, he'd recognized the freedom it would give him to come and go as he liked. It still did.

In the quiet night, his muscles loosened. He inhaled the familiar smell of rotting plants and sundried leaves. Insects buzzed around him. He swatted at a mosquito on the back of his hand.

How much freedom did he want, he asked himself, and what was he willing to pay for it? Those Watchmen tonight had reminded him how much he'd resented being "Gavun's boy," how much he'd squirmed in the role his father laid out for him as part of the Rhale Island kinship.

In this past year, roaming the Center Sea, he'd been able to earn enough to live on by straight up healing, not nudging. Without Gavun there making demands, he'd had no needs he couldn't meet. He'd been surprised by how good it felt to stand on his own, like he was proving something to Gavun, though his father was a hundred miles away.

On the other hand, he'd hated the absolute aloneness he'd felt on being apart from the familiar web of his kinship. No islander wanted to be cast adrift like that. Who could they rely on, cut off from kin?

In the end though, it hadn't been his shattering loneliness that made him come home. He'd come because, in Vaum, he'd once again encountered the smell he'd inhaled last year at Festival and again tonight in the Blue Whale. "Mage flower," a Vaum Hedge Mage told him. "It makes people suggestible." The revelation had all but stopped Fitch's breathing. The Winter Fire Nera drank had been spiked with this exotic Mage flower. She'd been suggestible. And Fitch had suggested she do something "exciting," but he hadn't known about Mage flower. To his enormous relief, what the Vaum healer said meant he wasn't the only person who had caused her death. Maybe he wasn't even the *main* person. The guilt that weighed him down could be shifted onto someone else. Fitch had come home hoping to find Mage flower in some Fire again, learn who put it there, and make them pay; pay in pain, maybe even in death.

But what if the person who'd done it was his father?

Mage Flower's wide presence tonight meant someone wanted a lot of people open to suggestion. That could include suggestions like what to buy and how much to pay. In other words, suggestions a smuggler might find extremely useful. Suggestions a whole lot like those Gavun urged Fitch to make by nudging people.

Jogging footsteps shook the dock, making Fitch jump. Loni's lean face split into a familiar grin, one Fitch had welcomed all his life from a playmate and fellow trouble maker. "Wake up, coz," Loni said, pushing the flop of curly dark hair out of his eyes. "There's money ready to sail home where it belongs."

Fitch rose. "You look pleased with yourself."

"Gavun will be pleased too when he hears how much I collected." Loni tossed a purse to Fitch. Fitch hefted it and whistled. "Tomorrow night, you should come with me." Loni jumped into the *Sea Wind* and settled on the bench by one of the oars. "It'd be like old times."

Fitch considered the weight of the bag of coins before he dropped them in his carry bag. "How'd you sell so much?"

Loni shrugged his broad shoulders. "My glib Rhale Island tongue. You think you're the only one who's persuasive? Gavun's been training me all the while you were gone."

Fitch grimaced. "Careful, Loni."

Loni bent his head and ran his hands over the oar. "You take him for granted."

Fitch thought of Loni's father, dead these past eight years, and decided to ask his question carefully. He untied the line and stepped over into the dinghy. "In the Blue Whale, I bought some Winter Fire that smelled different than the rest of this year's batch. Was it ours?"

Loni tightened his hands around the oar. "Of course not. Gavun would drown any supplier who sold him bad goods. What's got into you anyway?"

Fitch's tense muscles relaxed. "Nothing. Sorry." He didn't trust Evia, and even more, he didn't trust his devious father, but he trusted Loni the way he trusted himself. He tucked his carry bag under the bench and settled next to his cousin.

"Mama wants to know when you're coming to see her," Loni said. "She said, and I quote, she 'wants to be sure the little savage still knows not to eat while he's sitting on the privy.'"

Fitch laughed. After his own mother left, Loni's mother had cared for him until he was old enough to go to sea when Gavun did. "Little? She knows I've been pointing out the gray hair on the top of her head since I was twelve, right?"

"I think she was talking about your brain. I notice you're not contesting the savage part."

"Tell her I'll stop by once Festival is over. Gavun has work for me until then." And Fitch had work he'd chosen for himself if he was to learn who put the Mage flower in the Winter Fire. He took the other oar, and together they maneuvered the *Sea Wind* through the narrow channel to the bay. He found himself settling into an easy familiarity partnering with Loni. Small gods, he'd missed this.

Maybe Loni felt it too because he said, "I've missed you. Why did you have to leave? I know the girl died but *leave*? That's what I don't get. Blood of my blood, Fitch. And not just mine. Gavun was knocked out when you vanished. He kept talking about how much he missed you, how much he needed you."

Fitch suspected his father missed his ability to nudge more than his company. Customers bought more and paid more when Fitch was around. Still, he heard the pain in his cousin's voice. Of course Loni didn't get why Fitch left. He, too, had been born into the Rhale Island kinship. But Fitch didn't want to talk about Nera's death. She'd been his first serious girlfriend. In the secrecy of the night, he'd been practicing the word "love."

"I'm back now," he said as the *Sea Wind* emerged onto the bay's open water. Off to his right, the city glowed along the shore of the Winding River that fed into the bay. He shipped his oar and moved to the tiller while Loni hoisted sail. The boat heeled over, and Loni perched on the high rail, a line in his hand. He grinned at Fitch again, and Fitch grinned back. Maybe he'd come home because this was where he belonged. This, right now, was good.

# Chapter 3
## Dilly

I HADN'T EXACTLY been afraid during my lonely walk home, but I had to admit, I hurried. I'd always felt safe here when I was a little girl living with Mama, but I was sixteen now, and life on the streets had made me nervous. Plus, the drunk kiss-stealer had spooked me. It wasn't until I led Tuc through the gates into the Royal Fortress courtyard that the tension eased out of my back. I was home, and even better, I was returning Elenia's note to her. I flew up the steps and through the doorway into Elenia's quarters, then jammed to a halt. At night, the stained glass panels overhead looked dark from inside, but the room itself blazed with light. It also vibrated with tension. Nemay and Jessa sat on the padded bench, their eyes fixed on Elenia, who was glaring at Captain Jaf in the room's center. The room smelled of wine and expensive perfume.

"She must have gone off with a lover," Elenia was saying. "That happens at Festival you know. With normal people anyway. You probably dropped that note you stole from me. Serves you right. Didn't your mother ever tell you thieves never prosper?"

I backed toward the door. It was possible Elenia was talking about Tira going off with her man, but Tira had slipped away before Elenia produced her note, while I could easily have been the only one to touch Captain Jaf between the time he put the note in his pocket and the time he reached for it again. The man hadn't been chosen from the army to become a captain in Lord Suryans's household guard by being a fool. I groped for the door latch just as Tuc pattered up to Jaf and sniffed his boots.

Captain Jaf whirled. When he saw me, his face relaxed. "Give it to me." He held out his hand, then snapped his fingers when I failed to jump at his command.

Annoyance uncurled in my chest. Was I wearing a guard's uniform? No, I was not. I was one of Lady Elenia's attendants. He could go and snap his fingers at some helpless recruit. "Give what to you?"

"The note." He took two steps toward me but halted when Tuc let out a low growl. "Empty your pockets," he ordered from a yard away.

I held my arms out and pretended to examine my yellow and blue gown. "As you see, my costume doesn't allow for them."

"Your sash, then. Untie it."

"Captain," Elenia said, "I must protest this rude treatment of one of my women."

I cocked my head and smiled at Jaf.

"I'm sorry, lady," Jaf said, "but your lord father put his trust in me."

"I don't mind, lady." I unknotted the bow at my waist, held the sash by one end, and swept it out as dramatically as I could. Something small thudded to the patterned carpet. For a moment, I was more surprised than Jaf. Then I recalled the feel of the thing I'd slipped from the Hedge Mage's pocket when I tucked the coins in.

Jaf picked it up and turned it over. "What's this?"

I hadn't even looked at it yet. "A trinket I bought at Festival. That happens, you know. With normal people anyway."

With scarlet rising from under his collar, he made to hand me the thing, but Tuc snarled, and he tossed it to me instead. I closed my fist around it without taking my gaze off him. He eyed my costume's deep cut neckline, the fingers of one hand opening and closing. My body stiffened. Surely he wouldn't search me. I glanced at Elenia, silently willing her to speak up.

"That's enough, captain." Elenia caught his arm and aimed him at the door. "Please leave."

He resisted her push. "I have to tell Lord Suryan about the note."

"Tell him I'm sorry I did it and will never do it again,"

Elenia said briskly, which I guessed was a big, fat lie on both counts. Probably Captain Jaf guessed it too, but he didn't have many choices. He bowed to Elenia and left, closing the door a little too firmly behind him.

"The nerve of him," Nemay said.

"I'm sorry he treated you like that, Dilly," Elenia said. "I don't know what made him think you had my note."

"What happened to your wings?" Jessa frowned.

"The strap broke, and I had to leave them." Tangled up with a drunk, I did not add. I fished the note out of my neckline and held it out with a flourish.

"You really did have it?" Elenia snatched her note back.

"How clever of you, Dilly," Nemay said.

Jessa narrowed her eyes at me. "Captain Jaf said you picked his pocket. Is that true?"

"Don't be ridiculous, Jessa," Elenia said. "As if I'd have a pickpocket in my household."

I suddenly felt faint. "He dropped it," I said quickly, "just as Elenia said."

"Well, bless the Trickster." Elenia turned the note over. "Now how am I going to get this to Veren?"

"I'll take it to his ship tomorrow," Nemay said.

"Someone might recognize you," Elenia said. "My father doesn't even want me writing to Veren."

"I could wear my mask and costume." Nemay twitched the green silk tail of her mermaid costume.

"Even in disguise, you wouldn't look like you belong

on the docks," Elenia said. "You look too expensive."

"Elenia, you need help," Nemay said. "Let me do it."

I twisted my hands together. Somehow, I needed to make sure Elenia valued me enough to overlook any... peculiarities my past life had taught me. If I tried, I could easily look like I belonged at the docks. I'd roamed the ones in Rin City. But if I pointed that out, I might be marking myself as a changeling who'd snuck in where she didn't belong. Which was a surer path to safety? I took a deep breath and decided on courage. "I could take it. I'm new enough that people aren't likely to know me."

The three women turned to me. "She probably could take it," Jessa murmured nastily. "She'd fit right in."

Though I'd just been thinking the same thing, I shot her a look that had scared off street thugs in Rin City. To my dismay, I realized that on the bench next to her, even Nemay, who wanted to do this herself, was slowly nodding.

"Dilly," Elenia said, "I think you could."

I was torn between pleasure at being the one to help Elenia and fear that she, Nemay, and Jessa so easily agreed that I, unlike the rest of them, looked like a woman who'd be on the docks.

"He's expecting it tonight, right? Would you like me to go now?" I moved to the sideboard and poured half a cup of wine to unstick my dry tongue. The stem of the silver goblet nearly slipped through my sweaty fingers. Captain Jaf was already suspicious of me, and Lord Suryan would be furious if he knew I was helping his daughter defy him. Suryan knew my street history, even if Elenia didn't. He'd blame me, not Elenia, for any trouble and would toss me out on my backside. The thought left me unsteady on my feet. I took another sip of wine and told myself that *Elenia* was the one I needed to please at the moment.

"Not tonight," Elenia said. "I need to rethink when and where Veren and I can meet. Go on to bed, all of you."

Tuc and I followed Jessa and Nemay down the short hallway to the room I shared with Tira, who still wasn't back yet. Tuc immediately curled up in a nest of blankets he pawed together on my bed. In the moonlight falling through the window, I examined the Hedge Mage's trinket. I'd surprised myself by taking it. Until I lifted Elenia's note from Captain Jaf, I hadn't picked a pocket since returning to Lac's Holding. Maybe doing it with Jaf made it easier to fall back into old habits. My fingers had always itched to even the score when someone gave me trouble. Still, given the way Elenia just swore she'd never have a pickpocket in her household, I needed to stop.

The Mage's trinket was a blue and green abalone shell set in a silver oval. The narrow loop at the oval's top showed it was meant to be worn on a chain around the neck. I turned it over and held it to the light to make out the letters F and N twined together on the back. I ran a finger across the thin lines and felt a twinge of guilt that the Mage might have meant to give it to someone special.

*He can buy another. He shouldn't have been rude.*

Through the open window I could still catch the music and crowd noise of Festival, but only dimly because this side of Elenia's quarters looked over the river where a forest of masts rose from the docks. Tomorrow, I thought with a shiver of unanticipated excitement, I'd carry Elenia's message, meet Veren, and be in on whatever they were planning. Jessa would be wildly jealous. I'd have to watch my back. Rich girls carried little embroidery scissors rather than knives, but they could still cut you.

I raised the lid of my clothes chest and fit the shell in the top rack next to the fancy combs and silver bracelet Elenia had given me, then shed what was left of my costume before sliding under my covers. As I did every night, I inhaled their clean smell. Maybe someday, I'd take a clean bed for granted, but not yet. Tuc had just rearranged himself against me when Tira breezed in, smelling of Winter Fire.

"Oh, Dilly, you wouldn't believe the night I've had." The door hadn't quite swung all the way shut before she began pulling off her costume, letting it fall in a silken puddle around her feet. She climbed into bed and wriggled into her blankets, reminding me of Tuc. "I'll never be able to sleep."

"I could tell you a story." Eager to please, I'd offered a restless Tira a story the first night we shared a room. After I got too old for Mama to tell me stories, I'd always told them to myself when I couldn't sleep. Stories were comforting. In a story, events made sense. And a teller could make them end the way she wanted.

"A story would be lovely." Tira yawned. "Tell one about Festival."

I cast around for a tale and found being at Festival tonight had stirred memories. "In the time of times, there lived a woman named Aylen who was lucky enough to live in Lac's Holding, the most wonderful city in the world. The food was luscious. Music played all day and night. The sea lay at the city's feet, deep and changing. One night during Festival, Aylen met a man and fell in love. She'd loved other men but not the way she loved this one."

"Ah," Tira breathed a satisfied sound. "There's nothing sweeter than love."

"To Aylen's grief, her lover decided to leave Lac's Holding and take Aylen and her daughter to the capital."

"She had a daughter?"

"Didn't I say that? I forgot."

"Best not to forget something like a child," Tira murmured. She turned over onto her side and a moment later drew a deep breath and was still.

Alone at last, I felt my tense muscles soften. Of all the women, Tira spent the least time judging the others' actions, including mine. Still, it would be better if she never knew how I'd lived.

I watched the moonlight travel across the wall. *Best not to forget a child.* Truth enough in that. An adult who forgot might leave a child at the mercy of a cruel world outside any sense a story would make. *I don't live like that anymore. I'm one of Elenia's household.* So what had I been thinking when I volunteered to go to the docks? Why had I picked not one, but two pockets? *Just this once*, I thought, *to prove my value to Elenia. Then I'll never risk my place again.*

Tuc stood up, turned around to face me, and licked my chin. He always knew what I was feeling. It would be nice, I thought, if people were as sympathetic. But then, on second thought, maybe not. It was probably better if Elenia didn't always know what was on my mind.

# Chapter 4

## Fitch

BOWLINE IN HAND, Fitch hopped onto the dock and tied up. Loni climbed up next to him, eyes on the unfamiliar craft on the other side of Gavun's. He trotted toward it, looking for a name and evidently spotting a shield symbol instead. He frowned over his shoulder. "Fortress guards."

"Did you run into them tonight?" Fitch asked.

"I didn't even see any. They leave patrolling the streets to the Watch."

Fitch had seen guards, the two babysitting Lady Elenia, but he held his tongue about what happened in the shrine. Gavun had cautioned Fitch not to tell anyone else about his nudging, not even kin. He'd seen what Fitch's gift meant to his business and didn't want word to get out. Fitch running into guards tonight probably didn't matter enough to warn Loni anyway. Fitch was pretty sure the guard captain with Elenia hadn't identified him. Still, could the visiting boat have something to do with Gavun siccing Fitch on Lady Elenia?

"I'll go home the long way," Loni said. "Better cautious than caught. Want to come with me?"

Fitch shook his head. "Gavun's expecting me."

"You coming with me tomorrow night then?"

"It's up to Gavun."

"Take care, coz." Loni trotted along the beach to where a path led to the other side of the island.

Fitch started up the wooden steps wedged into the sand, ready to duck into the bushes on either side if he heard the Fortress guards coming. At the hilltop, he slid into the cover of flourishing elf grass, watching the door to his father's house and waiting for the guards to leave. They'd notice the *Sea Wind* at the dock but were unlikely to climb the hill again to question him. They knew who was in charge on any of the islands, and on Rhale, it wasn't Fitch. He was just Gavun's sometimes nameless boy.

He dropped his bag and sat cross-legged. The sea shushed in the night. Stars prickled the velvet dark sky. He breathed in the scents of Rhale Island, clean and peaceful after the frenzy of Festival. Eyes lifted to the stars, he probed his shirt pocket, pushing aside the butterfly girl's gull coins and the broken chain that had led him to stow the shell charm there, but his fingertips found only a fluff of lint. With a frown, he pulled the pocket as open as it would go and pressed his chin to his chest, trying to peer into it. He took the chain and coins out, palmed them in his other hand, and ran a finger all along the pocket's seam.

"Healer, help me," he breathed. Had he dropped it somewhere? Even as he scanned the dark grass around his feet, he knew the shell wasn't there. He felt again the brush of the butterfly girl's fingers and groaned. How could he have been so stupid? He'd seen her lift the note from the guard.

A crash came from inside the house, followed by a man's muffled cry. Jamming the coins and chain into his pocket, Fitch sprinted to the door, reaching it just as it opened, spilling light. A Fortress guard stalked out, almost running him over. A second guard loomed behind him. Fitch tried to back away, but the first guard closed a hand over his arm and ducked around him to wrench it up behind him.

"Who's this?" the first guard asked.

To Fitch's surprise, he felt the guard's anger through the touch, though it had been hours since he nudged the butterfly girl and he'd made no effort to enter the man's mind. He could see past the second guard into the house. Gavun sat on the floor, hair straggling loose from its usual tail, the table and a chair overturned next to him.

The second guard said, "It's Gavun's boy, the heir. Haven't seen him in a while." He drew his elbow back and punched Fitch in the stomach.

Fitch tried to double over around the pain, but the first guard held him tight. He fought off the urge to puke on the man's blue and red uniform. "What was that for?"

"For cheating Lord Suryan out of the custom payments you owe, which means cheating me out of my pay. Also for making me work during Festival." He drew his arm back again, but his companion loosened his grip and said, "Enough. Let's go."

Fitch braced his hands on his knees and watched them head for the steps, the shells of the path crunching under their feet. The guard who'd held him said, "Festival still has three more nights. We'll get there." They started down, their voices blending into the sound of the sea.

Fitch retrieved his bag and staggered into the house where Gavun had righted the chair and collapsed into it. As Fitch heaved the table onto its legs, Gavun wheezed, "Was that supposed to be you rescuing me? I can still take care of myself." He hooked his dark hair behind his ears.

"Next time I'll let you do that." Fitch felt like a fool, but at least the pain in his belly was letting up. He closed the door he'd left open. "What did they want beyond the chance to use their fists?"

"To tell me Lord Suryan was giving me a chance to heed his warning and take the entire kinship elsewhere." Gavun smiled grimly. "I told them we'd lived on this island when Suryan and his kin were squatting in huts on the other side of the sea."

"I can't imagine why they took offense."

"Suryan's prodded us like that before. He won't do anything." Gavun straightened up. "About time you got here. Did she show? Did you nudge her into defending us?"

Apparently they were moving on. "She showed. Along with a gaggle of women and two guards."

His father scoffed. "You thought she'd be alone? It's Festival, and she's Lord Suryan's precious heir. Of course he sent guards with her." He stiffened. "You didn't lose your nerve, did you?"

"I was ready to nudge her," Fitch said, resentment flaring at his father's scorn. "But before I got the chance, she tried to give me a note, and the guard swooped in to take it. After that, she stomped out."

"A note? What was in it?"

"I told you, a guard took it." Despite the payback he owed the butterfly girl for picking his pocket, Fitch decided not to tell Gavun about her. She was just a waiting woman trying to please her mistress.

"Stone it, Fitch. Whatever was in it might have been useful if you failed at getting her to call off her father."

Gavun looked ready to say more, but Fitch headed him off by dropping his bag on the table and fishing out the sack of coins. "From Loni." He tossed it across to Gavun.

Gavun loosened the drawstring, peered inside, and smiled broadly. "It's easy to see Loni is blood of my blood."

Fitch snorted.

Gavun raised an eyebrow. "What?"

"Nothing." Fitch refused to be jealous of Loni. "Some Fire I bought at the Blue Whale had an odd smell. Loni says it isn't ours. Aren't they buying from us anymore? Whose stuff is it?"

"What kind of odd smell?" Gavun walked to the shelves, pushed on the empty half of the top one, and stuck the bag in the space that opened behind it.

Fitch struggled to describe it. "Kind of flowery, only drier. Less sweet. It's an herb called Mage flower that grows wild in Vaum. It makes people suggestible."

"Loni's right that it isn't ours." Gavun moved the basket holding their mending in front of the hiding place. Fitch knew none of the coins would come out again until after Festival, when Gavun would pay out shares to each kinship member. "I have no idea who else Evia might be buying from, curse her." He turned around. "If another kinship is trying to undercut us, I'll sic the customs sharks on them."

"Tell me if you find out who it is. Nera had some last year. That night..." Fitch cleared his throat. "I think it made her take a wild risk when I sent her out looking for excitement. I'm going to find the bastard who gave it to her, or at least the one who supplied it, and make him pay. A customs fine isn't good enough."

Gavun shot him a look from under half-lowered lids. "No good comes of hanging on, Fitch. You're just making yourself unhappy. Let it go." When Fitch opened his mouth, Gavun sailed doggedly on. "I wonder what the lord's daughter is hiding. Let's see what the man you replaced has to tell us." He picked up the mask hanging on the back of his chair. "Where's yours?"

Fitch wrestled his thoughts away from Nera's death. "You have the Mage here? The one who should have been in the shrine?"

Gavun shrugged. "I couldn't let him wander loose."

"You had him in the house while the Fortress guards were here?"

Gavun grinned. Against his will, Fitch smiled. Gavun the Bold, he and Loni used to call Fitch's father when they were kids, as if he were a pirate. They'd played at being his crew – Loni the Gallant and Fitch the Fearless.

"Let's see if he's useful," Gavun said. "He doesn't know where he is. Put your mask on."

Fitch took his mask from his bag, picked up the lantern from the side table, and followed his father down a long hallway to the storeroom at the back of the house. Gavun unlocked the door and opened it on a darkened room. Even before Fitch hung the lantern from the high hook, he knew what the room held: Dolyan pottery and textiles, fragrant spices from the south coast of the Center Sea, obscene art from the Janda peninsula – all of it ready to be smuggled past the customs officers and sold at a sweet profit. There was no Winter Fire. That was stored aboard the *Shark's Teeth*, the Rhale Island schooner floating in a bay on the island's other shore. As long as all of it stayed this far from the mainland, it was just past the edge of Suryan's territory, and the customs bloodsuckers couldn't touch it. In theory, anyway.

New to the room was the man with a burlap bag over his head and rope around his ankles and wrists. The man's head lifted as Gavun's boots thudded toward him. Gavun yanked the bag off, revealing a man of middling age with a traditional, pointed Mage's beard. He squinted against the light. "What is this?" he asked in a high, tight voice. "Where am I?"

"You're where the Trickster put you," Gavun said. "Lady Elenia arrived at the shrine this evening with a note for you to carry. Who were you supposed to give it to?"

The Mage's eyes widened. He pushed with his bound feet, scooting back as if to hide in the corner. "I can't tell you that."

"Why not?" Gavun asked.

"He'd kill me." The Mage's voice shook, and the smell of fear sweat prickled in Fitch's nostrils.

Behind his mask, Fitch raised an eyebrow. Death seemed an extreme threat for naming a man getting a woman's note, even if she was the lord's daughter. His father must have had the same thought because he leaned close to the Mage, his sharp eyes trying to pin his captive. "What does this man want with Elenia?"

The man's beard twitched as he curled his lip. "What do you think?

Gavun tapped his fingers against his trouser seam. "So it's just a lover?"

The man shrugged.

Fitch had the fleeting thought that of course his father would dismiss a lover as "just."

Gavun beckoned to Fitch and stepped out of the room, closing the door behind them. "If she has to sneak around to see whoever it is, there'll be something there we can use on her. We need to find out who she's carrying on with. Can you get into his head?"

"Most likely not now. You've scared him so much that his fear would overwhelm anything else."

"You could try." Between Gavun's mask and the dark hallway, Fitch couldn't see his father's face, but he felt the sting of the scorn in his voice. "Sometimes I swear you're thwarting me on purpose. At the moment, I can't go to the privy without Lord Suryan's soldiers checking to see what I left. We need Suryan to call them off, and Elenia can make that happen. You failed to push her into it tonight. Maybe we can get her to press Suryan without that."

Fitch twitched his mask, looking for a fit that didn't rub his skin raw. "Blackmail her into it, you mean."

"Toughen up, Fitch. Loni acts more like my son than you do. Blood of my blood. Make yourself useful." Gavun opened the door to the lantern lit storeroom and waited. When Fitch finally nodded, Gavun's shoulders visibly loosened. "That's my boy," he murmured. Fitch blew out his breath and followed Gavun in.

The Mage's eyes flicked back and forth between them, but when Gavun moved aside, his gaze settled on Fitch. "I won't tell you anything," he gabbled.

Fitch was almost certain that was true. All he was doing was proving Gavun wrong. He took the lantern from its hook and set it in front of the Mage. "I'm not going to hurt you. If you let me, I can make you feel better." He crouched so he and the other Mage were face to face.

The man lifted an eyebrow. "You're a Mage?"

"I am." The Mage's hands were tied behind him, so Fitch lightly gripped his shoulders, the silk of the man's robe smooth beneath his fingers. The Mage flinched, sending a ripple of his terror into Fitch. *Not mine. It's not mine.* But the hardest part of nudging someone was always the way he shared their feelings, and this Mage's were affecting him more strongly than usual. He'd never tried to nudge another Mage before. And he still seemed to be shaken from nudging the girl. That must explain the strength of the washback. "I know you're scared and probably sore from being tied up, but if you focus on the lantern and calm yourself, I can help you with both those things."

The Mage tried to twitch out of Fitch's grip. "Get your hands off me. You're a disgrace to the power the small gods granted you, assuming you're not a liar."

Fitch heard again the old man in the shrine saying he abused his gift. Apparently it wasn't a night for old men to be pleased with him. Gavun cleared his throat, and Fitch took the hint. He groped for a thread of the Mage's mind, but all he found was a jumble of fear and anger that flooded back into him so wildly that he had to give up or fall over. He staggered when he stood up.

Gavun snorted and gestured Fitch back out into the hallway. "Shall I assume that was useless?"

"I told you." Fitch stiffened. He knew what his father valued in him or anyone else, and *useful* was high on the list.

"Put the bag back on his head and dump him ashore somewhere he'll be found. Wait until he's loose, and follow him." Gavun headed back toward the front room, certain Fitch would obey.

Fitch caught himself reaching for the storeroom door latch, without thought falling back into being Gavun's boy. He dropped his hand. Was this really what he wanted? For now, he decided, it was good enough. He couldn't leave Lac's Holding anyway, not before he learned who was spiking the Winter Fire. And as he'd been reminded when he touched the butterfly girl, a world without kin was a cold place to sleep. He pushed the door open.

# Chapter 5

## Dilly

I PICKED MY way along the docks, ships looming in a long row on my left. I was partly scanning for Veren's and partly making sure I didn't step in something vile left during last night's Festival. When Tira and Jessa dressed me, Jessa had smiled nastily, declared that even the clothes Tira borrowed from a servant were too good for me, and dug a tattered gown out of the rag bag. Then she'd said I needed to be barefoot if my disguise was to be convincing.

"Are you sure?" Tira had asked, wrinkling her brow.

"Absolutely. Unlikely though it is, given who we're sending, we don't want anyone connecting her to Elenia. Take your shoes off, Dilly."

It was payback for my pushing her into the fish chowder last night, but there wasn't much I could say. So now I stepped gingerly. I didn't mind the discarded mask that caught on my bare toe, but I skirted around a pool of dried vomit. Being a dog and therefore sometimes disgusting, Tuc sniffed at the puddle before abandoning it for a skewer with a rat-gnawed chunk of meat still on it. As far as I was concerned, he was welcome to the meat, but I didn't want him getting splinters from the skewer. I tried to yank it away, he held on until I said, "Let go." In that moment's distraction, my right foot came down on something sharp. I sucked in my breath and hopped while Tuc danced around me, whining for me to give him back the skewer. "No. You'll hurt yourself." I flung it into the river, patted Tuc, and limped on.

Despite the beating my feet were taking, I was enjoying the chance to wander the city on my own. In the sunlight, the pink, yellow, and blue paint of the waterfront buildings made them look like candies laid out on a plate. Crew members called to their shipmates, and the air smelled of fish and tar. It all struck me as lively. Obviously, I was lucky to live with Elenia, but in Rin City, I'd grown used to occasional adventures and, to my surprise, I missed them. Not the frightening ones, the Trickster forbid. But a girl likes a bit of excitement now and then. Look at how Elenia was playing around with Veren.

Elenia had said Veren's ship was docked near the foot of Caravan Street, but she hadn't said in which direction. I'd guessed south, and as I scanned the name painted on each ship I passed, I was beginning to think I'd made a mistake. Thank the small gods, the next ship turned out to be *Storm King*, the one I wanted, but when I started toward the gangway, I nearly tripped over Tuc, who'd planted himself sideways across it. I prodded his furry belly with the top of my sore foot. "Move, Tuc."

He looked straight ahead, pretending he hadn't heard me. When I poked him again, he looked up at me, and to my astonishment, he growled.

"Stop that!" I said. "What's wrong with you?"

He glanced at the ship and then at me. If a dog could look disapproving, Tuc disapproved of the *Storm King*, though neither he nor I had ever been near it before.

"You think I'm going to sail away and leave you? Is that it? I'd never do that. You can come aboard with me and make sure." When he stayed put, I picked him up and set him on the dock. "All right. Wait here if you like." With a pitiful whine, he sat, and I climbed the rest of the way.

The sailor at the top of the gangway scanned my rags and looked down her nose at me. "Can I help you?"

As soon as I thought of a good enough revenge, Jessa was going to be sorry. "I have a message for Captain Veren."

She put out a hand. "Give it to me, and I'll see he gets it."

"My business is with the captain, not you."

"He's busy. You'll have to come back."

I planted my sore soles firmly. Elenia had a right to choose her own partner, and neither Lord Suryan nor this sailor was going to keep that from happening. "Believe me, you'll regret it if you don't let me through to the captain."

"Are you threatening me? Get off this ship, and do it now."

I stiffened. "I'm not moving."

A second sailor came up behind the first one. "She giving you trouble?" he asked.

The sailor giving me a hard time turned toward her crewmate. Bless the Trickster after all. I ran limping along the deck, found the likely door to the officer's cabins, and started down the steep stairs.

"Hey!" the woman on watch sputtered.

I barely heard her. At the foot of the stairs, I stood frozen. I'd sailed down the river from Rin City on a ship smaller than this one, so I'd expected the cramped, dark hallway. What I hadn't expected was the far too handsome man coming toward me. The man who'd taken Mama and me to Rin City and abandoned us there almost two years ago. My heart clogged my throat. He spiked to a stop. "Dilly?"

"Sorry, Mr. Cole." The sailor grabbed my arm from behind. "She slipped past me."

"Leave her," Cole said.

The sailor's fingers loosened a hair's breadth. "You want—"

"Leave her," Cole repeated, his gaze locked with mine. "Go back to whatever you're supposed to be doing."

I heard the sailor retreating up the steps. My breath

came in puffs. I'd dreamed of meeting Cole again, imagined what it would feel like to carve gashes in his face so no woman would ever again go near him.

He waited until the deck door closed out the sunlight, leaving us in lantern-lit dimness. Then he edged toward me carefully, as if my dreams had reached out and touched him so he half knew what I wanted. The hoop earring in his left ear swayed. When he shuffled an inch closer, I leapt at him, aiming to put thumbs in his eyes but only managing to claw my nails down his face before he grabbed my wrists in one big hand and wrapped his other arm around my waist. I writhed in his disgusting grip. "Dilly! Calm down. Come and talk." He pulled me toward a cabin door, fumbling with the key ring on his belt. There was no chance I'd let him lock me in somewhere.

I kicked him in the shin, cursed my bare foot, and tried to knee him in the groin. He twisted to avoid the blow, loosening his grip enough for me to break free and scramble up the steps, jamming my hand against the door to fling it open.

"Wait!" His fingers brushed my skirt as he tried to hold me back.

I had to dodge around the door to head for the gangway and that gave him enough time to block me. I whirled to run and found myself penned between a barrel and a large wooden box, so I set my back to the box and faced him. At the sight of blood oozing from a scratch on his cheek, I felt a stab of savage glee. "Get away from me."

He halted a foot from me, darting looks in both directions. "We're in the open. Everyone can see us. You're in no danger." He touched his cheek, then looked at his red fingertip. "Neither am I," he said dryly. He drew a handkerchief out of his pocket and dabbed his face.

The sailor at the top of the gangway was watching us. So was a man holding a paintbrush he'd been sweeping over the deck railing. I could still hear the chatter of crew on other ships. It all felt normal, as if I'd escaped from the underworld into daylight. I struggled to draw in enough air to speak. "Mama's dead, thanks to you."

He winced.

"She got sick after you left. After a while, she couldn't even go into the bakery to work. I ran messages for people, but we had nothing."

"Keep your voice down. Veren doesn't know I had a woman with me during that stay."

"You had a woman and her daughter." I pressed away from him until the edge of the box cut into my back.

"Shh. The thing is I was on business for Veren, and he paid. He'd object to paying for extras."

"Extras?" My body twitched with the urge to attack him again. If I rushed him, could I shove him over the rail? Would he drown or float like the rest of the garbage?

"I just mean Veren will be upset if he thinks I cheated him."

What he was saying sunk in. "You're crew on this ship? You work for Veren?"

"He's my cousin," Cole said. "You know how the islands are. Blood of my blood, and all that."

"You think I don't understand blood of my blood? Mama and I were everything to one another!"

Cole stowed his handkerchief. "Dilly, I'm sorry about your mother. Truly. Sorry about everything."

"Right." I put as much sneering into my voice as I could.

Cole lifted his hands in a helpless gesture. "I meant to go back to you and Aylen, but a man threatened to kill me if he ever laid eyes on me again."

I drew a soft breath. "The neighbor?"

His eyes narrowed. "How did you know that?"

"He came by looking for you," I said quickly. "I guessed you were bedding his wife."

"No," he breathed. "You told him. That's how he knew. Stone you, Dilly. I should have realized." He took a half step toward me, and I smelled the hair pomade he'd always worn. It made me gag. "You made it too dangerous for me to stay," Cole said. "If things went bad for Aylen, it's your fault, not mine."

Familiar guilt twisted my gut. I pushed it back in the dark hole where I usually kept it. "You could have sent us word to meet you somewhere. Not that I wanted you to. You came after me as well as his wife."

"No, no," Cole said with a self-assurance that made me want to spit in his face. He truly thought any woman would believe whatever came out of his mouth. "You were just a kid. You misunderstood.”

“You kissed me.” I heard my voice rising. “You grabbed my breast.”

“Shh,” he said again. “I was drunk. It was a stupid moment.” He ran his gaze over my ragged clothes. “You need help? I’ll help you.” He shook his head. “Small gods, you look like her.”

“Crawl into a corner and die, Cole. I don’t need your help. I don’t need you. I’m one of Lady Elenia’s attendants.” He raised an eyebrow, and I had the pleasure of shrugging him off. “You can believe me or not. In the meantime, I have a note from Elenia to Veren.” Too late, I realized Cole might not know about Elenia and Veren, and I shouldn’t have mentioned Elenia’s name. Still, the risk was worth it when I saw the flicker of doubt in his face. I pushed myself out of the corner. “Tell me where to find him, then get out of my way.”

Cole studied me. He must have seen something other than the vulnerable girl he left, because he took a step back. “All right, but you’re not going on your own. And you better be telling the truth. Veren won’t appreciate one of your tricks.”

I followed him back down into the dark at a cautious distance. What did it mean that Elenia’s lover was the kind of man who’d hire Cole? Was I going to have to tell Elenia about him? The idea made me cringe. If I did, I’d have to say I spent three months as a street kid because he dumped us in Rin and Mama died. Elenia was bound to wonder what I might have done to survive. Anyone would. And she'd already made her scorn of pickpockets clear.

Cole knocked on a door. "Come," a voice called.

Cole opened the door and waved me through. I slid past him, keeping as far away as I could. In the cabin, two men sat on either side of a desk. The porthole stood open, letting in light and the cry of gulls squabbling over a fish.

"What is it?" the one behind the desk asked. Veren, I assumed. I'd heard Elenia and the other women talk about him often enough. He looked to be in his mid-twenties, with eyes the gray of a gull's back and features that would have been delicate if not for the way wind and sun had roughened them. Both men at the desk wore captain's stickpins on their lapels, but Veren's flashed with a large, red jewel.

"Girl says she has a message for you, captain," Cole said.

Veren shifted his gaze from Cole to me. "Good. I've been waiting for one." He looked back to the man across his desk. "You understand what your people are to do tonight?"

"You can count on us. I'll see you at tomorrow's meeting."

Veren rose. "Cole, show our Half-Moon Island friend out. Then make that visit we talked about."

Cole gave me one last appraising – or maybe warning – look, and then left, shutting the door behind him. I couldn't help smiling. That look told me he was afraid I'd tell his cousin the whole tale of our time in Rin City. His fear warmed my heart.

I pulled Elenia's note out of my pocket and handed it to Veren, who sank into his chair, slit the seal with a dagger, and held the message up so light fell on it. "Bless the woman." He leaned back in his chair. "Tell her tonight is good, but it has to be at the Eastway warehouse. Say we'll have complete privacy there." He tossed the note onto the desk amid the clutter of other papers weighed down by a ring of keys even bigger than Cole's.

I rocked from foot to foot. "Would you like me to wait while you write her back?"

His mouth curved in a tight smile. "Just repeat what I said." He bent over a chart on his desk.

"Cole won't tell you," I blurted, "but I knew him in Rin City."

He ran his gaze over my ragged gown. "Is that so?"

"Mama and I lived with him."

Veren raised an eyebrow.

"If you wondered why he always needed money, that was probably the reason."

Veren's mouth twisted. "The day Cole doesn't need money is the day I'll wonder." He pulled a paper out from under his keys and studied it.

More stories about Cole tried to slide out of my mouth, but I'd have had to tell them to the top of Veren's head. Clearly he didn't want to hear anything else now.

I backed into the corridor and climbed up the steps.

Cole was nowhere in sight. I didn't like his presence on the ship Elenia's lover captained, though maybe it didn't mean anything about Veren because, like the Mage boy said last night, kin weren't always a pure joy. And maybe Veren would think about what I'd told him and dismiss Cole. If he did, I hoped I'd run into Cole begging on the streets.

I headed for the gangway where the sailor who'd tried to stop me was waving an anxious looking man aboard. The sailor stepped out of my way but not fast enough to avoid my brushing against her, remembering too late that I'd sworn off pickpocketing. Mama would have said I needed my Guardian Dog. At the foot of the gangway, Tuc was turning himself inside out at the sight of me. *Even better*, I decided.

# Chapter 6

## Fitch

FITCH ENTERED THE cocoa shop across from the Mage's house and flopped into a chair from which he could watch the front door but stay mostly screened behind the other patrons. Not that the man was likely to recognize Fitch. He'd kept his Festival mask on the whole time they'd been together, and the storeroom had been only dimly lit.

He ordered a roll and a cup of cocoa, then waited, rubbing his palms over the fuzz on his cheeks. When the woman who ran the place brought his breakfast, he took a quick, grateful gulp of the hot drink, then grimaced at the bitterness. All the time he'd been away he'd craved cocoa, but it had always smelled better than it tasted. Still, he felt the rush of it to his brain, and he needed to wake up. He dipped the hard roll in the drink and chewed, still watching the Mage's door.

After following his father's captive here the previous night, Fitch had figured the man was tucked in until morning and caught a few hours restless sleep in the *Sea Wind*, alternating between slapping away mosquitoes and dreaming of Fortress guards punching him. He'd awakened at dawn and slogged back into town to take up his watch again. When Gavun said he should find out where the man went, he hadn't meant where he lived; that information wouldn't be much use to him. Gavun intended to make Lord Suryan back off and let the Rhale Island kinship smuggle in peace using any means he could, including blackmailing Suryan's daughter. For that to happen, he needed to know the identity of Elenia's lover.

As Fitch expected at this hour of the morning, the street was scattered with brisk stewards and housewives trailed by servants carrying shopping baskets, but his eye caught on someone pushing a cart through the shadows on the street's edge. He recognized Mesti from the Sera Island kinship and smothered a smile. He'd once moved spices with Mesti when Gavun and the Sera kinship head had briefly worked together. Mesti could kindly be described as slow-witted. He probably thought that slouchy shamble made him look innocent instead of out of place.

Fitch was about to hail him when a man called, "You with the cart. Stop!"

Mesti darted a look over his shoulder, dropped the

cart handles, and ran.

Small gods, the boy was dim.

Two men in bright blue uniforms pounded past after him. Not the city Watch, Fitch realized with surprise. Suryans's Fortress guards. Along with everyone else in the cocoa shop, he stood to see in time to witness one of the guards hurl himself at Mesti and throw him to the cobblestones. Fitch winced. The bruise on his belly throbbed sympathetically.

Shoppers screamed and scattered. The guard on top of Mesti seized him by the back of the shirt and hauled him upright, both of them panting. The other guard went back to the cart and pulled off the canvas covering its load. "You have customs receipts for this stuff?" he demanded.

"At home," Mesti squeaked, face gone red from the collar pulled tight around his neck. "I'll go fetch them."

"Tell you what," said the one holding him. "You stay with us until someone can fetch those papers." He dragged Mesti back toward the Fortress – or maybe the customs house, which sat on the river's bank half a mile or so downstream. His partner rattled the cart after them.

"Suryan's guards are jumpier than usual," said a woman at the next table.

"I hear he's fed up with smugglers," said the woman with her.

Fitch sank uneasily back into his chair. He'd never seen the Fortress guards take a smuggler off the city streets like that, for sure not while tourists were in town for

Festival. His bruise twinged again. Were his rough handling and Mesti's part of the same thing? If that was what Gavun had faced this year, no wonder he wanted a way to persuade Suryan to leave Rhale Island alone.

The Mage's door opened, and a man emerged, squinting into the morning sun. Fitch looked twice because the man was clean shaven, but he was sure this was the Mage his father had held captive the night before. His beard must have been fake. Fitch had to admire the quality of it though. Good fakery was hard to pull off. He gulped his cocoa, flung a gull on the table, and slipped out to follow the man, chewing on his roll as he went.

He had plenty of time to eat because the man dawdled, looking into every shop window and occasionally clutching his stomach. On Corsair Street, he ducked into a public privy. Nerves, Fitch judged, and leaned against a building ten yards away to wait. After keeping him out all night, the man had better lead Fitch to whoever hired him. He needed to get the lover's name for Gavun so he'd be free to snoop around some of the other island kinships and find who was selling spiked Fire. At that point, a good citizen would probably rat to the Watch, but after what he'd just seen, Fitch would have to be out of his mind to try that. The odds were good they'd arrest Fitch instead. Besides, kinships took care of their own business.

The Mage emerged from the privy. Fitch followed him down Caravan Street to the docks and eventually to the gangway of the *Storm King*, which as far as Fitch knew belonged to the Eastway Island kinship. Old Para Eastway had died shortly before last Festival. Fitch didn't know who headed the kinship now. As far as Fitch knew, Eastway ran a straight arrow import business paying every tariff Lord Suryan and the king imposed, much to Gavun's disgust. As a reward, they had the legitimate – and lucrative – contract to import Winter Fire, a fact that made Gavun a man to be avoided when he thought of it.

The Mage's shoulders heaved in a sigh before he made his way up to the deck. Someone on board must be the man Fitch was looking for. Sorting through ways of finagling a name, Fitch moved a few yards closer and saw what had been hidden behind a piling – a mongrel dog with one torn ear staring intently up the gangway.

His heart jumped. It was the mutt who'd been protecting the butterfly girl last night. Possibilities opened. The girl was one of Elenia's people. Elenia might be on the ship even now.

But what made his heart race was that if the dog was here, the butterfly girl was here. And she had Nera's necklace.

The dog jumped to its feet, tail wagging furiously. Fitch looked up the gangway and spotted a girl wearing a fancy dress that looked like it had been dragged through a thorn bush and trampled into a mud puddle. How one of Elenia's women could be out of the Fortress wearing it was beyond him, but the dog left no doubt she was the butterfly girl, now without the Festival mask she'd worn in the small gods shrine. He narrowed his eyes as she brushed against the sailor on watch and started down to the docks, setting her bare feet carefully. The high arch of each one flattened in a graceful move that made Fitch think the butterfly costume had suited her. Unexpected grief panged in his throat, and it took him an instant to identify the cause. Like Nera, the girl had red hair and honey colored skin. *Half the girls in Lac's holding have a variation on the same hair and skin*, he scolded himself. *Don't be a fool.*

He moved to block the end of the gangway. The girl stopped, her body visibly stiffening. A low growl made Fitch look down at the dog who had gone rigid, staring at him.

"Who's this, Tuc?" the girl said. "Do we know him?"

Keeping one eye on the dog, Fitch said, "We met last night. You have something that belongs to me."

Her gaze darted to his ears and recognition flickered in her face. She hunched one shoulder. "Get out of my way, please." The dog bared its teeth.

Fitch moved enough to let her reach the dog but still block her from leaving the docks. At the girl's approach, all the menace apparently fell out of the dog's head, and it danced around her feet.

"I want that shell charm," Fitch said.

She stooped to scratch the dog's ear, not incidentally he guessed hiding her face. "I don't know what you're talking about."

"Does Lady Elenia know you steal? Is that why you're dressed like that? You stole from her, and she threw you out."

She straightened abruptly enough that the dog growled in Fitch's direction again. "She did not throw me out. She wouldn't do that."

Fitch swept his gaze over the *Storm King's* deck. "Shall I go aboard and ask her if that's true?" It occurred to him that he'd told Gavun he didn't like manipulating women. Apparently he'd inherited the family flexibility on principles.

The girl relaxed again. "Go ahead."

So Elenia wasn't aboard. "The man she was writing to is there, right? She said his name but I can't remember it." He snapped his fingers. "It was…"

"Elenia never said it, and you're a bad liar."

"I'm quite a good one, actually, but keep your secrets. I don't need you to find them out." He leaned toward her. "But I want that charm. It belonged to a girl I loved," he found himself saying. Small gods, he must be desperate.

The butterfly girl stroked the dog. "Belonged? Loved? As in the past? Did she decide she'd be better off without you?"

"She died."

For a heartbeat, the girl closed her eyes. She opened them again. "I don't have it with me."

"Bring it to Festival tonight. I'll be at the shrine at whatever time you say." He felt lightheaded.

Chewing her lip, she glanced back at the *Storm King*. "I'm not sure I'll be able to go to the shrine tonight." She prodded the dog out of her way with one delicately boned foot. "I have to go."

"Wait." Fitch moved around to block her again. "If you can't bring the charm to the shrine, can you leave it at the Fortress gates?"

She scanned his face. "I don't want to leave it with anyone else," she said slowly, confirming Fitch's guess that she didn't want to explain how she came to have the charm. "But if it's so important, I'll bring it to the Eastway warehouse tonight as soon after darkfall as I can."

Fitch's whole body flooded with gratitude. "Thank you. I'll be there."

She turned and started away, the dog at her heels.

"You'll bring it?" he called.

She paused. "I said I would."

In Fitch's experience, people routinely said things they didn't mean. What could he do to be sure she'd show up? The girl started walking again. "What's wrong with your foot?" he called.

"I'm not used to being barefoot." She flushed. "This isn't the way I usually dress."

Thank the Trickster. He gestured toward a bench. "Sit down over there, and let me ease the soreness." He'd make her grateful and also take the chance to nudge her. Flexible principles, he thought again.

Her eyes narrowed. "I'm not going to tell you anything

about Lady Elenia."

"I'm not asking you to. I'm just offering Mage healing."

"You were doing more than that last night."

"Did I mention I have troublesome kin? One of them needed me to do that." He realized that he'd just admitted what she guessed was true. Gavun would have a fit if he knew. But Fitch needed her good will. "You have a long walk home. Let me take care of that foot."

Her eyes narrowed. "If I sense you doing it again, that's the last you'll see of me. I won't be pushed to do what I don't want."

Stone the girl. "All right. Sit. I promise I won't do anything without asking your leave." He'd have to settle for making her grateful.

She hobbled to the bench. "Asking my leave is all I really want, about pretty much anything," she said, her gaze on the *Storm King*.

Fitch picked up the foot she'd been limping on and examined the sole. The dog sniffed it, then licked a bruise. Fitch elbowed him aside.

"If you're going to heal me, don't you need a fire for me to look at?" she asked.

"Not really. For healing, I just need something for you to concentrate on so you let your guard down."

She jerked her foot out of his grip. "I am *not* letting my guard down for you. I don't even know you."

He had to admire how closely she had him pegged. "I

meant the way we all guard against other people. Haven't you ever been to a Hedge Mage before?"

"Not one who tried to make me give away a note. And I need to get home. Lady Elenia is waiting for me."

"I already promised I won't do what you don't want me to. Now concentrate on, let's see, the lighthouse on the breakwater." He reached for her foot, but she still drew it back. "You are the most untrusting girl I have ever met. Come on. I'm paying ahead of time for you bringing that charm."

The dog poked his nose at her foot. "Oh, all right." She let Fitch cradle her heel in his hand.

"Look at the lighthouse. Relax. Breathe deeply." When the girl obeyed, Fitch tried to slip his gift's healing energy into her bruised foot. He closed his eyes and waited but felt no gods-given rightness flow from him to her. Instead, he felt empty and found himself caught in the tide of her eagerness to get back to the Fortress. Behind him, a gull cawed as if in scorn.

"Is that it?" The girl pulled her foot away. "You're bad at this, and I have to go."

"Sorry. I'm usually better than that." For a moment, he stayed in his crouch at her feet. He wasn't just *usually* better than that. He *always* was. His gift was strong. The girl must have been resisting him. He stood when she did, shoving his hands in his pockets.

"Maybe you need to practice healing without taking advantage of people. Come, Tuc." She limped away.

"Tonight," he called. "The Eastway warehouse." He watched her and the dog until they turned up Caravan Street before he walked back to the *Storm King*. He didn't recognize the woman on watch, which probably meant she wouldn't recognize him either. That was good. The Eastways would get their backs up if they knew Gavun's boy was nosing into their business. He strolled up the gangway. "The girl who just left says she lost a knife that belongs to me," he told the sailor. "She had it when she came aboard. Can you check wherever she went for me? Or tell me, and I'll look."

"Bother the captain? Not on your life. Not on *my* life. Get its worth from the slut."

For a moment, Fitch wondered if he should tell the sailor the girl had picked his pocket, but in the end, his smugglers' blood stirred unhappily at the thought. Besides, she hadn't yet brought Nera's charm back. At least, he now knew Elenia was sending notes to the ship's captain. Gavun would know who that was and be pleased Fitch had found out. It was too early to visit the alehouses looking for the source of the spiked Fire. He'd deliver his news, get some sleep, and come back when they were open.

IT WAS BRISK on the bay and the *Sea Wind* scuttled across the water, sending spray into Fitch's face. He was hungry and irritated. When he'd got back to his dinghy, he found a Watchman bending over it, watching another toss around the ropes, oars, and other gear Fitch had tidily stowed. They'd ignored his protests, but eventually had to admit they'd found no contraband and left him to straighten up. The biggest loss was the secrecy of the landing place. Gavun had others, but it was still annoying.

Once again, he found a strange boat next to Gavun's on Rhale Island. The bruise on his stomach reminded him it was there, and he took a good look at the unfamiliar vessel but saw no guards or Watch insignia. He shrugged. Gavun always had visitors during Festival. People came from all around the Center Sea to cut deals. Right now, Gavun was probably cursing Fitch for not being there to sweeten his bargain. He climbed the steps and let himself into the house.

Gavun sat at the table, leaning forward so his head was inches from that of a second man whose back was to Fitch. They jerked apart when Fitch entered. The man turned, showing a handsome face marred by a scratch on his left cheek. Fitch stopped just inside the doorway waiting for Gavun to signal if he wanted Fitch to join the meeting.

"Fitch," Gavun said, "this is Cole of Eastway Island. Cole, this is my son, Fitch."

At the mention of Eastway, Fitch's attention sharpened. Maybe his father already knew which family Elenia's lover belonged to. How he could have found out, Fitch couldn't imagine, but Gavun had resources known only to himself.

Cole nodded to Fitch, then rose and picked his cap up off the table. "Let us know about joining us for the rest, Gavun." He nodded again to Fitch and left.

Fitch watched him until he started down the steps before he closed the door, softening the sound of waves. "What was that about?"

"A deal the Eastways are trying to work for themselves," Gavun said. "At the moment, I can't see how they'll pull it off. I'm always happy to make a sale, but now Cole's pressing for more." He shrugged, then scowled at Fitch. "It's about time you turned up."

"The Watch were searching the *Sea Wind* when I went back to it." As Gavun swore, Fitch went on. "I hadn't left anything on it, but we can't use that dock for a while."

Gavun swiped his hand down his face, then shrugged. "It can't be helped. It's not as if that's the first time. Where did that Mage go?"

Back to business, Fitch saw. "Home and then to the *Storm King*." Fitch jerked his thumb at the door through which Cole had vanished. "Their ship."

Gavun's eyebrows shot up.

"Is Cole their captain now?" Fitch asked. "Because if he is, Elenia is writing to him."

"Veren is captain."

Fitch tried to remember if he knew Veren and came up with a stiff-backed jerk maybe ten years older than himself. If he had the right man, he'd once seen Veren throw an Eastway cousin overboard into the filthy water at the docks. Lady Elenia had picked herself a real winner there.

Gavun rubbed his jaw. "I should have guessed. Veren's no fool. Of course he's the one romancing her. Wish I'd known that before I met with Cole."

"What are you talking about?"

Gavun drummed his fingers on the table. "You should like it. It's a way to get Suryan off our backs without blackmailing Elenia. I thought it sounded too risky. Your news changes the balance. I'll take a trip over to the *Storm King* and see what I can negotiate."

"How risky? I just told you the Watch is stirred up enough to search the marsh. What's more, those Fortress guards weren't fooling around last night, and I saw them arrest Mesti Sera on the street this morning."

"Suryan's just flinging threats he can't carry out. I'll make sure we're on the winning end of things. Don't be a baby."

Fitch blew out his breath and told himself not to rise to the bait. "Well, count me out. I have things to do." He circled the table and started toward the larder. "First, food and sleep."

"I need you to collect our takings at Festival tonight," Gavun called after him.

"I can't." He stuffed a chunk of cheese in his mouth and tore off a hunk of bread, too tired to make an actual sandwich. "I told you I want to nose around to find out who's feeding people Mage flower."

"Let this Mage flower craziness go, for gods' sake. You have work to do for the kinship."

"Loni can collect. He did a good job last night."

"I want Loni to deliver some goods."

Over his shoulder, Fitch glared at his father. This kind of thing was one reason he'd left. Infuriating him still further, he felt himself beginning to give way. Loyalty to the kinship apparently nested in his blood and bones in a way he hadn't appreciated until he'd spent time away. "All right. I'll go early and take some time to look around, too."

Gavun leaned back, nodding. "Good. I need you."

"To nudge people into paying more, you mean."

"No," Gavun said. When Fitch popped his lips in scorn, Gavun added, "Well, yes, but not just that. I need my heir. I need *you*."

Against his better judgment, Fitch felt a flash of gratification. *I am such an idiot.* "Let me know who to collect from," he said, starting down the hall, bread in hand. He'd do it after he reclaimed Nera's charm, of course. And while he was collecting money, he'd ask where people were getting Mage-flower-laced Fire.

# Chapter 7
## Dilly

CLUTCHING THE ORNATE iron railing, I dragged myself up the stairs, the marble cool under my sore foot. The Mage boy really wasn't good at healing. Tuc's claws clicked behind me. The guards at the gate and side door had at first seen only my rags and tried to bar me out. They'd recognized me eventually or, in one case, recognized Tuc, which put me in my not-entirely-certain place. Then I'd had to dodge around a swarm of their fellow guards I'd been surprised to see drilling in the side yard, like they expected an invading army. Tuc darted right through their lines, making an officer swear.

The Glass Chamber was empty and quiet, with patches of colored light flooding through the ceiling onto the pale wooden floor. The smell of winter roses drifted through the open balcony door. I stepped out and looked over the railing into Elenia's garden below. Through a screen of trees, I glimpsed blue, yellow, and green gowns. All the way home, I'd pictured Elenia reacting to Veren's message. She wouldn't want to wait. I limped down the spiral stairway and then cut across the soothingly damp grass. Tira, Nemay, and Jessa all sat on a bench near the fountain. Their heads swiveled toward me.

"Where's Lady Elenia? I have an answer from Veren."

"Shh." Tira tipped her head toward the other side of the fountain, and I saw what I hadn't spotted from above. On a bench next to Elenia sat Lord Suryan, his hair the same red as his daughter's, his face considerably more weather beaten.

Trickster save me. Maybe the splash of the fountain had drowned me out. If not, maybe I should just drown myself.

Elenia crossed her arms over her chest, and I saw her skirt twitch where she must be tapping her toe. Her voice rose. "It's my ship. I choose where it goes."

"You'll lose money," Suryan said.

I tried to shrink back toward the stairs, but Tuc pattered up to Suryan, and he lifted his gaze from the dog to me. Raising one eyebrow, he stood, so of course everyone else did too. As he came toward us, we all curtsied. I dropped my eyes as if that would somehow hide me. Instead polished shoes stopped on the patch of grass right in front of me. Tuc pressed against my leg, ears alert.

"What's this?" Suryan asked coolly.

"It's Dilly." Elenia surged forward to take her father's arm. "You remember."

"The pickpocket," Jessa purred.

"Nonsense." Elenia shot her a sharp look that warmed my heart. "She's dressed like this because we're making her a dust fairy costume for tonight's Festival. Very convincing, don't you think?"

Suryan kept quiet for a heartbeat too long. I had time to hear the gulls crying over the river beyond the Fortress wall. I looked up from under lowered lids to find him still eyeing me. "You know Captain Veren?" he asked me.

Small gods, he'd heard me blab that I had Veren's reply. I had no idea what to say, but Elenia saved me the trouble of answering. "No, she does not. Leave her alone, Papa. If you want to pick on someone about Veren, pick on me."

His hawk's gaze shifted from me to his daughter. I felt as if a weight had been lifted from my chest, leaving me free to catch a breath. "I am not *picking* on her, or on you either," Suryan said. "I am trying to save you and Lac's Holding a great deal of grief. Veren isn't fit to rule here, which means he's not a fit partner for my heir."

"*Fit to rule* means different things to different people." Elenia shrugged. "There are people who think I'm unfit. Besides if by *partner* you mean *husband*, I'm not planning to marry for a long time. Maybe never."

Thank the Trickster. Elenia marrying Veren would bring me much too close to Cole.

"Elenia, all I ask is that you stay away from him for a week or so while I carry out some investigations." Suryan's eyes swept over Nemay, Jessa, and Tira. "I now give you all the same warning I've given my daughter. Some of the Winter Fire on the streets last night was contaminated with an herb called Mage flower. This herb gets into your head and opens you to suggestions. Be careful what you drink." His gaze circled back to me. "And stay away from Veren."

I swallowed hard.

Elenia took her father's arm. "Veren had nothing to do with that. The Fire on the platform last night was fine, and that was Eastway's. His family has imported Fire for the Festival for years with no problems. He's not going to change that now."

"I can't yet prove his involvement one way or the other," Suryan said. "But I will tell you now, Elenia. I'm done tolerating the lawlessness of the island kinships. Their leaders think they're rulers of their own territories. I intend to show them they're not."

I thought about all the guards drilling in the yard. Was that why they were there?

"Veren's kinship doesn't smuggle," Elenia said. "Besides, doesn't legend say the small gods come from the islands? The kinships are the islands' keepers."

"They're criminals who evade paying what they owe," Suryan said.

Tuc went rigid. An instant later, the ground rumbled

and trembled under my feet. I staggered and groped for the back of the bench. Under the trees next to us stood an old-fashioned cairn to the small gods. The first time I'd come into the garden, Nemay told me the cairn had been there before the Fortress was built and, worried about intruding, Lac's Holding's new ruler had left it alone. The fist-sized rock on top shivered and rolled off. The ground steadied, but we all stared at the fallen rock.

"Small gods save us," Nemay whispered.

Suryan snorted. "It was just an earth tremor."

We all nodded as if we agreed.

"Take care at Festival tonight." Suryan kissed Elenia's cheek and departed through the gate to the yard, leaving silence behind.

As soon as he was gone, Elenia turned to me. "Dilly, what did Veren say?" The other women crowded close to hear, sending a cloud of perfume swirling around my head. Tuc sneezed.

"He wants to meet, but at his warehouse. He says you'll have privacy there."

"Ooh." Tira giggled. "Privacy."

"Hush," Elenia said, but she laughed too.

"Will you meet him?" Nemay asked.

"Of course," Elenia said as if Nemay had asked her if she meant to let her heart keep beating.

"Even after what your father said? He's right that islanders make trouble," Nemay said.

"Everybody makes trouble," Elenia said in the tone she

used when she came back from her father's weekly council meetings. "Papa's prejudiced against the islanders which, I have to say, is not *fit* for him as a ruler. They're our people too. And the Trickster enjoys a little lawbreaking. All the small gods do."

I looked sideways at the stone that had fallen from the cairn. That looked like a comment on Suryan's treatment of the islands to me.

"Prejudice is wrong," Tira said. "And Veren *is* quite good looking."

We all laughed again. Despite my doubts about a romance that meant being around Cole, I found myself enjoying the mutual womanly understanding, the kind I'd felt when it was just me and Mama. In Rin, my street friends had been boys.

"And he's interesting," Elenia said. "He's been everywhere. I can learn a lot from him."

"Ohh," Tira said, straight faced. "He's *interesting* and you're *learning*."

"Stop." Elenia grinned. "The question is how to do it. I'll have to give the guards the slip." She snapped her fingers. "One of you should go out wearing my costume. I'll wear something else."

I had to give Elenia credit. Mama might have said it takes one to know one, but to me, Elenia was a true Trickster's child.

"I'll go with you," I said. "I promised to meet someone there anyway." Four pairs of kohl-lined eyes turned my way.

"Meet someone?" Jessa said "Now where could you know him from? The docks?"

I bit back my denials. Letting them think I had a lover was better than explaining I was meeting the Hedge Mage because I picked his pocket. Besides, going with Elenia might give me another shot at prodding Veren to get rid of Cole.

"Leave her alone," Elenia said. "It's Festival."

Jessa smirked at me. "You should change your clothes, Dilly. And for gods' sake, put on shoes."

"Why are you barefoot?" Elenia frowned. "You could step on something sharp."

"Jessa said—" Tira started, then squealed and rubbed her arm. "Stop pinching me." She glared at Jessa.

On my way to the spiral staircase, I picked up the rock that had fallen and put it back on top of the cairn. My rich girl companions might feel safe in the hands of the gods. I did not.

I limped up the stairs and down the hall to my room, where I fished out what I'd taken from the sailor on the gangway at the *Storm King*. It turned out to be a tiny statue of the Trickster, mouth gaping with laughter. I made a face at her. *Aim that laugh at someone else, please.* I dropped it in my box along with the spool of scarlet thread I'd just picked up passing through the Glass Chamber and took out the shell pendant the Mage boy had given his dead girl.

It would be a lie to say I didn't know why I sympathized with him. When I ran into him, I'd just seen Cole, and Mama was fresh in my mind. I knew what it felt like when the person you loved most in the world died. I put the charm under my pillow, ready to take with me that night.

I touched the side of the lidded water pitcher, found it was warm, and filled the basin. I'd noticed that Tira never tested the temperature before she poured, but I still couldn't believe how servants brought hot water in throughout the day. I was thrusting my hands toward it when I spotted a dark line under my right index fingernail. Cole's blood, I realized, and found myself smiling like a savage. I decided to leave it there for a while as a kind of promise to myself. I dabbled my fingers carefully so as not to disturb it and changed into a gown made of wool soft enough to wrap a baby.

Back in the Glass Chamber, I found the other women turning over cushions and poking into drawers. Tuc flopped down for a nap in a patch of blue-tinted sunlight. "I can't imagine where I left it," Jessa said.

"You drop things wherever you are when you're done using them," Nemay said. "Aha!" She held up a spool of red thread she'd dug out of a chair.

"That's not it," Jessa said.

"It's red," I said.

"It's not what I'm using to embroider my vest," Jessa snapped. "I can't change color in the middle."

I sat down at the card table to enjoy watching. It felt surprisingly good to be once again, uh, removing things belonging to annoying people. Too bad no one here was likely to share my satisfaction. Elenia was humming a cheery tune though, so at least one person appreciated the results of something I'd done.

"Stone it," Jessa cursed.

And at least one person didn't. I hugged myself.

"It will turn up." With a yawn, Tira moved to the card table. "What shall we play?" She tapped the deck of Waterfall Cards against the table.

"I'm sick of cards," Nemay said. "Tell us a story, Dilly."

"Do." Elenia settled on a cushioned bench. "Make it romantic." Everyone else sat down too.

I was sorry to give up the search for the missing thread, but I wasn't in charge of the entertainment here. "All right. A romance." I gathered my thoughts.

With Mama and Cole on my mind, I knew romance could make people do things they regretted. Maybe this was a chance to slip in a warning about Veren without too much risk of annoying Elenia. Mostly it was Cole I was worried about, but Veren kept him around and that made a prickle run down my spine. "In the time of times," I started, "a woman from Lac's Holding fell in love with a sailor."

The women all laughed. "That is such a Lac's Holding beginning," Tira said. "Did he sail away and leave her?"

"No," I said. "He left Lac's Holding, but he took her with him."

"Didn't you already tell me this story?" Tira asked.

"Yes, but Lady Elenia hasn't heard it."

"I like it." Elenia leaned back. "She chose her own way, and she chose love."

"Like you, lady," Jessa said.

I strained my eyes trying not to roll them. "The problem was that once she was away from home, she had to rely on the sailor. And while love is sweet, it can be fleeting. She picked the wrong man, something every woman has to be careful of."

"Are you suggesting something about Veren?" Jessa asked.

Small gods curse her. I swear she could smell that I was trying to sneak a message to Elenia.

"I hope not," Elenia said sharply. "I won't be lectured by anyone about this."

"I meant nothing," I said hastily. "It's just a story." I should have kept my mouth shut. What would I do if Elenia threw me out? But then, what would I do if she chose to keep romancing Veren and I had to be around Cole?

Frowning, Elenia jumped to her feet. "Everyone help Jessa look for her lost thread."

I opened and closed a drawer, and decided I'd have to find a way to get rid of Cole on my own, the way I got rid of him in Rin City. After that, I'd feel a lot better about Elenia's future. And my own.

# Chapter 8

## Fitch

FITCH HAULED THE crate from the back storeroom down the steps to the dock. The awkward size made the wooden corners dig into his arms, but at least it was light. He handed it over to Gavun, who stowed it in the boat next to a second, identical box.

"I thought Loni took the small stuff over earlier," Fitch said. "What are you dealing?"

Gavun gave him an easy grin. "Extra special honestly imported goods. Get the line, will you." Fitch untied the rope on the dock and tossed it to his father. "Set up somewhere along Corsair Street," Gavun said. "Keep track of who shows up and how much they pay. Anyone who stiffs me tonight will be sorry." He hoisted sail.

Without waiting to see Gavun off, Fitch jogged back up to the house, ducked into his room, and gathered his

Mage gear. He needed to hurry. Gavun had kept him so busy all afternoon that he hadn't been able to get to town early the way he'd planned. He went back toward the front room, then jammed to a halt. The front door stood open and a slim woman stood silhouetted against the afternoon sun.

"Fitch?"

He took an uncertain step. "Who's asking?"

"Oh gods." She came far enough in that the banked fire in the hearth flickered over her red-gold hair and high cheekbones. "Don't you know me?"

Fitch dimly remembered being roused from his bed and urged down the same steep steps to the dock he's just been on. He'd been slow because Mama was carrying things, so she couldn't hold his hand, and he was afraid he might fall. At the dock, Mama lifted him into an unfamiliar boat and began to pull lines. He'd been enthralled by the idea of sailing at night. His father's shouts were the first confusing sign that things weren't right.

Mama had grabbed the oar to push against the dock, but Gavun leaped into the boat and snatched Fitch in a grip rough enough to pinch. Fitch had started to cry. "He's mine," Gavun shouted. "Blood of my blood. Rhale Island kin."

"You're not fit to raise a kitten," Mama shouted back.

Gavun handed Fitch off to Loni's papa on the dock, and Loni's papa carried Fitch up toward the house. Back at the dock, his parents screamed at one another.

"You and your kin and your gods-forsaken island," Mama cried. "No sane person could live here."

"Go," Gavun shouted. "I'm thrilled to be rid of you." Over his uncle's shoulder, Fitch saw Gavun jump from the boat to the dock. He saw the sail on the small boat fill with wind. He watched until its white glimmer vanished. He never saw his mother again.

Until now.

"Mama," he whispered.

"Look at you!" She was crying as she stumbled toward him. "You're taller than Gavun. I knew you would be." Her voice rang with satisfaction, as if she'd bested his father at something. He stood paralyzed as she put her hand up to touch her fingertip to his cheek. An unfamiliar warmth and possessiveness leapt from her hand like a spark. He jerked away. Healer help him. He was still as sensitive as he usually was right after he'd nudged someone.

Her hand fell. "What's wrong?"

"What are you doing here?" His own voice sounded far away. He felt as if he might be dreaming.

"I'm here for you, of course."

"Now? After all this time?"

Her smile faded. "I couldn't come before. We were living on the South Coast and I'd have had to make the crossing by myself. Besides, Gavun would never have let me near you. I wanted to come. More than anything. But I didn't dare."

"Are you telling me you're that scared of Gavun?" He took half a step back. "Did he hurt you?" Fitch couldn't believe it. Gavun had occasionally swatted him but had never used anything harder than the back of his hand. Yet what other reason could be strong enough to make his mother abandon him at age three? Unless she didn't care, of course. The pain of that made him inhale sharply.

"No. But everyone on this island hates me. You must know that." She shuddered. "I think the island itself does."

Fitch realized the feeling flooding his veins was rage, shocking in its strength. "In fourteen years, you couldn't manage to get a single word to me? You couldn't find *someone* Gavun wouldn't know to carry a message?"

Her brown eyes widened, and she reared back as if he'd slapped her. Her shock added fuel to his fury. How had she expected this meeting to go? "I thought hearing from me would just stir things up," she said. "I thought it would unsettle you."

"I used to imagine you turning up, maybe as a surprise on my name day." His voice thickened, and he looked away. In the scrub outside, he glimpsed a broad shouldered man facing the steps down to Gavun's dock. The man jiggled his left leg. Nervous. Keeping watch. "Who's he?"

"That's Brend."

Fitch squinted at the man. "I know him. He used to come around sometimes. He brought honey drops." *We* were living, his mother had said. He turned to her and jerked his head at Brend. "You didn't leave because you were scared of Gavun. You left because you wanted him." *More than you wanted me.*

She flushed. "I couldn't stay here. Rhale Island was sucking the life out of me." She swiped her fingertips under her eyes. "I was wrong. I made a mistake. I've made lots of mistakes, but none bigger than leaving you. Now I want to set things right. There's been a bit of trouble, and Brend and I are headed for the Dolyan Islands. We can hide there. I want you to come with us."

"What?"

"Come with us. Our boat is in that cove on the south shore. If we go now, we'll be long gone by the time Gavun realizes you're missing."

"I can't go with you. I don't even know you."

"You do! I'm the one who sang you to sleep, the one who kissed your scraped knees, the one who wouldn't let Gavun throw away that ratty stuffed dog you loved. What did you call it? Fofo, that was it."

Fitch had a sudden memory of the panic he'd felt when the toy went missing. "I don't remember," he lied, keeping his face blank.

A shadow fell across the floor. Brend had come to the doorway. In the years between Fitch's hazy memory of him and now, his wide shoulders had been weighed down by a round belly. "Fitch? I'm not sure I'd have known you. If you're coming, we should get going. We don't want any of your kin to spot us."

His deep voice stirred Fitch's instant resentment. The idea of being part of a *we* that included Brend made him want to punch someone.

His mother looked at Fitch beseechingly. "Fitch?"

Fitch shook his head, as much to try to straighten out his thoughts as to say no. "I can't." And yet, he knew he could. He'd already left Lac's Holding once. He could do it again and leave Gavun's boy behind. Was that what he wanted? He found he didn't know.

"Why not?" His mother's delicate features puckered. "I truly am sorry, Fitch. Can't you be even a little forgiving?"

"There's something I have to do." He needed time to think, and in any case, he couldn't go until he'd found Nera's poisoner. He grabbed onto that thought like a life buoy.

Her face lit up. "After that? How long will it take?"

"We can't stay here, Laell," Brend protested.

"Until Festival is over," Fitch said. He had to find the Mage flower supplier before then and do whatever he had to for Nera's sake. *Kill him?* whispered a voice in his head. If he had to, he told himself. After that, he might have to leave anyway. "Then maybe."

"We can stay that long," she said. "Gavun is always frantically busy during Festival. He won't have time to notice anything else."

"You won't tell him, right?" Brend asked Fitch. "That

way your mother can wait."

Fitch felt as if the man was once again distracting him with honey drops. He shook his head stiffly.

"We'll dock the *Escape* in town where all the visiting boats put up," his mother said quickly. "I'll be there, waiting. Come tonight, even if you haven't finished what you need to do. I have to see you again. This little corner of time isn't enough."

"I'll come if I can."

Before he could avoid it, she grabbed him in a hug. Her joy and hope flashed through him, startling in how welcome they felt. She pulled back, her hands on his shoulders. "I've dreamed of this day. I won't leave without you, Fitch. I won't do that again."

Brend put his hand on the small of her back and propelled her out the door. They ran around the side of the house to the path leading to the south shore. Fitch was left staring at the empty space where she'd been. He felt as if he were once again three years old, trying to understand what had happened.

# Chapter 9

## Dilly

I HELD STILL behind a set of steps, watching the other women go out the gate with two guards in tow. Darkness was deep enough between the circles of torchlight that I couldn't see them clearly, but I had to admit Jessa looked convincing in Elenia's Festival Queen costume and mask. Why not? As she showed me every chance she got, the woman thought herself entitled to a queen's treatment.

I caught myself looking around for Tuc before remembering we'd left him snoring loudly, full of sausage laced with Nemay's sleeping powder. I felt a little guilty, but knocking him out was the only way I could think of to leave without him, and since the guards had proved more likely to recognize him than me, his presence would have given us away at the gate.

Next to me, Elenia laughed softly. She was having a good time. I guessed life as a lord's daughter didn't present many chances for adventure, including slipping around to see a forbidden lover. I understood. I was grateful for life with Elenia, but a girl could take only so many afternoons playing cards and pretending to search for lost thread.

We waited until a knot of servants came out of the Fortress on the way to Festival adventures of their own. Elenia adjusted her mask, put up her hood, and led me out of the shadows to join them. I hitched up my boy's trousers and patted my pirate hat to make sure my hair was safely tucked underneath. At least no one tried to stop me from wearing shoes tonight. My heart sped as we crossed the dozen yards of cobblestones to the open front gates through which I could see the street gradually filling with Festival goers. Three guards were on the gates tonight rather than the usual two. I didn't know how they'd react if they realized Elenia was leaving a second time, but I was sure they'd at least report their confusion. Suryan might be inclined to blame the "pickpocket" for his daughter's escapade. At that point, adventure could turn into catastrophe, accompanied by a Trickster belly laugh.

"Gates will be locked at midnight," one of the guards announced.

Elenia turned as if to question him. I caught her arm, and a woman in a milkmaid costume saved Elenia from acting like the lord's daughter when she'd gone to such trouble to disguise herself. "Why?" the milkmaid asked.

"The crowds are restless," the guard said. "They say Winter Fire is flowing like high tide."

"It always is at Festival," the milkmaid said, "but you usually leave the gates open all night."

"The Fire is stronger this year," the guard said. "You be careful. Rumor is some of it is spiked."

Suryan hadn't issued any warnings about Mage flower to everyone then. Maybe he was hoping to trap whoever was contaminating the Fire.

As if sharing my thoughts, Elenia murmured, "Veren had nothing to do with that."

"Of course not," I said. Maybe it was even true. Elenia knew the man better than I did.

At Elenia's side, I plunged into the night beyond the gates. For a hundred yards, Elenia followed the crowd along the fancy apartment-lined street toward where music and a hubbub of voices marked the presence of Festival. Then she steered me into a deserted side-street leading down to the harbor.

As soon as we were by ourselves, Elenia let out a long breath ending in a laugh. "We did it!" she crowed, taking my arm. "You are a brave and useful girl."

Now that my heart was slowing to its normal rate, I had room to feel warmth at the praise and affectionate touch. Mama used to take my arm like that when she was gleefully excited too. I prodded Elenia into the middle of the dark street where we'd be harder to reach if anyone lurked in the inky shadows between the torches on the buildings.

"So you saw Veren," Elenia said. "What did you think? You have to admit he's good looking, but then all those Eastway men are. Still, what really strikes me about him is how wide his vision is. He's not going to captain a single ship all his life. He'll need a fleet to carry out the kind of trade he has in mind. And what he wants will make Lac's Holding even more prosperous. He's the one who set up that grain shipment I sent to sea. He knew of someplace where there'd been a blight, and said I could make a great deal of coin."

"Lord Suryan stopped it, I think?" I spoke cautiously. I didn't want to get between two people looking for a bit of power over one another. Even – especially? – if they were parent and child.

"He tried, but Veren had my authorization." She shook my arm. "He is not a *wrong* man."

My heart jumped again. I never should have told that story. "I'm sorry. It's not really my business." Except for Cole.

"No, it's not," Elenia said.

Right. I would never, ever criticize Veren again. Not out loud anyway.

Elenia led me along the deserted docks to where the *Storm King* sat, looking abandoned. As Elenia reached the warehouse kitty-corner from it, a figure emerged from the shadows. Even before he was fully in the light of the lantern hanging by the door, the self-satisfied tilt of his head told me it was Cole. I'd spent too much time watching his every move to mistake him. I couldn't help stiffening.

"Fair evening, lady." Cole's teeth flashed. "I see you brought a friend." He raised an eyebrow, looking for all the world as if he'd never met me before. It occurred to me he was mighty sure I hadn't told Elenia about him. Since this was Cole, he probably thought he'd charmed me into it. I controlled the urge to shove him against the side of the building.

"This is Dilly." Elenia pulled off her mask. "She's my chaperone." Elenia grinned over her shoulder at me. "In case I run into the wrong man."

The woman knew how to hold a grudge.

"The captain is waiting." Cole opened the warehouse door and gestured Elenia inside.

Tugging my own mask off, I followed her. I hadn't asked if Elenia wanted me to stay with her, but I meant to keep watch over her and also see if I could find a lever to pry Cole loose. He escorted Elenia across a huge room, half full of barrels of what I guessed was Winter Fire, then rapped on a door and opened it. Elenia swept in. I reached the doorway in time to see her step into Veren's embrace. In the room behind him squatted a polished wooden desk, a rack of charts, and an ornately carved bench piled with cushions.

"Ah love," Veren said. "I've been waiting."

Cole backed into the big storeroom and flicked his

finger at me, telling me to move from the doorway. Instead, I darted into the office. "Where would you like me to wait for you, lady?"

Elenia gave an exasperated click of her tongue. I cringed.

"You don't have to loiter here," Veren said. He let go of Elenia long enough to push me toward the door, making me stumble. I braced my hand against his chest, my fingers brushing his captain's pin and, well, he shouldn't have pushed me. "Cole volunteered to take you to Festival," he said. Maybe I'd grown too skittish in Rin, but I was sure there was an edge of menace in Veren's voice when he turned me over to Cole. My chest tightened. I'd vowed long ago never to be alone with Cole again.

"Go on to Festival, Dilly," Elenia said. "Didn't you say you were meeting someone?"

"Talking to him will only take a moment. Other than that, I can sit right outside this door."

Elenia frowned, and Veren exchanged a look with Cole. I was suddenly certain Cole had told Veren about me and Mama. Or told him some version of it anyway, and Veren believed that version over what I'd told him that morning, a sign he trusted his cousin in a way I didn't like. In my head, I heard Veren saying Cole always need money. Would he believe Cole stole from him? Like, stole a captain's pin in order to sell it? I would, and I was a pickpocket, so you might say I knew the type inside and out. Opportunity was knocking. All I had to do was make sure Veren found the pin in Cole's possession.

"Cole will take care of you, Dilly," Veren said. "I'll get your lady home safely."

Cole grabbed my arm, and my brain melted into panic. He dragged me out, closing Elenia in with Veren.

I yanked free, gagging at the smell of his hair oil. For a moment, I thought I might vomit. "Get away from me."

"My captain just told me to escort you to Festival. Don't be like this, Dilly." Cole raised both hands as if that would convince me he'd never touch me again and maybe that I was mistaken in thinking he ever had. "Surely you don't think Elenia needs you to guard her. She's an adult making her own choices. And she and Veren are in love."

"You and Mama were in love too. Or she was, anyway."

He smiled his polecat smile. "The difference is Veren plans to marry Elenia."

My breath caught. Was that true? Was this more than a romantic game to Elenia? Surely not. If she tied herself – and me – permanently to Veren, she'd tie us both to Cole too. Any regret I'd had about taking Veren's captain's pin fell down a deep well. "I don't believe you. She talks about him all the time, but I've never heard her say she'd marry him. Lord Suryan would object. He doesn't even want her *writing* to Veren."

Cole cocked his head. "Are you claiming Suryan has the right to decide who his daughter marries? That's not the Lac's Holding way, and you know it." He stepped closer. My heart kicked at my ribs, and I fought the urge to pound on the office door and demand Elenia come out. "But I'll tell you what, Dilly. If you foul up Veren's plans, he'll make you regret it. Elenia probably will too. He's not forcing her. She wants what he's giving her. Suryan's objection is probably part of the attraction."

I struggled for enough breath to say, "Women get forced in a lot of different ways."

"*People* get forced. Don't believe anyone who tells you different." He leaned in so I felt his breath on my cheek. "But your mother chose."

"I didn't." I whirled away from him and ran for outside with his quick step right behind me. I slapped my hand on the door and shoved. A nail on my right hand still had Cole's blood under it. What a joke it was to think that showed I was fierce. To my shame, I'd been too afraid even to touch Cole and plant Veren's pin.

# Chapter 10

## Fitch

FITCH HURRIED TOWARD the Eastway warehouse, his mind churning with his mother's reappearance. He couldn't seem to put together a single thought that didn't go crooked before he finished it. He'd grown up without her, grown used to her absence, been sure he didn't need her. He'd have sworn he was too small when she left even to have clear memories. But that mental glimpse of a stuffed dog meant he'd maybe just tucked them in a dark hole because it hurt too much to look at them. Some part of himself must be tangled up with her, the same way part of him was tangled up with Gavun. And now she wanted him to go with her.

With an effort, he shut down the storm in his head. When he reached the warehouse though, she hadn't shown. He let his simmering anger flare, glad of a new target. The stoning girl had lied to him when she said she'd be there.

The warehouse door burst open, and a boy in a pirate's hat surged out with a man chasing him. "Dilly, wait," the man called.

Fitch narrowed his eyes. Not a boy. A girl. The butterfly girl, whose name was apparently Dilly, pursued by Cole, the man who'd been meeting with Gavun this morning. Ignoring Cole's plea, she rushed out, nearly ramming Fitch. When she skidded to a stop, Cole caught up.

"Don't go wandering around by yourself, Dilly. Let me keep you company."

Fitch had never heard *keep you company* sound like a threat before. Judging by the way she hunched her shoulders, the girl felt the same way. "Fair evening, Cole," Fitch said coolly. "You're not bothering Dilly, are you?"

Cole looked quickly back and forth between them. "Of course not. It's Fitch, right?"

Fitch could almost hear the questions sailing through Cole's head. Cole had proposed some scheme to Gavun, who'd then visited the Eastways, trying to work a better deal for himself. Was Fitch's presence part of some sly move to boost Gavun's part of the bargain? He was enough his father's son to enjoy the other man's confusion.

"Gavun sends his regards. Is there anything you'd like me to tell him?" Fitch tried to make *regards* sound even more ominous than *keep you company*, and must have succeeded because Cole stiffened and shook his head. "Come on, Dilly," he said. She took the arm Fitch offered, and he knew he'd judged Cole rightly because, in what seemed to be his permanent post-nudge state, her fear was strong enough to kick at his heart.

As he strolled away with the girl, a glance over his shoulder showed Cole watching them, rubbing his mouth. Fitch hoped he hadn't blown a hole through one of his father's schemes, but if Gavun wanted Fitch to tread lightly somewhere, he should have shared his plans.

He turned Dilly up Caravan Street, and as soon as they were out of Cole's sight, he freed his arm from her touch. He had enough unhappy emotions of his own tonight without inviting the washback of hers.

"Thank you. I hate that man," Dilly said.

"I gathered that. What did he do?"

Her voice was hard. "Romanced my mother and then left her to die on her own in Rin City."

He cringed. "I'm sorry." The thought of his own mother slipped from the corner he'd shoved it in. People left. Who knew why?

Dilly took a deep breath, then fumbled in the pocket of her boy's trousers. "I brought it, like I promised." She held out Nera's pendant.

Hand trembling, he stowed it in his shirt pocket, then cleared his throat. "Where can I take you?" Needling Cole had been satisfying, but obviously he couldn't just leave her here. The few torches along Caravan Street left large pools of darkness, and only two people meandered ahead of them, doubtless on their way to Festival.

She bit her lower lip. "I guess I should go home." She looked wistfully toward where music and lights rolled over the rooftops.

"Don't be silly. Let me take you to Festival. I have to work, but maybe there's someone you know there who I can leave you with?" Memories of their last meeting made him grin and add, "Elenia, maybe?"

"I'm not telling you anything about what Lady Elenia is doing."

He tried not to look smug. "I already know that, more or less."

She put her hands on her hips. "How?"

He grinned again. "I'm not telling you anything," he echoed.

Her mouth quirked. "Then we'll have a quiet walk. I'm not saying where Elenia is, mind you, but her other attendants are at Festival. Maybe we can find them." She pulled off her pirate's hat and shook her red curls loose. "I do hate to miss Festival."

In the dark street, the lights of an alehouse pierced the night as the door opened and a group of shouting men spilled out. Fitch put himself between them and Dilly just as one of them took a swing at another. He missed, but his momentum carried him into Fitch, who pushed him away. The man whirled, fists already punching at the air, as if to search for this new enemy. The men around him jeered. With a roar, he lowered his head and charged.

Fitch stepped aside, realizing too late that the man was heading straight for Dilly. As she skipped back, Fitch lunged, and the man went down with Fitch on his back, grabbing at his carry bag at the last instant to keep it from crashing to the cobbles. The man's friends groaned, while Dilly shouted, "Stop!"

Enough was enough, Fitch thought. He shoved the man's shirt collar aside and pressed his hand directly against the skin of the man's neck. He sharpened his focus and probed for some feeling, some wisp of thought he could nudge in the direction of calm. A whirl of emotions washed back through his touch. Anger, fear, desire flickered into being, then blew away into blackness, taking Fitch's feelings with them. It was as if a riptide was dragging him under. Panic choked him. Which part of this was his?

"Fitch!" a girl shouted. "Stop."

He yanked his hand back. The man under him went limp. He rolled off the man's back and lay on the cobblestones, staring up at stars that seemed to move farther away, then closer, then farther again. A girl bent over him. The one who shouted maybe. He blinked. Dilly.

"Are you all right?" she asked.

"I think so."

In the distance, at least two Watch members blew their whistles. The other men who'd been fighting were fleeing into the dark, which Fitch reckoned was what he and Dilly should do too. Fitch staggered to his feet, tried to bend to check on the unconscious man, and had to brace his hands on his knees to keep from falling over. The man reeked of spiked Fire.

Dilly held her hand under the man's nose. "He's breathing," she said.

A Watch whistle sounded in the next street.

"Let's go," Fitch said.

"He's hurt."

Fitch grabbed the pleated back of her pirate shirt and towed her into a side street. Away from the man, she gave in, faced forward, and ran at Fitch's side, Fitch certain at every step that he was about to trip over his own boots. His brain still felt blurred from trying to nudge the Mage flower addled man.

Where the side street ran back onto Corsair, he gestured toward a café. "I need to sit for a moment. Everyone passes this corner. We can watch for your friends." He collapsed into a chair as Dilly settled across from him, breathing heavily. Without waiting for an order, a waiter dropped mugs of Winter Fire in front of them and rushed away. Good guess, Fitch thought. He sniffed the drink which seemed clean enough. "This is all right, but some of the Fire is spiked with an herb called Mage flower."

"So I heard." She raised an eyebrow. "What do you know about it, *Mage*?"

"You think I'd give that poison to someone?" She drew back in her chair, and he realized his voice had been sharper than he meant. He licked his lips. "I'd never use it."

"Because you don't need it, you mean. You think I don't know what you tried to do with that man back there? You tried it on me, remember? I know what it looks like."

"I didn't damage that man. Mage flower did. I was trying to *help* him."

"Is there a difference between muddling someone's thinking with an herb and doing it with Magery?"

He opened his mouth but found he had no answer. "The Watch will get him some help." Assuming something *could* help the mess in that man's head. He shuddered.

He took a drink, the fruity taste bursting to life on his tongue, and mentally crossed this café off the list of places he'd ask about their Fire supplier. He'd go back to that alehouse where the mush-brained man had collapsed though, as soon as he got rid of Dilly.

He dragged his fingers through his hair. "What a night. Before I met you, my mother turned up for the first time since I was three." He frowned at passers-by, celebrating a yard away. Celebrating was probably easier if you hadn't just poked into the head of a man who'd gone brain soft. Judging by the way he was now emptying his own head out for Dilly's inspection, the encounter had shaken him even more than he'd realized.

"Small gods." Dilly took a drink. When she set her

mug down, she caught the edge of the table and slopped Fire onto a floor already pockmarked with puddles. "That would be… hard to take in."

"That's one way to put it. She wants me to go with her when she leaves again."

For a handful of heartbeats, Dilly watched the crowd. "That's a big decision." She swirled her drink so flecks of lantern light shimmered on the surface. "You might think about it. The islands could be unsafe if Lord Suryan gets sick of smugglers."

His gaze snapped up from the table. "D'you know something *I* should know?"

She stood up. "I'm trying to be friends and now you're prying"

He jumped up, slapped coins onto the table, and followed her to the street. "I didn't ask anything about Elenia." She kept marching. He hissed in exasperation. "If you don't want to stay with me, I understand. I have work to do anyway. But you shouldn't be by yourself." Nera had died alone, the way Dilly said her mother had. If he'd been with Nera, his life might be different now. "Is there some place in particular the other attendants are likely to be?"

She thought a moment. "Maybe the music stand on Merchant Street. Nemay was talking about that." She grimaced. "I didn't mean to be touchy, but I had a bad time in Rin. It's nice to have someone worry about me for a change."

Fitch pointed her in the right direction, still

wondering what she'd meant by Suryan getting tired of smugglers. Unless he pried into her head, though, she would tell him nothing. He had to admit he was tempted, but he found he wasn't ruthless enough to do it. Maybe he wasn't totally Gavun's boy. Not yet, anyway.

And sure enough, she kept a foot away from him as they walked in silence among Festival goers from all around the Center Sea. A pair of women tossed juggling balls back and forth. A man with multiple braids piped a song Fitch had first heard a hundred miles away.

"You know Cole, I take it," Dilly finally said. "Do you know Captain Veren too?"

"I don't really know either of them. Just the Eastway reputation." He reminded himself she served Elenia. Maybe he wasn't the only one fishing for information.

"Is the Eastway reputation good? Are they trustworthy?"

Into his head popped a picture of the Mage he'd followed to the *Storm King*. The man had genuinely feared Veren might kill him if he talked. "I've always heard they were pretty straight arrow, but I wouldn't want to get on Veren's bad side."

Ten yards ahead, he spotted a figure he recognized despite the Watch uniform and mask. His father had been wearing the stolen uniform as a costume when he left Rhale Island. Fitch was sure Gavun thought it was clever. He was equally sure the real Watch would disagree. Forcibly. As Fitch watched, Gavun pulled a pouch out of his carry bag and slid it over a window counter, where it was immediately scooped out of sight. Gavun turned and walked down the street, his back to Fitch.

Long experience with his father made Fitch freeze. That plus the quick way the merchant tucked Gavun's goods away. Suspicion he couldn't quite kill flared to life. Obviously, Gavun hadn't been delivering a barrel of anything, but what if Mage flower was added to the Winter Fire *after* it was in the barrel? Delivered as an herb, it wouldn't take much space, and there were ways to breach a barrel.

"Something the matter?" Dilly asked.

*Careful*, Fitch reminded himself. Who knew what she'd pass on to Lord Suryan or his daughter? "I don't know. Wait here, and I'll find out." He approached the booth where Gavun had lingered. The scent of exotic pipe fillers spilled out from behind the counter. Fitch recognized the tall, skinny proprietor. "Fair evening, Donyn."

"Fitch! I heard you were back. Your father was just here." Donyn waved a hand in the direction Gavun had gone.

"I'm sorry I missed him," Fitch lied. He laid his hand on his own carry bag and spoke low. "I thought I was supposed to deliver to you though. Did Gavun give you all you ordered?"

"I haven't looked yet." Donyn pulled the pouch from a shelf under the counter and loosened the drawstring.

"Seems like it." He shook a few flakes onto his palm.

Fitch knew right away it wasn't what he was worried about. The knot in his chest loosened. He shouldn't have doubted. Loni wasn't a fool, and he'd told Fitch the Mage flower wasn't theirs.

"This stuff comes from halfway around the world," Donyn said with awe in his voice. "Even Gavun charges a tower an ounce for it, and of course that's without the tariff we're supposed to pay Suryan. Curse him." He tucked the pouch away. "I'm glad you stopped by." He opened a cash box, counted out towers and handed them to Fitch. "You've saved me the trouble of hunting you down later."

Fitch dropped the coins into his bag rather than mix them with what was in his pocket. Gavun always kept delivery of his goods separate from payment on the theory that it made his smuggling less obvious. Fitch had found keeping his own money separate from his father's was also a good idea. He turned to find Dilly's just a yard behind him.

"Is your father in charge of a kinship?" she asked.

"Yes." Fitch saw no point in lying. Everybody knew Gavun.

She shifted her weight. "Like I said, maybe you should think about going with your mother."

"That's the second time you've suggested that. As you say, it's nice to have someone worry about me, but what are you trying to tell me?"

She shook her head and marched away.

They turned into Merchant Street, but the crowd seemed to be swirling around some obstacle. The people in front of them parted, and he saw a man set his bag down and bend over a woman sprawled on the pavement.

Next to him, Dilly let out a cry. "Tira!" She rushed to the woman's side and dropped to her knees. The woman lolled, loose-limbed, unconscious, and smelling of spiked Fire.

Fitch's heart clutched, and once again he saw Nera's body on the beach. He grabbed the arm of the man bending over her. "Did you give it to her? Who did you get it from?" He closed his other hand around the man's throat and tried to reach into the man's mind and rip out the answer. Terror from the man's head washed back over Fitch. The man gagged and clutched at Fitch's fingers. Fitch's bag slid off his shoulder. He heard his glass globe shatter.

"Tira, talk to me." Dilly slapped the woman on either cheek. "Fitch, can you help her?"

The man yanked loose and bolted into the crowd. Fitch cursed, but the woman came before the Fire seller. He crouched next to the collapsed Tira, wiping his palms on his thighs. When he gripped Tira's hands, they lay in his like dead sea creatures. She was so deeply unconscious that he felt no emotion from her at all. She was worse off than the man he'd fought with earlier. He tried to send healing warmth, a simple sense of comfort and ease, one of the first things his Mage training had taught him, but her body felt closed to him.

"Can you do anything?" Dilly clutched his shoulder, sending her fear flooding into him. "If you can't, we need to get her to the Fortress. There's a doctor there."

"I can do it," he said, resenting the implied insult.

"I don't think you can. Let's go."

Reluctantly, he rose, dragged Tira to her feet, and drew one of her arms around his neck, but she slumped against him, and he wound up having to pick her up. How could he have failed to send even warmth? "Grab my bag," he called over his shoulder. His globe was likely in shards, but there was a chunk of Gavun's money in that bag. He started for the Fortress with Dilly scrambling after him. Healer help him, Fitch thought, his gut twisting. Nothing like deliberately going into the Fortress.

# Chapter 11

## Dilly

"GET OUT OF the way," I shouted. Ahead of me, Fitch slithered between the people crowding Corsair Street with Tira in his arms. Silhouetted against the rising moon, the Fortress loomed at the end of the street, but it seemed miles away. I'd expected folks to be going the other way, back toward the music stand and alehouses and cafes, but most people drifted along the same way Fitch and I had to go. Staggering and pushing, they clogged our path.

"Who you telling to get out of the way?" A woman shouldered me aside. "We got as much right as anyone to be here."

"My friend is sick. Too much Fire." I gestured ahead at Fitch and Tira, her head bobbing on his shoulder like a puppet with cut strings. My chest swelled with fear for her but also with fury. How could she have been so foolish after Lord Suryan warned us?

"Oh honey, everybody's had too much Fire." The woman laughed shrilly. "It's Festival."

Someone to my right shouted, "Winter Fire is king! Winter Fire is king!"

The woman who shoved me took up the chant. "Winter Fire is king."

I slipped past her and caught up with Fitch. Two men blocked his way with their arms around one another's shoulders. They chanted in clashing cadence. "The Watch are thieves, thieves, thieves."

I glimpsed a black and gold uniform: a Watchman shoving with his lowered wooden stave. "Back off," he shouted. "Go home or back to Festival. Anyone still here will be arrested."

One of the chanting men moved his arm, and a knife flashed in his hand. The Watchman swung his stave, and the knife wielder staggered. The woman next to him shrieked as his blade cut across her sleeve. Screaming people pressed out of the way, bumping me so I almost fell. My already thumping heart drummed faster as I pictured myself under the feet of the crowd.

Fitch looked back, face grim. "This is dangerous. Can you go ahead and open the way for me?"

I slung the strap of his bag across my chest, where it tangled in my loose hair, then slid in front of him. "We have a sick woman," I shouted. "Let us through."

We scuttled out of range of the Watchman's stave, but now the crowd was picking up speed and carrying us along. A boy stood on the edge of the road shouting. "Suryan is a thief. He makes us pay for his army and fight in it too." The crowd swept us past him. I couldn't have stopped if I wanted to, not without being trampled by the people behind me.

An ugly murmur ran through the crowd and burst aloud into—"Suryan is a thief, thief, thief."

Fitch pushed up next to me. "They're going to the Fortress," he shouted over the noise. "The guards won't be playing around. Where else can we take her?"

I looked back. The crowd filled the road for the score of yards I could see in the dark. "We can't go back. We'd never get through." Apartment buildings lined the left side of the road shoulder to shoulder, torches flaming over each door. I grabbed one latch and pulled, but it was locked. At this time of night, they probably all were. A solid river of people penned us in from the right. "There's nowhere else."

"What?" He leaned his head closer, trying to hear.

"She needs the Fortress doctor. The gate guards know me. They'll let us in." I hoped. I put a hand on Fitch to push him toward a gap. The muscles in his back were trembling. "Is she too heavy?"

"No." He tightened his mouth and hefted Tira into a more secure grip. "I can't avoid bumping people, and I feel their anger and fear. I'm trying to block myself off but there are too many of them."

"Small gods. Hang on." When I looked ahead, I realized we'd reached the place where the road opened into the square in front of the Fortress gates. Over the heads of the crowd, I saw they were shut. They felt immensely far away. The mob poured into the space, packing tighter against one another. People in the front flung themselves against the gates. "Thief, thief."

"We'll never get through," Fitch said. "And the guards would be fools to open for us and risk letting the crowd in." A muscle jumped under his ear. If he hadn't told me he felt what the crowd did, I wouldn't have noticed. No surprise he was struggling. If I'd had other people's fear added to mine, I wouldn't be standing, much less carrying an adult woman.

I could see guards on the wall looking down, crossbows in their hands but not yet raised. The thought of those bolts being fired into the crowd made me dizzy. The square smelled of danger.

"Is there another way?" Fitch asked.

Before I could answer, new voices cried, "Back, back!"

I had to stand on tiptoes to see them, but Fortress guards were streaming around the corner of the building, flowing along the base of the Fortress wall. All of them carried staves and all of them swung the staves freely, sending people screaming and reeling. The crowd retreated toward us. A man reeking of Mage flower stomped on my foot, making me cry out. I couldn't hear

Fitch swallow over the shouting people around us, but I saw his throat convulse.

"Left," I pointed Fitch. "Where the guards are coming from. There's a postern gate." Arms extended to shelter Tira, I herded him along the edge of the square until the crowd was too packed to let us move. I scrambled up onto the base of a statue of Suryan's father, Lac. Fitch turned so Tira was between him and the statue's base. Driven by staves and panic, the crowd shoved past him, jostling him. He flinched and clamped his mouth shut. His shoulders heaved with his breath.

From my perch a yard in the air, I saw guards still swinging at everybody they passed. A man fell and vanished under pounding feet. Then a few yards away, I spotted Captain Jaf as he let a woman go but brained the man next to her. I waved my arms, calling, "Captain Jaf! It's me, Dilly, with Tira. Help us. Tira is hurt."

He squinted my way and started toward me.

"Dilly, I'm worried I might drop her," Fitch said through clenched teeth.

I glanced down and saw what looked like shame in his flushed face. I jumped to the ground. "Put her down."

"She'll be trampled."

"I'll keep them off, and a guard is coming to help. Leave."

His breath came in great heaves. "Are you sure?"

"Go."

For a moment, I feared he wouldn't do it. Then he

said, "I'm so sorry." He set Tira down and eeled his way along the edge of the square, using his elbows to ward people off. I put myself between Tira and the crowd. A running man brushed too close and shoved me so I lurched to my knees, catching myself on spread arms so as not to land on Tira. Someone stepped on my hand, sending pain knifing through it. The man tripped and went sprawling. A swarm of people tried to claw their way over the top of his flattened body. A booted foot crushed his cheek. Another one stepped on his arm and snapped it. I screamed, but the noise was swallowed by the people jammed around me. As I staggered to my feet, I was crying.

"Thought you were a boy until I saw your hair." Captain Jaf handed me his stave, picked up Tira, and lumbered toward the side of the Fortress. Still gasping with tears, I ran to get ahead of him, swinging the stave as I'd seen the guards do. I clouted one man in the ribs. He cried out, and I cringed. *I didn't break a bone, did I?* The crowd shriveled as the guards chased people back down the road to town. Fallen people moaned on the cobblestones. I followed the narrow path along the base of the wall until I reached the postern gate, but the latch held firm. I looked around wildly for Jaf, who'd been slower with Tira to maneuver.

"Open for a guard captain," Jaf bellowed.

The latch rattled, and the gate inched open. I flung my shoulder against it and tumbled into the arms of the guard manning it. Captain Jaf came right behind. "Lock up," he ordered. He forged through a side door and up two sets of stairs.

I followed, my knees so weak with relief that I had to cling to the banister. It was like my body couldn't believe my danger was over, that I'd escaped with just a bruised hand after seeing what had happened to that man who fell. I thought he was dead. He looked dead.

I flung open the door to Elenia's quarters, and Jaf carried Tira in. Nemay and Jessa were there, Nemay still in her costume and Jessa still in Elenia's. They jumped to their feet when I burst in followed by Captain Jaf. Tuc rushed to greet me, tail wagging furiously. I felt an instant of gratitude at how thrilled the dog was to see me even after I'd betrayed him with drugged sausage. I didn't deserve him.

"This way, Captain." I ran toward the room Tira and I shared. "Send for the doctor," I called over my shoulder. Jaf laid Tira on the bed I pointed to. I handed him his stave. "Thank you. You can go." It felt astonishingly good to be giving orders. I felt like I was turning a terrifying chaos back into the tidy life I'd grown used to in the Fortress, like maybe the dead man outside was something I imagined.

Captain Jaf hesitated. "I'll have to tell Lord Suryan about this. I'll speak to Lady Elenia first, of course."

"Elenia's not here just now," Nemay said as she entered the room. "We'll tell her." Captain Jaf looked skeptical but left, probably planning to go straight to Suryan. "What happened?" Nemay pulled Tira's mask over her head and undid the buttons on her costume.

"A man was trampled to death." I heard my voice shake, and I had trouble gripping the knob on the lamp to turn it up.

She glanced at me, brows drawn down. "I'm sorry. What happened to Tira?"

"I don't know. Wasn't she with you?" Indescribably glad to have something useful to do, I bent to help drag Tira's dress over her head and realized I still had Fitch's bag slung across my chest. I dumped it next to the bed. I'd have to figure out how to get it back to him later. I worked Tira's high heeled shoes off and threw them on top of the bag. Tuc sniffed at the pile.

"She was meeting someone," Nemay said. "I assumed it was her man. Or one of them. You know Tira."

"She was a fool tonight," I said. "We found her collapsed like this."

"You and Elenia? Where is she?"

"I left her with Veren. Thank the small gods. At least she's safe there." *Safe like Mama was with Cole maybe.*

Jessa hustled in, accompanied by the plump Fortress doctor, whose name I couldn't recall. He bent over Tira, inhaled, and grimaced. From his bag, he pulled a vial of greenish liquid that he handed to Jessa. "Mix that with an equal amount of water."

I grabbed the jug and cup on the bedside table, and

after Jessa poured the green stuff in, I diluted it and gave it to the doctor. "Will that bring her around?"

"Depends on how much Mage flower she had," the doctor said. "It was clearly more than it takes just to make a person pliable. Enough of it can wipe your mind out for a while, or even permanently."

A chill slid down my spine. Lord Suryan hadn't told us that. Maybe I got ahead of myself when I thought I left danger behind.

The doctor held Tira's head up and trickled the medicine into her slack mouth. Some of it ran down her chin, and I caught myself wiping my own tickling chin though it was dry. I heard footsteps in the hall and turned in relief, expecting to see Elenia, but it was Lord Suryan who entered. Suddenly the room was too crowded. I curtsied as best I could in trousers and tried to slip behind Nemay.

The doctor looked up from his work. "Mage flower."

Lord Suryan swore. "I called all the guards in from the outskirts, and everyone I can spare is helping the customs people stop it in the harbor. The Watch are trying to control it in the streets but it's as unstoppable as the tide. The island kinships just thumb their noses at me. I've had enough." He scowled at the death-pale Tira. "I warned her, and she drank it anyway. I'm not sure I want her around my daughter."

The threat his words implied sent a shudder through me. At least Tira had a family to go to.

The doctor propped Tira's head up with pillows. "I'll be back in the morning. Someone should stay with her in case she vomits."

"I'll be here," I said.

The doctor left. The rest of us looked at Tira's pale and sweating face. Even Tuc put his front paws on the bed and studied her.

Lord Suryan stirred and scanned the room. "Where's Elenia?"

My breath caught. The floor creaked as Nemay and Jessa both shifted their weight.

"I asked a question," Suryan snapped. "Where is she? I assume you all went to Festival with her. Keeping her company is your function." His gaze landed on Jessa, wearing Elenia's Festival Queen costume. "Where did you leave her?"

Jessa raised an eyebrow at me. "Dilly?"

Curse Jessa anyway. My mouth was sand dry. "I was the only one with her. She hasn't come back yet."

Lord Suryan seemed to grow even taller. "Are you telling me she's still at Festival? By herself? People are being trampled, not fifty feet from the Fortress gates. Could she be caught in the mob?"

"No." *Though I was. Thank you for asking.* "She never went to Festival."

"Then where is she?" He bit off each word.

My stomach flipped over. I tried frantically to think of what I could say that would reassure Suryan but not betray

Elenia.

Suryan's eyes narrowed. "Never mind. I know where she is." He raked his eyes over us, even Tira. "You have all failed her. You have failed me. If I didn't have more trust in the guards than you, I'd make you all go out and bring her home." He stalked from the room.

I collapsed to sit on my own bed and was grateful when Tuc jumped into my lap. I looked up at Nemay and Jessa. "It's Lac's Holding. Elenia has a right to choose her own man."

Nemay grimaced. "Only if Suryan says she does."

"You were supposed to stay with Elenia," Jessa said. "Why did you leave her, Dilly? This is your fault."

Old guilt sprang to life in my heart. "She told me to leave."

"You abandoned her."

"That's enough, Jessa," Nemay said. "Out." She steered Jessa out of the room, following on her heels.

I stroked Tuc, allowing his warmth to erase the vision of the trampled man. Tira's breath rasped in and out. She'd gone with a wrong man, sure enough. My words to Cole about Mama came back to me. Having the right to make your own choice didn't help if you chose badly.

# Chapter 12

## Fitch

FITCH STUMBLED ALONG Corsair Street, shoving his trembling hands in his pockets so he wouldn't have to see how shaken he'd let himself get. Folks around him staggered as if they'd just come off a two-day drunk. Even the strings of Festival beads stretched overhead seemed to sag. A horn player tucked in an alcove next to a cake shop actually seemed to be playing a funeral dirge.

He hoped Dilly and her friend were all right. What a useless fool he'd made of himself. Not only in the riot, but in healing Tira too. He'd been eleven when a Hedge Mage he'd gone to for a sick headache told him he had the gift of Mage healing. Gavun grudgingly consented to his being trained, a decision that looked better to Gavun when he learned Fitch's gift included nudging people into doing what he wanted. But tonight he'd been unable to help Tira at all. When he thought of it, he hadn't even been able to heal Dilly's foot that morning. Instead, he seemed permanently condemned to be flooded by the feelings of anyone he touched, whether he nudged them or not. What was *wrong* with him?

At that moment, he spotted his father, fidgeting in front of a jeweler's shop that was shut tight. The sight jarred Fitch into slapping a hand against his empty hip. He groaned. Dilly still had his bag holding the money he'd collected from Donyn, the only money he'd taken tonight. Gavun was going to spit fire.

"Where have you been?" Gavun demanded. "I had to collect one payment myself. I hope you got everyone else."

Fitch set his jaw. "Just Donyn."

His father looked incredulous. "Small gods and stupid boys. I delivered to a dozen people tonight, and you're off enjoying yourself? This is business."

"In case you didn't notice, there was a riot. A woman collapsed on the street, and I helped get her home." Best not to say "home" was the Fortress.

Gavun cursed loudly enough that a man in a turban skirted around them. "Give me what you got from Donyn. You'll have to go after the rest." He held out a hand.

Fitch blew out his breath. "It's in my bag, which someone else has. I'll get it tomorrow."

Gavun flung his hands up. "If you don't, you'll pay me anyway."

"I said I'll get it." Fitch hadn't expected anything

different. Once Gavun decided a coin was the kinship's, he never let it go, not even to his son. "But I have other things to do too. Folks in that riot were fired up on Mage flower. Whoever's supplying it has a lot to answer for, and I mean to make them do it."

"Why are you wasting your time on nonsense instead of collecting what we're owed?" Gavun's gaze shot over Fitch's shoulder. "Just get those payments." Fitch turned enough to glimpse a pair of Watchmen. Gavun smoothed his hand down his stolen Watch uniform and backed away. "I'll see you at home tomorrow." He vanished as only he could do, leaving Fitch to slide away from the Watch on his own. He supposed he could take that as a sign of Gavun's confidence in him. If he tried hard enough.

He walked the length of Corsair and then the streets around it, collecting from half a dozen of Gavun's buyers, most of whom seemed to be looking for him. Nobody wanted to risk stiffing the Rhale Island kinship and having their supply of smuggled goods cut off. Fitch repeatedly brought up Mage flower under the cover of shocked talk about the riot, but no one admitted to knowing who supplied it.

It was somewhere between very late and very early when he concluded Gavun's remaining customers had given up waiting for him. In light of Gavun's annoyance, Fitch should probably hound them at home. He headed toward the docks where he knew one man lived. The man must have been asleep because no light leaked around his shutters. Fitch had to knock three times and when he appeared, the man was loosely wrapped in a blanket, his breath smelling of sleep. As soon as the man saw Fitch, he said, "Wait. I'll get it." He padded away, came back, and thrust a small bag in Fitch's hand. "I'd have brought it tomorrow," he said sourly and waited for Fitch's nod before he closed the door.

Fitch shoved the bag into his bulging pocket and looked toward the foot of the street, beyond which rose a tangle of masts. His mother would probably be asleep. But she'd said to come any time, he silently argued. Maybe she even meant it. Without having finished the mental argument, he found himself trotting toward where she said she'd be. She was his mother and, unbelievably, she was right here in Lac's Holding.

The docks were quiet except for the slap of water against the river bank. He strode along the wharf toward the visitors' slips, scanning names as he got close. There it was. The *Escape*, with a light showing dimly in the cabin. He wiped his damp palms on his trousers, then edged partway up the gangway, cleared his throat, and called, "Ahoy, *Escape*."

The cabin door opened at once, revealing his mother, washed in yellow lantern light. She swung the door wider and stepped aside. "Come in, Fitch."

Brend appeared behind her in the doorway. Fitch clenched his fists. "It's a nice night. Why don't you come out?" Without honey drop man, he wanted to add.

Maybe his mother wanted to be alone with him too because she threw a shawl around her shoulders and exited, pulling the cabin door shut. Ear cocked for the whisper of her steps, he led her to the wharf rather than offering her his arm. If there was one thing he didn't need, it was the emotion that would come with her touch. He gestured toward a bench, and they sat side by side. He caught a whiff of half-forgotten vanilla perfume that left him dizzy.

"I'm glad you came," she said.

He felt as if he'd been listening for that voice everywhere he went. "Sorry I'm so late."

"So have you decided to come with me?" she asked.

Longing spurted through him, strong enough that he surprised himself by saying, "Maybe."

The curtain twitched in the porthole on the *Escape*. Brend must be watching, Fitch thought. Of course he was. Years ago, Fitch's mother had chosen Brend over her family. He must see Fitch as an unwelcome intruder. He probably thought of Fitch's mother as his to claim. What did his mother care enough about to claim as hers? Fitch edged away on the bench to where the air smelled only of coming rain. "I don't know. I told you I'm working with Gavun."

"You don't even call him Papa. He can't be much of a father."

Fitch shrugged. "I've always called him by name, I

think because Loni did. He never asked me to call him anything else."

"And is working with Gavun what you want? You want to be a smuggler?"

Fitch had long ago accepted what his kin all were. He'd been fine admitting it to Dilly, but the distaste in his mother's voice made him grope for something else to call himself. "I've trained as a Mage healer too."

"That's wonderful!" she cried. "You can do that anywhere and be welcome."

Assuming he could still heal, of course.

"Come with me now, Fitch. We can set sail as soon as the tide turns."

"I can't. I have to do this thing for a girl I used to know."

In the flicker of a harborside torch, he saw her smile. "A girl. My, you have grown up."

He cringed at how trivial she made Nera sound. He shouldn't have brought her up.

"How long will this *thing* take?" She played with the fringe on her shawl. "We can't stay past the last night of Festival."

"Why not?" His resentment flooded back. "You've been gone for fourteen years and now you give me three days to decide whether to uproot my life?"

"The thing is Brend is wanted by the Watch. That's one reason we had to leave and he didn't dare venture back. As long as Festival is going on, they're too busy to notice him, but once it ends, the danger for him here is too great."

"Wanted? What did he do to make the Watch still want him after fourteen years?"

She grimaced. "It was an accident, but he killed the brother of a Watchman."

Fitch pushed to his feet. "You've got nerve scorning Gavun for breaking the law." Small gods. Where had that urge to defend Gavun come from?

"Wait." She jumped up, grabbing at his arm and catching only a fold of his sleeve when he yanked it away. "Gavun is what he is, and I don't just mean that he's a smuggler. Blood and bone, he belongs to the kinship, and I couldn't fit in. But this is about you and me, Fitch. I have never in my life regretted anything as much as I regretted leaving you."

Fitch felt as if half-a-dozen people had all bled their feelings into him at once, but he knew the feelings were all his. "I have to go. Let me get you back onto the *Escape*." He snorted at the name. He'd thought his mother had been flaunting her feelings about Lac's Holding and Gavun. Now Fitch thought maybe Brend had named the boat. His mother apparently couldn't resist law-breaking men.

She followed him. "Think about it. Let me know tomorrow, and please, let your answer be yes." She ran lightly up the gangway.

Fitch walked away. Meeting with his mother had left

him feeling more ragged than being caught in a rioting mob while carrying a sick woman and following the red-haired butterfly girl.

# Chapter 13

## Dilly

WHEN I WOKE the next morning, rain sang against the shutters. I rolled over to look at Tira, who'd vomited twice in the night but seemed to be sleeping normally now. My eyes drifted shut again. Even apart from getting up with Tira, I'd slept badly. My dreams had been disturbed by Suryan's voice saying we'd *failed* him; by visions of Elenia, angry over being escorted home by Fortress guards; by images of Fitch, still caught in a crowd, buckling to his knees. I felt my world tipping toward danger.

I shuddered, and thought instead of Elenia and Veren. I didn't like that Veren had sent me off in Cole's company when he had to know the kind of man his cousin was. And what had Cole meant when he talked about Veren's *plans* for Elenia? The whole thing made my street-kid nerves tingle.

So what to do? Trying again to put Elenia off Veren was a risk I didn't want to take. But if I could get rid of Cole, that would at least take care of my strongest worry. All I needed to do was convince Veren that Cole had stolen his captain's pin.

The sound of guards drilling in the yard told me it was late. When I moved, Tuc jumped off the bed and stretched. I shrugged into my robe, warm against the damp that had shouldered in with the rain.

After closing the bedroom door softly so as not to disturb Tira, I padded barefoot into the Glass Chamber with Tuc charging ahead, nose in the air. I halted in the doorway. Elenia sat at the table, looking pale and disgruntled. The morning servants had already vanished. None of the other attendants were around either. Unlike me, they knew enough to lay low. Tuc crouched at Elenia's feet, looking adoringly at the toast in her hand. A string of his drool barely missed the toe of her slipper.

"Fair morning, Dilly," Elenia said coolly. "As you see, I arrived home safely, unharmed by any *wrong man.*"

"Lady, truly I didn't tell your father you were with Veren. He guessed."

Her gaze bored into mine. Then her shoulders eased. "Good. I thought Jessa was mistaken."

Jessa needed her head held down in the privy. "Did Lord Suryan send guards to fetch you?"

"He sent them," Elenia said, "but I was halfway home

when they found me. Luckily, Cole was with me, not Veren, and Cole turned out to be good at disappearing."

*If only he would.* I speared bread from the sideboard, laid it on the brazier, and slid the resulting toast onto a plate before joining Elenia at the table. I poured a cup of cocoa, the fragrant steam curling into the morning air.

"You know Tira is ill from Mage flower?" When Elenia nodded, I said, "Your father threatened to throw her out."

"Nonsense. I won't allow it. I govern my own household."

"I thought so." Rain streamed over the colored glass dome overhead. The room felt cozy and safe. Suddenly hungry, I crunched my toast, prodding Tuc away with my bare foot. None of Elenia's ladies was going anywhere without her consent, which she wasn't about to give, and that included me. "So what will you do now?"

"What do you think?" She set her cup down hard enough that cocoa slopped into the saucer. "I'll do whatever I choose. I'm not a child, and this is Lac's Holding. My father thinks enough of my good sense and knowledge to name me his heir. He ought to trust me about Veren, too."

*Maybe,* I thought, but it seemed to me that ruling and romance came from two different parts of a person. Mama was as sensible a woman as you ever saw about most things, and she'd still been a fool over Cole. Still, Elenia knew Veren far better than I. And as for Suryan, if Elenia thought he'd accept her right to her own choice, who was I to say he wouldn't?

Elenia laid her hand over mine on the table. "I need help, Dilly, and you're the only one who can give it."

It took me a moment to realize that what I felt was happiness. It was a stupid thing to feel, given the hornet's nest Elenia was poking, but there it was. "Anything."

"I need you to carry word to Veren."

"Of course." I'd carry Veren's pin too and stick it where it would cause Cole the most pain.

"It's important." Elenia's eyes gleamed. "I want you to tell Veren I agree to marry him. I have no intention of letting my father think he's won."

So Cole had spoken too soon when he claimed to know Elenia and Veren would marry, but now, small gods help me, it was true. Maybe Elenia could deal with Veren as well as Suryan, but Cole went out of his way to scare me every time he came near.

Demonstrating to myself that I'd shed enough of my street kid ways to stop hoarding food, I fed the last of my toast to Tuc. I went to our room and checked on Tira, who lay asleep, mouth open, smelling faintly of vomit. I cracked the shutter and tucked Tira's blankets around her before I reached for the trousers I'd worn the previous night. I paused, fingering the rough fabric. I'd just been thinking women should be able to choose their own actions. Disguising myself as a boy to do it seemed cowardly. I could wear the ragged evening dress I'd worn to the *Storm King*, but when I looked at it, folded in my clothes chest, the idea of putting it on again made me feel like the girl who lived for months on the streets of Rin City, and that was the stuff of nightmares. Jessa had enough spiteful instinct that she'd known what would bother me most when she sent me out in that gown.

I didn't need to disguise myself to go out the gates in broad daylight anyway. I shook out the blue dress King Thien had supplied when I traveled from Rin City to Lac's Holding. It was pretty but plain enough that it wouldn't obviously mark me as Elenia's if someone saw me on the docks. Besides, in the rain, the chances were no one would look too closely. I took Veren's pin from the chest and put it in my pocket, then slipped into my jacket with the oiled hood. After one last look at Tira, I went back to the Glass Chamber where Elenia waited.

"When? Where?" I asked, feeling a little squashed by the weight of what I was helping Elenia do.

"He'll be at the warehouse this morning, but the marriage needs to be on the *Storm King*, so a captain can perform the ceremony," Elenia said. "Tomorrow night. I'll be there soon after darkfall."

I took a deep breath, drawing up all my courage. "Come on, Tuc." The dog tore himself away from sniffing for crumbs under the table and followed me through the rain to the front gate.

One of the guards on duty lowered his pike to block my way and peered under my already dripping hood.

"Lord Suryan asked us to warn everyone going out to be careful, miss. After last night's riot, he's worried about the household's safety. A man was trampled to death right outside the gates here."

I smothered the memory of the man I'd seen die. "I have an errand to run for Lady Elenia."

His brows drew down. "Maybe you ought to ask her if she's sure about risking you like that?"

"She's not risking me. I'm a member of her own household! Besides, that mob won't be around this morning. They'll be sleeping it off." Hidden at my side, I flicked a finger at Tuc, and he raced out the gates. "Excuse me. I have to catch my dog."

The guard grimaced but lifted his pike. "Your choice of course. Take care."

I swept out, scanning the street for Tuc, and bracing myself to do whatever it took to get rid of Cole.

# Chapter 14

## Fitch

F ITCH WAS HUNCHED over his morning porridge when Gavun came into the front room. Fitch had been late, but Gavun had been enough later still that Fitch hadn't heard him come in. Gavun poured himself a mug of small beer and dropped into the chair across from Fitch, fingers rasping over his stubble. He yawned, showing Fitch the place where he'd lost two teeth in an encounter with pirates off the Janda coast. Gavun laid his hand palm up on the table and wiggled his fingers.

Fitch shoved the pile of coins across to him. "I'll get the rest today." He watched his father count them, trying to ignore the insult.

Gavun got up, hid the coins in the space behind the bookshelf, and returned to his ale. He hadn't tied his hair back yet, and it straggled over his ears. "I have something to talk to you about."

"I'm guessing it's whatever you have going with the Eastway kinship."

Gavun took a deep drink and seemed to pick through what he wanted to say. Fitch waited. Silence stretched, broken by the drum of rain against the shutters. "You going to be true to the kinship and keep it to yourself?" Gavun asked.

Fitch raised an eyebrow. "It must be pretty bad if you have to ask me that."

"It could get us all hanged."

Fitch stopped breathing. His father had been defying the law for all of Fitch's life. Gavun had twice spent a few months in jail and paid several fines, but Fitch had never seen him as serious as he was now.

"You have to swear not to tell," Gavun said. "Swear on pain of being banished from the Rhale Island kinship."

Fitch looked into the abyss. For an islander, a kinship was home. It fed you, clothed you, taught you, cared for you if you were small or sick or old. Being without one would be like drifting alone in a rowboat in the middle of the ocean. He'd been antsy about being squeezed back into his role as Gavun's boy. Now it seemed his choice was to do that or live alone. Unless, of course, he chose to leave with his mother.

"I want you to be part of this," Gavun said. "Loni's been willing to do what he had to in order to replace you, but I want you back. You're mine."

"That's what you said the night Mama left." Fitch realized he'd said it out loud only when he saw the startled look on Gavun's face. "You said *he's mine.*"

Gavun drew in his chin. "What put that in your head?"

"I just—" Fitch shrugged. "I've just remembered some things lately. Why did she go?"

Gavun's mouth twisted. "She was a city girl. She missed living near shops, if you can believe that." He shrugged. "I should have known better."

Fitch felt grudging admiration for Gavun's withholding the fact that there'd been another man. It was possible Gavun didn't know about Brend, but given how many kinship eyes watched island events, Fitch doubted it. Well, if Gavun could keep quiet about Brend, Fitch could hold his tongue about whatever Gavun was up to. "I swear on pain of being banned from the Rhale Island kinship that I won't tell anyone what you're about to tell me."

Gavun leaned back, looking pleased. "I told Veren you'd be with us." He took another drink, then leaned close as if to keep anyone from hearing them, despite there being no one else in the house as far as Fitch knew. "Veren has a plan to get us all out from under the customs Lord Suryan collects," Gavun said.

"He's taking up smuggling?" Fitch heard the disbelief in his own voice.

"No. He just wants to import goods without paying customs."

"You mean do what smugglers do."

"He wants to do it legally."

Fitch couldn't imagine how Gavun managed to say that with a straight face. He thought about what his father had told him. "That's why he's romancing Elenia. He thinks the same thing you did and plans to get her to work on her father."

Gavun shifted. "Not quite."

A buzz of caution ran down Fitch's spine. "What does that mean?"

"He plans to remove Suryan as ruler and replace him with Elenia. That's the scheme Cole came to tell me about yesterday. I thought it was mad until you brought news that Elenia was secretly writing him. That told me she's in deep. Veren's been working for weeks on getting her to marry him."

Fitch realized his jaw had sagged. "You want to risk hanging over that plan? And I'm using *plan* very loosely. Even married to Elenia, Veren would be just a ship captain, an island head. Suryan has an army."

Gavun flapped his hand impatiently. "Suryan's grown old and weak. You saw how folks went after him last night."

"Was that part of this? Never mind. Stupid question. I assume Veren's people were there leading the chants and urging people on. I saw it. I saw how the Fortress guards drove them back too."

"Some well-placed bribes would take care of them."

"We'd be better off lying low and letting Veren jump off the dock by himself. I hear rumors Suryan is getting ready to move against the kinships," Fitch said.

"Where? Who from?"

"I don't remember. Here and there." Thank the small gods Fitch hadn't told Gavun about Dilly. If he had, Gavun would be on him to use her for his ends.

"All the more reason to act against Suryan now. And don't forget we'll have Elenia. Some of the guards might choose her side."

"She'd never turn on her father. He's blood of her blood."

"Veren says they're quarreling," Gavun said. "And city folks don't care about kin the way we do."

*Dilly cared*, Fitch thought.

"Besides, she might turn." Gavun licked his lips. "With a little nudge."

Fitch's chair scraped over the floor as he jumped to his feet. "That's why you want me. I won't do it. This isn't just getting someone to pay more for smuggled goods. This is treason."

"Calm down." Gavun patted the air. "You don't have to decide what you will or won't do now. You might not even *need* to nudge her. She's already handed over managing her ship to him, which should tell you how much she's put herself in his hands. Veren says she's in love."

Only Gavun would say *love* in that scornful way, Fitch

thought. "What about King Thien? He chooses the lords for each province of Rinland. I don't see how he can let Veren interfere without stirring up trouble elsewhere too."

"Thien let Suryan name Elenia as his heir, so he's thinking about what he wants when Suryan is gone. He might be sick of the trouble Suryan makes."

Fitch paced, then cracked the shutter open, looking for air. Rain misted the hand he set on the window sill. Rhale Island seemed to rush through and claim him – the rain-blown smell of salt roses and fish, the wash of waves he heard as his mother rocked his cradle, the whisper of clean wind in the grass. Every day he was gone, he'd missed this place. Every night he'd dreamed of it. He leaned one hip against the window sill, then pulled away when rain seeped through his trousers. "Last night, I wound up helping a woman who'd collapsed from too much Mage flower. And flower was sure part of what caused that riot last night. Its presence looks mighty convenient for someone wanting to overthrow Lord Suryan."

Gavun looked away and back. "You think I'd ask you to join in if this involved Mage flower? No one knows better than I that you're not rational on the subject. Flower is around. I can't argue about that. But you know the Eastway reputation as well as I do. They'd spit on feeding people Mage flower."

"You can't tell me the folks in that riot would have acted that way *without* flower."

"Of course not." Gavun rubbed his mouth. "It was a

coincidence, a lucky one, but just a chance."

Uncertainty bubbled up in Fitch's chest. Gavun could smell someone cheating him a mile away. It beggared belief that Veren was putting one over on him. "You sure Veren will let the rest of us keep smuggling, not claim everything for himself?"

"There'll be arrangements," Gavun said.

"What does that mean?"

"If we support Veren, we'll have a one-fifth share."

Fitch closed the shutter. He had no choice but to – well, not trust Gavun exactly. Trusting Gavun demanded stupidity beyond what Fitch hoped he was capable of. But he would join his father because Gavun was right. Fitch belonged to this kinhip and this island. If Suryan threatened his kin and home, he had to stand behind them. "What do we have to do?"

Gavun's shoulders eased. "I'll kick in some of the bribe money, and we may have to contact and pay some people. Then all the kinships bring their crew into the city and help Veren and his new wife take over the Fortress. Not that she knows that yet, of course. But Veren says she'll go along."

"When?"

"Tomorrow night. The last night of Festival. New Year's Eve."

Fitch coughed a short laugh. "On the good side, that leaves less time to worry about what a rope around my neck would feel like."

Gavun rose. "Bring the *Sea Wind* across and meet me at the dock you used last night."

"I'm collecting the rest of your money this morning. You want me to put that off?"

"I have a little time before I'm supposed to meet with Veren. You and I are going to persuade some of the Watch that they prefer Elenia to Suryan as ruler. You can collect what I'm owed afterwards."

"Persuade? You mean bribe?" Fitch was pretty sure bribery wasn't what Gavun meant. Or not only bribery. And in his head, he heard Dilly asking if it mattered how a person messed with someone else's mind if the effect was the same.

"I'll offer the coin. You nudge them to take it in good faith."

"You don't need me. You're a champion at bribery."

Gavun flushed. "You've been nudging people for me for years. And you swore you'd be faithful to the kinship."

Fitch took in his father's wide eyes and quick breath. Gavun wasn't joking about the risk the Rhale Island kinship had entered into. He jerked a nod. *Blood of my blood*, he reminded himself. Wanted by mother and father both. Why didn't it feel like he'd always imagined it would?

# Chapter 15

## Dilly

I FOUND TUC sniffing a butcher's cart sheltered under an overhang. Hunched against the rain, I walked briskly with him at my heels until I came face-to-face with the scarred door of the Eastway warehouse. I rapped, and had raised my hand to do it again when it cracked open to show a bearded man I didn't know. "I have business with the captain," I said.

He glanced over his shoulder, then frowned at me. "The captain's busy."

"I have to see him."

"You'll have to wait."

"Here? In the rain?" I wrapped my arms around myself and rubbed my damp shoulders. "Can I wait inside where it's dry?" When he still hesitated, I snapped, "Do I look dangerous to you?"

"I guess not." He opened the door to let me step through, but blocked Tuc with his foot. "Not the dog. We have goods in here."

"Sit, Tuc." He did, but I could still hear him whining pitifully after the bearded man shut the door.

He'd told the truth when he said there were goods. A stack of crates had been added to the barrels full of what I assumed was tonight's Winter Fire. Two men grunted as they loaded the barrels onto hand carts. They turned to eye me.

"Keep at it." The bearded man clicked his fingers. "And check every cork. Those cobbles are rough. The captain will have your hides if there's Fire all over the streets. That's money in the gutter." They bent to their task. The bearded man turned back to me. "Sit." He pointed to a bench outside Veren's office and went to help move the barrels.

Feeling like Tuc, I obeyed, then pushed my hood back and looked around, fingering Veren's pin in my pocket. If the Trickster wasn't set on amusing herself at my expense, I'd spot a jacket or something else belonging to Cole where I could leave the pin, but, of course, nothing like that was in sight. I'd have to plant it on Cole when I saw him. What was the worst he could do if I got near him? Nothing that couldn't be fixed or forgotten. My stomach twisted anyway.

Male voices had been rumbling in Veren's office. Now, as clear as good glass, I heard one say, "Elenia."

I froze, pin clutched in my hand. Was that Veren? If so, he'd sounded amused, and not in a nice way. I slid as close as I could to the door's end of the bench. The bearded man frowned at me, but when I widened my eyes and smiled, he turned away. As if I were resting, I leaned my head back just beside the door. A second and then third male voice said things I couldn't make out. Veren's mentioning Elenia was odd. He should be trying to keep his and Elenia's plans private if he didn't want Lord Suryan to interfere.

"You're sure about Elenia?" said a man I didn't recognize. It sounded as if he'd moved closer to the door.

"Oh, yes," Veren said. "She believes my experience and advice will make Lac's Holding more prosperous. Also, she's quite taken with me."

The other men all laughed. I wanted to reach through the closed door and slap every face in there.

"I grant you," Veren went on, "I'm not sure how to manage Suyan, but I'm hoping Gavun will give us the thing we need."

Someone knocked loudly on the warehouse door, and a man called, "It's Gavun."

I grabbed for a scrap of memory and recalled that Fitch and the merchant he'd collected money from had talked about *Gavun*. This must be Fitch's father.

The bearded man opened the door, let a man in, and shut Tuc out again. Curious, I eyed Fitch's father. Like his son, Gavun was tall, and shared the same dark, curly hair and the same wide mouth. He strode across the warehouse floor, knocked once on the office door, and entered without waiting to be asked.

"You're late," Veren said. "What's the word? Will your boy help us?"

"He's all in," Gavun said. "He nudged at least a dozen Watchmen for me this morning." He shut the office door, muffling whatever else he had to say.

Fitch was *nudging* Watchmen for Veren and the other men who'd laughed? What did that mean? If it was what he did to me in the shrine, the thought of it made my skin crawl.

I was leaning toward the office when the warehouse door opened, and Cole walked in. He took two steps before he spotted me and his jaw fell open. He swooped down on me, grabbed my arm hard enough to hurt, and dragged me to my feet. "What are you doing here?"

At his touch, my heart sped up. The men working with the barrels all stared at us. "Let me go," I said. "The man told me to wait here. I have a message for Veren." Hand low, I slid the pin toward his pocket. My fingers brushed his damp wool jacket.

He let go of my arm, seized my wrist, and twisted until it felt as if the bones would break. I cried out and opened my hand. We both stared at Veren's pin, its red gem glittering in the lantern light. Cole pried it out of my grip.

He smiled nastily. "I knew it. Now *would* be a good time for you to talk to the captain." He turned to the watching men. "Get those barrels on their way." As they scrambled to obey, he hauled me to the door, knocked, and opened it without waiting.

I was breathing so hard I thought I might faint, but I peered in to see five men, including Gavun and Veren, standing or seated around Veren's desk.

"Look who I found." Cole's hand pinched around my arm. "And look what she had." He held up the pin.

Veren moved quickly to the doorway. "Excuse me a moment, gentlemen." He stepped out into the warehouse, shutting the door behind him.

I swallowed as much spit as I could find. "Captain, please tell your man to let me go. I came here with a message for you. I'm one of Elenia's ladies, so this man has no right to abuse me. That pin fell out of his pocket. I knew it belonged to you. I was going to return it to you."

Veren shifted his gaze from me to Cole. One corner of his mouth lifted. "You heard the *lady*." Cole snorted but let go of my arm. Veren took his pin from Cole and shoved it into his lapel. "See to our guests, Cole."

"I'd swear she was listening at the door," Cole said in a low voice. He disappeared into the room with the other men, snapping the door shut behind him.

Veren stood a finger's width too close, his back to the three men loading barrels, who all hustled faster with him there. My heart clawed its way up into my throat. "I'll bet Cole meant to sell your pin," I heard myself babble. "Because he needed money, like you said."

"I missed that pin after you left the warehouse last night," Veren said. "My cousin says you're a pickpocket."

"Why would I take it?" I said. "Lady Elenia gives me what I need."

"Nobody likes living off someone's charity. We islanders know it's important to have control of our lives." He cocked his head and looked at me from under hooded eyelids. "Control of other people, too."

"I'm happy with Elenia." My tongue stuck to the roof of my dry mouth.

"Then you'll have to be happy with me and my kin," he said. "At least, I assume that's what the message Elenia sent will mean." A silent moment passed before he raised an eyebrow. "The message?"

I sucked in what air I could. "Lady Elenia says yes." Judging by his satisfied smile, Veren had expected no less. I felt a flare of hatred so strong it startled me. I should have known. He and Cole were kindred spirits as well as kin.

"Anything else?" he said.

I managed to spit out Elenia's instructions for when and where the marriage would take place. Despite the chill of the rainy day, I had to scrub my sweaty palms against my skirt.

"Tell her I'll arrange it." Veren closed the space between us so he could keep his voice low. "What did you hear before Cole found you?"

"Nothing."

"You're not someone who'd spread private business around, I hope."

"Of course not." I felt strangely breathless, though what I said was the absolute truth. I wasn't the one who'd talked about Elenia in a roomful of men.

"Good. Because Cole takes care of blabbers for me, and I'd hate to send him after a pretty little thing like you." He grabbed my shoulders and squeezed. "If you ever take anything of mine again, you'll regret it." He released me and went back into the office without giving me another glance.

"I WAS STARTING to worry," the gate guard said when Tuc and I hurried back into the Fortress.

"Sorry." I rushed into the building and up the stairs. On the way home, the rain had stopped, but my wet shoes squished against my feet and left damp footprints. Veren had finally showed me that my street-sharpened uneasiness about him was right. If I'd met him in Rin City, I'd have taken care to stay out of his way. His threat to sic Cole on me made me want to throw up, not least because he'd known exactly how much that would scare me. Elenia needed to be warned. She wouldn't like it, but I couldn't help that. Street kids weren't the only people who survived by sticking together. I needed to look out for her the way she'd promised to look out for me.

I paused outside the door to Elenia's quarters. Tuc seemed to sense my worry and rubbed his wet fur against my leg. I petted him. "Courage," I advised him and opened the door to the Glass Chamber. Everyone but Tira was there, looking excited.

"What did Veren say?" Elenia asked gleefully. "How did he look when you told him?"

Small gods. I couldn't say anything bad about Veren now, not with everyone else here. I'd have to catch Elenia alone. "He said he'd make the arrangements. He looked… glad."

The other women crowded around Elenia, chatting about what she should wear. Jessa took the time to curl her lip at me. "You look like you rolled in puddles, Dilly."

Tuc bounded across the room and put his muddy paws on her skirt. "Curse you, Tuc," she cried.

I managed to smile at her on the way to my room to change out of my soaked things, mind busy with how to hold a private talk with Elenia in a household full of women, one of whom was Jessa.

My room smelled oddly flowery. I paused, trying to take in the fact that Tira's bed was empty though I could hear her raspy breathing. Tuc pattered out of sight around Tira's bed and gave a low woof. I followed him to see Tira sprawled on the floor, one arm flung over a carry bag with its contents sliding out. Fitch's bag, I remembered at the same moment I realized that an uncorked jug of Winter Fire was spilled on the floor. The room's smell snapped into place. The Fire was full of Mage flower.

I opened my mouth to call for help, but clamped it shut again, mind racing. I'd brought that bag into the Fortress, and everyone had seen me do it. Would the other women believe it wasn't mine? Would Suryan? I set the jug on the table and snatched up the bag. Its weight made me look inside. Trickster take me, there were two more corked jugs. I looked frantically around for a place to hide it and finally dropped it into my clothes chest. It couldn't stay there, but for now, it was out of sight.

Then I called at the top of my voice. "Help!"

Footsteps ran down the hall as I thought with fury of Fitch and the lies he'd told and the damage he'd done. And he was helping Veren! If there was one thing I thought I learned in Rin City, it was to stop being stupidly trustful. I was a fool ever to have thought he might be someone I could grow to like.

# Chapter 16

## Fitch

FITCH TOOK THE merchant's money, tucked it into the pouch tied to his belt, and checked the woman's name off the list Gavun had given him. A mental list, of course. Gavun didn't believe in putting things in writing. Fitch's damp shirt itched against his shoulders, but at least the rain had stopped, and it had raised a pleasant, flinty smell from the cobblestones. Sauntering along Caravan Street to his next name, he thought again about the plans Gavun had laid out for him, then hastily pushed it aside. This whole thing made him sweat if he thought too much about it.

His body still echoed with the anger at Lord Suryan that his nudging had called up in the Watch members that morning. *Not mine*, he kept telling himself. *His* fury was for the Mage flower dealer, and though he meant to keep his vow to help the kinship, his first goal had to be tracking the dealer down. If he couldn't find the slime bucket before the end of Festival, Winter Fire would be gone from the streets, and he'd have to wait a full year to try again. Time was slipping away from him.

Last night, he'd seen again the damage flower did. Both Dilly's friend and the drunk outside the alehouse had been unconscious with it. He hoped Dilly had reached safety after he left her, but he couldn't have stood the crowd's touches much longer without collapsing even more humiliatingly. He would call at the Fortress gates later, ask after her, and send word for someone to bring his bag to the gate. Maybe Dilly would bring it herself. He wouldn't mind seeing her again. Sharing danger with her had left him feeling a connection to her.

He felt a twinge of guilt at that thought.

The café he'd been looking for appeared on his right, but as he started to turn in, an old man tottered out, blocking his way. Fitch waited for him, but the man stopped in the doorway, looking straight ahead and shading his eyes against the watery light.

"Excuse me," Fitch said.

The old man creaked his head toward Fitch. "How are you?" he asked as if the two of them were old shipmates.

"I'm fine." Fitch tried to think where they might have met but came up empty.

"Learn anything yet? Take my word. You'll be sorry if you don't."

As Gramps shuffled away, Fitch caught the mixed smells of dust and mint, then smothered a laugh. It was the old codger who'd come into the shrine after Dilly picked his pocket. What a loon. At least he'd given Fitch his first laugh in what felt like a month.

He ducked into the café, collected Gavun's payment, asked about spiked Fire, and ducked out again, no wiser than when he'd gone in. That had been the story all morning, even at the alehouse which had spat out the flower-addled man. In the back of his head, he heard Gavun say *useless*. He was starting to think maybe his father was right.

Across the street lay the Blue Whale. At late morning, it might be empty enough that Evia would tell him something. He paused in the doorway of the Whale, letting his eyes adjust to the dim light.

"Fitch!" Loni called.

A man jumped up from a table and dashed out the back door.

Fitch bolted after him. He was almost sure it was the man who'd been bending over Dilly's collapsed friend, the one who'd maybe given her the flower-spiked Fire. He hit the back door, bounced off, and rammed his shoulder against it to burst out into the alley. A boot vanished around a corner to the left. Fitch tore after it and swung into an adjoining alley, only to see his prey teeter on top of a fence and drop to the other side. He ran, grabbed hold, and pulled himself up. But, hanging from the top, he saw no one, just a beaten dirt corner where three narrow paths met among a tangle of apartment buildings. He couldn't even hear feet retreating, which meant the man had probably ducked into a building.

"Trickster take you," he spat and dropped to the ground. He leaned against the fence, catching his breath. Gavun had trained Fitch early never to run from the Watch. Running screamed guilt. So what was the man guilty of? Fitch had probably scared the runner so badly last night that he'd blown any chance of ever finding out. "Useless," he muttered.

He headed back to the Whale. Inside, Loni once again hailed him. He waved but went first to where Evia tended the counter.

"What can I get you, Fitch?" she asked.

"Winter Fire if you have some that's not spiked. Who was the man who ran out when I came in?"

"He works for the Eastways. And the Whale sells only legit stuff, straight from their warehouse."

"I had Fire in here the first night of Festival, and it was full of Mage flower."

She flicked him a quick look, then filled a mug from one of the barrels behind her. She shoved it into his hands. "Try that."

He sniffed and sipped.

"Satisfied?" she asked.

"I guess. But you did have spiked stuff. Where did it come from?"

"Let it go, Fitch," Evia said sharply. "If you can't, you'll have to leave."

"Fitch," Loni called a third time.

"Stick with whichever smuggler sold you the good batch," Fitch said. No way Evia would have bought from the Eastways when smuggled stuff was cheaper. Fitch ought to know. He'd delivered enough Rhale Island goods to her to predict what she'd pay to the exact gull. He joined Loni at the table, where his cousin was eating a mess of the sour herrings his mother refused to fix. Fitch jerked his head at the back door. "Do you know who that was?"

Loni looked amused. "The one you chased after? What did he do? Go after your new girl?"

"What new girl?"

"The one I saw you with last night. The one in the pirate costume. Those trousers looked good on her."

Fitch twisted his mug on the table, making a pattern of rings that looked like a chain. "She's not my girl."

"Sorry to hear that. I hoped you were moving on. I don't know the man who bolted."

Fitch slumped in his chair. "I can't move on. Not until I figure out how Nera died. Otherwise, it's just my fault, and I don't know if I can live with that."

Loni frowned. "What do you mean *your fault*? She fell off the break wall."

Fitch took a drink, struggling with an urge to tell Loni what really happened. "She drank Winter Fire that was spiked the same way this year's is," he finally said, keeping his gaze on the shimmering drink in his mug. "It makes people suggestible, and I told her to do something exciting." He darted a look at Loni, searching for his reaction.

Loni half hid his face behind a raised mug, but Fitch saw his brows draw together. As if he felt Fitch's eyes on him, he looked up, sighed, and put his drink down. "So what do you mean to do about it?"

"Find the supplier and make him pay."

"There's spiked Fire all over," Loni said. "You'll never find who did it. You should move on, like I said."

Fitch shook his head. "That's what Gavun says, but I can't. I feel responsible."

"At least come with me tonight," Loni said. "It'll be easy selling. Somehow Gavun got hold of saffron and pepper. Also pipe filler." He gave a grin that Fitch thought looked forced. "Gavun never misses a trick."

"I can't." Fitch rubbed his face, then leaned closer to his cousin. "You know about this thing he has going with the Eastways tomorrow night?"

Loni slid his eyes sideways. "Some of it. You know Gavun. He's close-mouthed. You probably know more than I do."

"I doubt it." He grimaced. "I picked an exciting time to come home."

"I'm glad to have you. So's Gavun, you know, even if he doesn't say."

Fitch shrugged.

"Really he is," Loni said. "He told me yesterday that, at first, your Magery spooked him a little – which I don't understand since it's just healing."

"Nice to know." Fitch took a long drink. Of course Gavun had been spooked when he realized Fitch could nudge him.

"Don't be that way. He said he used to think you were more your mother's than his, but not anymore."

Fitch stopped tracing a finger through the wet rings on the table. "What put my mother in his head?"

"Beats me."

Fitch kept his gaze on the table. Could Gavun have caught wind of his wife's presence in Lac's Holding? If so, he hadn't said when Fitch brought her up. But then, he wouldn't. "Do you remember her, Loni?"

"Nope." Loni cocked his head. "You all right?"

"Yeah, I'm good." Fitch drained his mug and rose. "I better get back to collecting the kinship's coin." He looked down at Loni's open face and felt a surge of affection. Here at least was someone he could count on. "This thing we're doing is dangerous. I hear rumors Suryan is ready to take action against the kinships. Take care, coz."

"You too." Loni lifted his drink in salute.

Outside, Fitch held still for a moment, blinking in the late morning sunshine. Even Loni thought he should forget about Nera's death. Maybe he should, he thought bitterly. He wasn't making any progress in finding the dealer.

"Fitch," a woman said softly.

He spun to find his mother in the shadow along the Whale's wall. "What are you doing here? I thought you were staying on the *Escape*."

"I took a chance and hoped you might show up here. I knew it was a Rhale Islander place, or at least it was in my day."

"Loni's inside. You need to move if you don't want him asking me questions." He waved her into an alley out of sight, dodging shallow puddles. A barrel along the Whale's wall reeked of fish guts.

"Little Loni?" Her face lit up, and she looked back over her shoulder. "I wish I could see him, but we don't have time. You have to come with me right now." She took three quick strides, then stopped when Fitch stood anchored to the spot.

He could see shoppers passing the end of the alley behind her. In an apartment somewhere overhead, someone was singing "The Sailor's Girl." The scene felt unreal, as if his mother and ordinary Lac's Holding life couldn't exist in the same space. "I can't," he blurted.

"Why not?" Her voice was urgent.

"I have to collect some money for the kinship."

"Money." She puffed out a scornful breath. "Let it go. Come on!"

"Why? What's the hurry?"

"Brend went out to buy supplies and got in a fight

with a Watchwoman."

"What? How does anyone even *do* that?"

"I have no idea. He knocked her out, but we have to leave before they track him to the *Escape*."

Standing in the alley, facing the idea of leaving that very moment, Fitch suddenly knew he couldn't do it. "I told you I have to do something for a girl I knew. I owe her." It didn't matter what Gavun or Loni urged Fitch to do. If he gave up now, he'd be ashamed of himself for the rest of his life. "Can't you wait until tomorrow?"

"You won't come now?"

"I can't."

She rocked from foot to foot. "All right. I'll get Brend to hide the *Escape* in one of the old places Gavun stopped using, assuming I can still find them. Tomorrow night, when the tide turns, we'll be back at the docks." She stepped closer. "Please come," she whispered and pressed her lips to his cheek. She hurried away, leaving him with his fingers touching the spot she'd kissed. He felt her worry. He just couldn't tell if it was for him or Brend. He cleared his throat, surprised to find there were tears in his eyes.

He shook himself. Everybody wanted something from him, even Nera from the grave, and he couldn't seem to be able to satisfy any of them. He'd go retrieve his bag from Dilly. He could use a friendly face.

# Chapter 17

## Dilly

I STARED AT a patch of green-tinted sunlight on the skirt of Nemay's yellow dress. My rain-damp gown flapped around my calves, and my feet were wet and cold, but the Glass Chamber felt so stuffy I could hardly breathe.

"What is taking that doctor so long?" Lady Elenia slapped the table, making all of us jump.

"Tira is such a fool." Nemay stared down the hallway leading to the bedrooms.

"Where did she get that jug of spiked Fire?" Lady Elenia asked.

"Maybe she had it on her," I offered.

Jessa scoffed. "In that costume? We'd all have seen it."

I clasped my hands together to keep them from shaking. Curse Fitch. This was his fault. How could he have stuck me with that spiked Fire? What a gullible baby

I'd been to trust him. To like him even. Hadn't life taught me better? Tuc leaned against my legs. I unknotted my hands to pet him.

A door opened and closed, and the doctor came into the Glass Chamber. Elenia rose to speak to him. "How is she?"

"Very ill," the doctor said. "She's had enough Mage flower that her mind believes she can't do without it."

"We'll take care of her," Elenia said.

"You have to make sure she has nothing with Mage flower hidden away," the doctor said. "I gather you didn't know she had that jar."

"I'll have the place searched," Elenia said.

"Just so you know, I'm going to Lord Suryan now." The doctor bowed and left.

I felt faint. I had to get Fitch's bag out of there.

Elenia went to the door and spoke to the guard. A moment or two later, Captain Jaf appeared. "I need someone to search these chambers," Elenia said.

He blinked, but to his credit, spoke coolly. "I'll get my lieutenant to help and do it myself."

"Whoever you get needs to be discreet enough to keep quiet," Elenia said. "I don't want to damage my attendants' reputations. You'll be looking for anything with Mage flower in it."

"Of course." He bowed and left.

Elenia motioned the rest of us to be seated. We waited in silence. I felt as if I might puke along with Tira.

A knock sounded at the door, and Jaf entered with another guard. "Beg pardon," Captain Jaf said, "but I have to ask you all to go to your rooms and stay there. We'll search in here first and then come to each room."

Elenia rose. "You heard him." We all shuffled down the hallway, sending glances back over our shoulders.

With Tuc at my heels, I slipped inside my room. Tira's breath was raspy and uneven. I bent over her as Tuc nosed her limp arm. "You're tempting the Trickster, Tira," I murmured. "Take it from someone who's seen it happen. She'll hold her hand over you for only so long before she takes it away."

Tira snorted.

"I assume that's an accident, not a comment. I'm glad you're still breathing." I opened my clothes chest and took out Fitch's bag, looking inside long enough to see it still held two more corked jugs. Then I set it on one side of the door. Tuc sniffed it. "Smell that?" I scratched behind his ear. "You must never, never drink that."

I pressed my ear to the door. Voices came from the Glass Chamber, along with the sound of cupboards and drawers being opened and closed. At last, booted feet clomped into the hallway. Someone rapped on my door. I opened it just wide enough to see Captain Jaf. Behind him, the other guard entered Jessa and Nemay's room. Tuc started out, but I grabbed his collar.

"Captain, I'm sorry," I said, "but Tira is vomiting. Can you search one of the other rooms first and come back?"

Prodding the bag out of sight with my toe, I opened the door a bit more so he could see Tira, who obligingly moaned.

"Of course." He backed away.

I put my ear to the door again and waited until I heard Elenia's voice. When I cracked the door, Jaf was disappearing into Elenia's room. "Now," I murmured to Tuc. I grabbed the bag and tiptoed out to the Glass Chamber, cringing at the click of Tuc's claws. I needed a hiding place where one of the other women wouldn't stumble across it. Better yet, I could pour it out under a bush in the garden. I cracked the door from the Glass Chamber to the balcony. From below came the sound of the Fortress gardener calling to his helper. *Stone it, stone it, stone it.* I eased the door shut and looked around.

Since the guards had already searched this room, they were unlikely to come back. I hoped. My breath came fast. I was taking too long. Jaf wouldn't poke around in Elenia's room too hard, so he would soon get back to mine.

A knock sounded at the Glass Chamber's door. I froze, then looked down the bedroom hallway. No one came out of any of the rooms. They probably hadn't even heard. Whoever it was knocked louder. I yanked the door open and found a footman, fist raised to knock again.

"Just the person I'm looking for," he said brightly. "Someone is at the gate asking for you to please bring his bag. Says his name is Fitch." His gaze dropped to the bag on my arm. "Is that it? Shall I take it for you?" He stretched out his hand.

I nearly let him have it. I'd be rid of the spiked Fire without having to leave Elenia's quarters. But I couldn't take a chance on the footman peeking into the bag because he was curious about what one of Elenia's attendants was up to with a boy. Besides, in putting Fitch within my reach, the Trickster had smiled on me. A girl would have to be downright sinful to reject the gift.

"I'll take it." I flew past the footman and down the stairs with Tuc racing ahead. Beyond the gate, the street teemed with people who'd finally rolled out of bed after a rainy morning and late night at Festival and were now looking for amusement. Well, I planned to amuse myself too.

"Dilly!" Fitch straightened from where he'd been lounging against the Fortress wall.

Cold fury filled my chest. This boy had stuck me with spiked Fire that left Tira sick and opened me up to deep trouble.

Fitch's smile faded when I halted in front of him and he took in whatever waves of enmity I was giving off. Even Tuc growled at him. He looked down at the dog and then up at me. "Is that my bag?" he asked uncertainly.

Behind him, I spotted a pair of Watchmen coming out of a cafe. The Trickster must be as annoyed at this boy as I was. I thrust the bag at him. "You bastard," I murmured.

"What?" He drew back, clutching the bag.

I marched around him and approached one of the

Watchmen. He politely stopped, head inclined to listen, which is what happens when a girl wears respectable clothes and lives in a good part of town. He thought I was on the side of the law, Trickster help me, and at the moment, I was. I pointed at Fitch. "That boy tried to sell me spiked Winter Fire. He has it in his bag." I whirled and strode back through the gate. Behind me, I heard Fitch protesting. Good. He was a liar. Men who lied to women walked through the world leaving trouble in their wake. I was done with Fitch of Rhale Island. Done.

And thank the small gods, I was rid of the spiked Fire. Worried as I was about Tira, I breathed easy for the first time since I found her on the floor.

Inside, I hustled up the steps with Tuc right behind me, stepped into the Glass Chamber and halted. Captain Jaf and the other guard were gone. Backs stiff, Elenia, Jessa, and Nemay sat around the table. But I was only dimly aware of them because Lord Suryan stood between them and me.

"Where were you?" Suryan asked.

At the ice in his voice, my heart turned over. "Tuc had to go out."

Suryan looked pointedly at the door to the balcony with steps leading to the garden. "The doctor informed me that Tira was once again ill from Mage flower. When Captain Jaf entered your room to search it, you were missing. At that point, Jessa remembered something." He tipped his hand toward Jessa.

"I'm very sorry to have to say it." Jessa's mouth crunched around a smile. "But you had a bag with you when you brought Tira home."

"You and Nemay may go," Suryan said.

The two of them rose, but Jessa paused. "She's a pickpocket too, my lord."

Suryan waved them away, and they fled down the hall. He turned to me. "Jaf couldn't find the bag Jessa described. If I questioned my household right now, would I find at least one person who saw you leaving these quarters with it?"

"It wasn't mine," I blurted. "The boy who carried Tira home gave it to me to hold, and I forgot to give it back."

"So you were at Festival with someone who dealt in Mage flower?" Suryan said.

"I didn't know! I met him at Veren's warehouse."

Leaning forward in her chair, Elenia shot a look at her father before speaking to me. "Are you claiming this dealer is one of Veren's men?"

"No! Fitch is from Rhale Island, not Eastway."

"Dilly, I want to trust you," Elenia said. "But how can I? This Mage flower is poison. I won't be part of letting it hurt my people. What's more, you brought it into my own quarters! What happened to Tira is your fault."

The room faded in and out. "But I'm telling the truth! Why don't you believe me?"

"You are no longer welcome here," Suryan said.

Breath coming in pants, I took a step toward Elenia.

"You said you wouldn't let one of your attendants be thrown out." How could she betray me like this?

"Daughter, you may go too," Suryan said. Elenia pressed her lips together but obeyed. Suryan turned back to me. "I gave you a chance because King Thien asked it. But perhaps you can't leave the streets behind. I want you out of here within the hour." He swept from the room.

I sank into a chair that was still warm from Elenia's body. I'd told the truth, and she hadn't believed me. Instead, she was sending me to find food and shelter in whatever way I could scrounge from the streets. My chest was so tight, I couldn't breathe. I had to put my head between my knees to keep from passing out.

Someone knocked, and without waiting for an answer, Captain Jaf entered. "I'm sorry, Dilly," he said, "but Lord Suryan just ordered me to escort you out of the Fortress. Do you need help gathering your things?"

My stunned brain slowly worked through what he'd said. I rose on unsteady legs. "I can manage." I started down the hallway to my room, sliding one hand along the wall to be sure I didn't collapse. When Jaf followed me, I repeated, "I can manage."

"I'm sorry," he said again, "but under the circumstances, I need to make sure you don't take anything that isn't yours."

My face got hot, but I could hardly blame Jaf. I did pick the man's pocket.

In my room, Tira snored on while Jaf watched from

the doorway. I found my satchel and picked through the clothes in my chest, struggling to figure out what to take. If I was on the streets, would any of it be useful? I was already wearing my plainest dress, and I put my rain-damp jacket on over it. I stuffed my satchel with a change of underclothes, my boy's trousers and shirt, and my cloak. In a moment of clarity, I reached for the bits of jewelry Elenia had given me. Those would be saleable if only to a fence who'd be sure I stole them. A hand clamped around my wrist.

"Leave those," Jaf said.

"They were gifts from Elenia. You can ask her."

"I'm not going to bother her now. Leave them."

I let the jewelry go. I also left the box with my stolen treasures, including Jessa's spool of red thread. She should sew her mouth shut with it.

As Jaf waited, I checked on Tira one last time. "Be more careful," I murmured. "The world isn't as safe as a rich girl might think." I pulled her covers up and used the sheet to mop a thread of drool on her cheek. Then Tuc and I followed Jaf back to the Glass Chamber.

He escorted me to the gate and eyed the street beyond. "The small gods keep you," he said, and Tuc and I walked out into Lac's Holding.

# Chapter 18

## Fitch

"I T'S NOT MY bag," Fitch said again.

"Of course not. It never is." The Watchman shoved Fitch into a cell, slammed the door, and turned the key.

The Watchman's partner still held the bag Dilly had thrust into Fitch's hands. He fished out a jug, uncorked it, and sniffed, just as he'd done on the street. Fitch was a yard away, but he could still smell the Mage flower. "You're Gavun Rhale's boy, aren't you?"

"Smugglers." The first man spat on the jail floor. "Always thought Gavun was the one bringing the Mage flower in."

"You're wrong," Fitch said. "And that bag isn't mine. I wasn't selling anything to that girl. She's the one who gave me the bag."

They both laughed. "The Fortress girl? She was ticked off at you," the first man said. "You picked the wrong target." They both walked back to the front room.

Fitch dropped onto one of the two shelf beds and tried to make sense of what happened. The Watchman was right enough that Dilly was ticked off. *Bastard*, he heard her again. He'd handled the bag she gave him for no more than a moment before she sent the Watch swooping down on him to grab it and lift the flap. He'd been stupefied at the sight of the jugs. The Fire obviously wasn't his, and when he looked, neither was the bag.

Elbows propped on his knees, he buried his face in his hands and tried to think. Maybe she believed the bag really did belong to him. He pictured the events of the previous night – strolling with Dilly, collecting for Gavun, finding Dilly's hurt friend. He lowered his hands and frowned at a patch of green fuzz growing on the wall opposite. The man who'd been bending over Tira, the one Fitch had just seen in the Blue Whale, he'd run off when Dilly and Fitch approached, but hadn't he left a bag behind? Fitch had dropped his carry bag to pick up Tira, and Dilly had grabbed it for him. Could she have picked up the wrong one?

"Hey, Fitch," someone called.

He shoved to his feet and went to look through the bars into the cell across the way. It held two boys about his own age from the Half-Moon kinship, a family whose head, Owun, Gavun sometimes took as an ally. Fitch recognized the boy with the sea serpent tattoo on his neck as Owun's son and heir, Royce.

"Welcome to the Mage flower sellers club." Royce leaned back, feigning a relaxed state that his jiggling knee put the lie to.

"You Half-Moon islanders the ones bringing it in?" Fitch asked as casually as he could. Owun Half-Moon was a target he hadn't considered.

"Just selling it," the other boy said. *Erald*, Fitch thought. "We didn't run it past customs. That was Gavun, wasn't it?"

"No."

Erald giggled. "Whatever you say." Fitch judged he'd been drinking his own wares. "Did they tell you we're being taken to the Fortress to be questioned by Suryan himself?"

Fitch tightened his fingers on the bars. Why was Suryan taking a personal role in this? Maybe last night's riot had been some sort of final straw for him. If that had worked Suryan up, he'd be trying hard to find out where the Mage flower was coming from. Fitch was all for that. He just didn't want to be the one Suryan squeezed to cough up the information. Fitch had heard talk of hot irons, whips, hooks.

On the other hand, maybe Suryan suspected the plot Gavun had laid out for Fitch. Dilly had hinted that the Lord of Lac's Holding was planning some action against the kinships. Did he suspect they were plotting to remove him? If that was so, Suryan might resort to torture to find out what was up. Even if he didn't, Suryan sent young men and women he was unhappy with to serve in his army. Fitch had already avoided the army once and didn't want to have to figure out how to do it again. In either case, Fitch had to get out of here.

He pressed his face against the rusty bars and looked sideways down the hall. The Watchmen who'd brought him in had gone, but he could see the booted foot of the jailer who'd been lounging on a bench when they dragged Fitch past. Maybe he could nudge the man to believe he was supposed to release Fitch. "Jailer," he called.

The man appeared at the end of the hallway. "What?" Behind him the front door opened, and he turned back as three Fortress guards barged in.

The woman wearing a sergeant's sash said, "You have some island trash for us?"

Fitch cursed. He should have acted more quickly.

The jailer led the guards down the hall, unlocked the door of the cell across the way, and herded Royce and Erald out. Royce's throat knot bobbed. Erald swayed and hummed a Festival tune. Fitch edged into the shadows of his cell and held his breath. Then the jailer shoved a key in the lock of Fitch's cell. "Is he ours too?" the sergeant asked.

"Just came in." The jailer swung Fitch's cell door open.

"If I'd known there'd be three, I'd have brought another guard." The sergeant entered the cell and cuffed Fitch herself.

"You wanted island boys, right? This one is Gavun Rhale's," the jailer said.

"Is he now?" The sergeant raised an eyebrow. Both of her underlings turned to look.

"That bag wasn't mine," Fitch tried.

All three guards and the jailer laughed. The sergeant planted her palm in Fitch's back and shoved, leaving him no choice but to stumble out of the cell and out into the street after the rest. The guards elbowed a path through shoppers and strollers. Not that much elbowing was needed. People saw the uniforms and scattered like rats.

Fitch thought frantically, fishing for a way out of trouble. He'd have to convince Lord Suryan he hadn't been selling spiked Fire. Or, Healer help him, conspired in treason. Although of course he had. Maybe he could nudge Suryan, though the thought of pawing around in the mind of the Lac's Holding Lord made his stomach churn.

The sergeant greeted the Fortress gate guard as she shoved Fitch through and around to a side door into what looked to be some kind of guard room. Pikes and swords were neatly stowed, and the room smelled of leather and oil. At the sight of the weapons, Fitch gave up any faint hope of having his hands freed. The guards wouldn't want anyone in this room except them to get hold of something sharp and pointy.

"Fetch Lord Suryan," the sergeant ordered. One of her men vanished through an inner door.

Fitch gulped deep breaths, trying to relax enough to drag some clever ploy up from his smuggler's brain. Erald was humming again. If he didn't quit it, Fitch might save the guards some trouble and club him silly with his cuffed hands.

Suryan must have been nearby because they waited no more than a handful of moments before brisk footsteps echoed, the door opened, and he strode in. Fitch had seen Suryan around the city, but this was the first time he'd been close enough that, if he wished to, he could have priced the green gems dangling from the lord's hoop earrings. The way he moved made Fitch think of Gavun. They both walked as if everyone else would get out of the way. The sergeant shoved, and Fitch landed on his knees with a painful thud in a line next to Royce and Erald.

Suryan leaned his hips back against a desk, crossed his arms, and studied them. He held his silence long enough that Fitch had plenty of time to panic. Erald giggled. Royce elbowed him, and he hiccupped and fell silent.

"Names," Suryan said.

"Royce and Erald Half-Moon," Royce choked out.

Suryan's gaze slid to Fitch, who was having trouble making his mouth work. The sergeant kicked Fitch in the back. He caught himself on his cuffed hands. "Answer Lord Suryan."

Fitch pushed himself erect. "Fitch of Rhale Island."

Suryan raised an eyebrow at the sergeant who pointed first at the Half-Moon boys. "Son and cousin to the family head. And this one—" She pointed to Fitch.

"I know," Suryan said. "Gavun's boy."

Fitch would have expected Suryan to know who led each island family. It was his business to know that. But to know Fitch, who'd been away for a year? That made him shift uneasily. Suryan had to have been studying the island families closely to know that.

"I understand you three were selling spiked Winter Fire," Suryan said.

"No, sir," Royce said. "We'd never."

"Maybe a little." Erald smiled as if he'd given a good answer to his tutor.

"I wasn't," Fitch said. "Not last night and not today either. The bag wasn't mine."

The sergeant kicked him in the same spot, forcing a grunt out of him.

"Where did you get it?" Suryan asked.

Silence. Of course there was silence, Fitch thought. Royce and Erald were contemplating the impossibility of betraying kin. Fitch was contemplating whether to implausibly but more or less truthfully say he'd found it. He felt the sergeant shift her weight onto one foot before Royce said, "We found it."

The sergeant gestured to the guard behind the Half-Moon boys. He punched Royce in the side of the head.

Good thing Fitch had been slow to speak then.

Suryan strolled to stand a foot in front of Fitch, close enough for Fitch to smell the pipe filler the man smoked. From Parda, he thought. "Was it Gavun?" Suryan asked.

Fitch cricked his neck to meet Suryan's hard eyes. "My father swore to me he's not bringing it in, sir."

The sergeant kicked him again, in the shoulder this time, sending him sideways so he wouldn't crash into Suryan's legs. The pain in Fitch's elbow competed with the pain in his back. The sergeant seized his shirt collar and hauled him to his knees again.

"I know how these cursed island kinships work," Suryan said. "You pups wouldn't have made a move without approval. What do you know about last night's riot?"

Erald smiled dreamily. "That was amazing."

Suryan bent so his face was close to Erald's. "That was treason," he said softly. Fitch's mouth went dry.

Erald cocked his head. "You're not angry at us, are you?"

Suryan straightened. "The kinship heads have been meeting for three days. What are they up to?"

"If you know how the kinships work, you know the heads aren't likely to have confided in us," Fitch said steadily.

Suryan studied him, then stepped back. "Sergeant, take them to the cells. See if you can't persuade them to tell us what's afoot." He swept out of the room.

The sergeant grabbed Fitch's arm and dragged him to his feet, which was good because Fitch wasn't sure he could have risen by himself. His back and arm throbbed. But he'd have worse than bruises by the time Suryan's jailers got through with him.

# Chapter 19

## Dilly

I WALKED AWAY from the Fortress, vaguely aware of passing other people who laughed and sang and seemed happy. I felt numb, alone on the streets with just myself and Tuc to rely on. I bumped into a woman because my vision blurred with tears. "Sorry." I blinked hard and wandered on.

Finally I stumbled, braced my hand on a wall, and found my feet had taken me to the entrance of the small gods shrine. I made my way down into the cool dark surrounded by statues of the gods. They were all there – the Trickster, the Sailor's Guard, the Healer, the Guardian Dog, and dozens more. I circled once before collapsing on the bottom step.

"Thanks a lot," I said.

Tuc sniffed in the Guardian Dog's bowl and came up

as empty of comfort as I did. I stripped off my shoes and stockings and rubbed my feet on a dry spot along my skirt's hem.

The dazed state began to clear out of my brain. This was Fitch's fault, no doubt, but Elenia's betrayal hurt even more. I'd served her faithfully. How could she believe I'd bring something harmful into her quarters? Curse Elenia anyway. I didn't need her. Rin City had taught me a lot.

Tuc rested his chin on my knee. I stroked his head, flooded with a memory of the day I'd found him. Or maybe the day he'd found me. The disease destroying Mama had finally left her unconscious. Unable to bear the sight of her one more moment, I'd gone out to sit on the steps in front of the house where we rented a room. The filthy street swam in and out of sight. And then a wet nose had pushed under my hand, and Tuc had whined, sharing my grief. I'd buried my face in his smelly fur and wept.

Late that afternoon, Mama died. When a street kid who'd befriended me heard and came to invite me to join up with him, Tuc glued himself to my side. The kid had laughed and said, "Him too. The Powers only know how much street kids need a watch dog." Tuc and I had gone with him, and I found myself with friends who looked after one another.

"Just you and me this time, Tuc."

He shook himself and looked up the steps to the street.

"You're right. Moping here isn't going to help. I need to look for work." That sounded like a plan, and I felt better for saying it. "One of the alehouses might need extra help for the last two nights of Festival." I considered my satchel. It would look better if I weren't carrying it like a homeless person, even though I was one. Again. I circled the shrine, finally spotting a space behind the Trickster. My god, Mama always said. I fished dry stockings out and tucked the satchel in the gap. Maybe I could even sleep here. The small gods might take me in. I put my shoes back on, brushed my hands over my skirt, and went up into the city with Tuc at my heels.

I'd looked for work in Rin, but I'd forgotten how discouraging it was to be turned away from place after place. Midday came, and I finally realized that I was losing hope partly because I was hungry. Now there was a feeling that brought back memories. And panic. I needed work and I needed it now. The next alehouse on Corsair Street was a place called the Blue Whale, but the woman at the counter gave me the same answer everyone else had. She didn't need a serving maid. When I turned away, I stumbled and had to grab a table to stay upright. It was too much. I burst into tears.

"Are you all right?" The counter woman appeared at my side. "Here sit down." She pulled out a chair.

"I'm fine."

She cocked her head at me. "Sit." She pushed me into the chair, and Tuc huddled against my legs. "I may have spoken too quickly. I might need someone after all. Here, you rest a bit while I think." She brought a slice of cheese pie and a mug of small beer, waving away my protest. "We'll talk about it later."

I broke off a corner of the pie for Tuc and had settled down to eat when Tuc stiffened and growled.

"Fair afternoon, Dilly." The voice sent a chill through my body. "You all on your own?" Cole sat in the table's other chair. "Did Elenia throw you out?"

"Not Elenia. Lord Suryan." Still stupidly loyal to my lady, that was me.

Cole leaned back in his chair, pursing his lips. "I didn't know you saw much of Suryan."

"More than I wanted to."

"Enough to know what he's up to these days?"

I tried to take a bite of pie, but my stomach curdled. "Get away from me, Cole."

He rose. "Come with me. I'll look after you."

"I'd sooner go with a scorpion," I spat.

Grabbing my arm tightly enough to make me cry out, he dragged me to my feet. "Forgive my wayward daughter," he called to the woman at the counter.

"I'm not his daughter!" I twisted in his grip.

Tuc didn't make a sound, but from the corner of my eye, I glimpsed a blur of grey and brown fur hurtling toward Cole.

Cole kicked him hard, sending him flying into a corner where he collapsed in a boneless heap, twitched once, and lay still. "Tuc!" I cried.

The counter woman had started toward us, but now

she backed away, eyes wide, hands raised to show she was staying out of this. "You have to help me," I begged. Cole clapped a hand over my mouth and hauled me out of the alehouse.

# Chapter 20

## Fitch

THE SERGEANT SHOVED Fitch out of the weapon storage room and into part of the Fortress yard obviously given over to the guards. On one side, a squad of them practiced fighting with staves. The sergeant aimed Fitch toward a small outbuilding set against the outside wall. Far enough away that the household wouldn't have to hear any screaming, Fitch thought wildly. Or the shouts of protest Royce and Erald gave now as the guards dragged them over the threshold. He tried frantically to nudge the sergeant holding him into letting go, but her mind was on only one thing: loosening Fitch's tongue. He glimpsed her mental image of him hanging by his arms from the ceiling. As far as he could tell, she took no enjoyment from the idea. She had the same feel Gavun had when he declared something was only business. Trickster help him.

Another guard ran up. "Sergeant, a messenger just came and said the sentry is missing from the side gate."

Swearing, the sergeant handed Fitch over to the new man. "Put him in a special cell," she said and jogged away.

"This way." The guard dragged Fitch away from where the Half-Moon boys had vanished, between two low buildings that looked like barracks.

Fitch fought against panic that rendered him unable to even try entering this man's mind. "Aren't I going with them? I don't need someplace special really."

"Shut it if you want to stay in one piece," the guard said. He swept off his cloak and flung it over Fitch's head. Fitch struggled for air. His knees hit something solid, and with a shove from the guard, he landed in what felt like a box. He'd heard of prisoners held in spaces so small they couldn't move. With his face covered, he already felt suffocated. When the guard grabbed his legs, he kicked and the man swore and jammed Fitch's knee against a wall. A light weight settled over Fitch's back. After a moment, he heard the clop of a horse's feet and the box moved.

Not a box, Fitch realized. A horse cart. Breath shallow, he lay still. Was he better off or not? The cart halted and through the cloak and whatever else lay over him, Fitch heard the guard say, "I'm off to visit my parents."

"During Festival?" another voice said. "You're a good son."

The cart moved again, jolting over cobblestones that

sent pain flaring in all Fitch's ripening bruises. Around them, cheerful voices sounded. The cart turned into a quieter street and after a moment, it stopped.

"You have him?" a familiar voice asked.

"You have the money?" the guard asked.

Coins clinked, and Fitch found himself being hauled to his feet. The cloak and a blanket fell away. Fitch sucked in a deep breath, relieved to find that his legs would hold him after all. The guard cut unlocked his cuffs.

"As always, a pleasure doing business with you," Gavun said.

"This is the last time," the guard said. "I intend to be well away from here before Suryan knows your boy is missing." He threw the blanket and cloak into the cart, climbed onto the seat, and drove off.

Fitch rubbed the welts on his wrists as his father steered him into Caravan Street, leading down to the harbor. He drew a long cool breath filled with the smell of sausage and Festival cakes. "How much did I cost?"

"Five kings."

Fitch had to snap his mouth shut. "That's… a lot."

"There are times when I'm not sure we're the biggest law breakers." Gavun grinned widely. "Who'd have thought it? Fitch the Pure selling spiked Fire."

"Not so," Fitch said stiffly. "That bag wasn't mine."

Gavun laughed out loud. "That's my boy. Anyway, I'm glad to get you out of there. We have a meeting with Veren and the other kinship heads."

"I'm not sure we should go. Suryan knows the islanders have been meeting. He's watching for trouble. Hanging out with Veren is dangerous."

Gavun made a rude noise. "If we stick together, Suryan is finished."

Fitch tried to read his father's face. Gavun was the smoothest liar Fitch had ever met. Even having watched his father all his life, he couldn't tell if Gavun believed what he was saying. "You're sure Veren is a good bet?"

"Are you so hot for Suryan's rule? What do you think would have happened if I left you to his tender mercies?" Gavun jerked his thumb over his shoulder. Fitch grimaced. "If that's not enough," Gavun said, "think about how much better off we'd all be if Elenia were ruling with Veren to teach her about the needs of importers."

"Us, you mean?" Fitch said. "You flatter us. We're smugglers."

"We wouldn't need to smuggle if the customs weren't so high."

"You'd do it anyway," Fitch said. "There's always a gull to make by undercutting the legit importers."

For a moment, Gavun looked as if he might claim to be insulted. Instead, he laughed and clapped his hands together. "All I'm asking at the moment is that you come to this meeting. For me, for the kinship. Surely you're islander enough for that."

Fitch felt the pull of what his father offered – a home, people who'd known him his whole life, people who accepted him as theirs. What was his alternative? Go with his mother and Brend? She wanted him, or said she did. But she'd been happy enough to leave him alone for years, while he'd grown up learning to fit in with his island kin. He was Gavun's heir. He and Loni knew one another like they knew themselves. He was a skilled smuggler and a convincing liar. What would he be if he *weren't* those things?

At Gavun's side, he threaded through streets where people were beginning to gather in the cocoa shops, cafes, and alehouses. It was too early for there to be much music, but a lute player plucked a hopeful song with a bowl at his feet for coins. At the bottom of the street, they turned onto the docks, and Fitch followed his father up the gangplank onto the *Storm King*. The woman on watch glanced at Fitch but let them pass.

Gavun obviously knew where he was going. He led the way below and knocked on a cabin door. "It's Gavun," he called.

"Come."

When Gavun obeyed the invitation, Fitch saw four men seated around the table of the ship's mess. He recognized three of them – heads of the kinships from Half-Moon, Westway, and Sera Islands. The fourth man must be Veren Eastway, though Fitch had never known him well enough to be sure. They must have been here a while. The room smelled of wet wool and leather. Fitch's nerves prickled. He'd never seen all the island heads working together before.

"Sorry I'm late." Gavun pointed at Fitch with his chin. "I had to spring Fitch here from the Fortress."

Every head snapped toward Fitch.

"The Fortress had you?" Veren asked. "What for?"

"They thought I was selling spiked Winter Fire."

"Were you?" Veren asked.

"No." Fitch nodded at Owun Half-Moon. "Royce and Erald were though. Suryan told the guards to find out what they could from them and then ship them off to the army. Also, he knows you've all been meeting, though he doesn't know why, so he's keeping a close eye on you."

"Suryan has my boys?" Owun cursed. "He's getting ready to take over the islands. You can see it."

"That's more or less what the Fortress guards threatened would happen when they came calling two nights ago – the first night of Festival," Gavun said.

"They gave me the same message," Owun Half-Moon said. "Gave it to all of us, I guess."

"Will your boys talk?" Veren asked Owun.

"They don't know anything," Owun said.

"That may be true," Fitch said, "but Erald at least had been drinking spiked Fire. He'll agree to anything Suryan suggests."

Veren glared at Owun. "I warned you about keeping them under control."

"You should have sprung them when you did Fitch, Gavun," Owun said.

"They're not mine," Gavun said. "I'm not made of money."

That was Gavun, Fitch thought. What had Owun expected? Fitch himself still couldn't take in what Gavun had paid for him. Coin might not be a good measure of a *normal* father's… Fitch groped for a word. Regard? Value?… Love? Whatever it was, coin told him the measure of Gavun's. What was he supposed to make of that?

"I'll see if I can get them out." Owun rose and left.

Gavun took his empty chair. Fitch hooked his foot around the leg of a stool and pulled it up next to his father. He found Veren frowning at him.

"Gavun told us you'd help sway the Watch and Fortress guards to our side. If they picked you up and held you, will they know you? How useful will you be in influencing them?"

"Hard to say," Fitch said. "Depends on which ones I run into. They're busy, and only some will know I'm supposed to be in a cell. The Watch might even think Suryan let me go."

Veren rubbed his jaw and then shrugged. "We'll have to rely on bribes for those." He cocked his head. "You said Suryan told the guards what to do with you. Does that mean you saw Suryan?"

"He questioned us himself," Fitch said.

Gavun swiveled to look at Fitch. "You didn't tell me that."

"I didn't think to," Fitch said.

"What exactly did he want to know?" Veren leaned forward.

Fitch's back gave a painful throb at the memory of the scene with Suryan. "He asked about Mage flower. He wanted to know where it came from. He believed it was part of what kicked off the riot last night. He thought someone used it deliberately, probably one of you." He scanned the men still at the table and wished he could see how Owen Half-Moon would have reacted.

"The man's not a fool," Veren said. "I'll give him that."

Fitch snapped his gaze back to Veren and took in the man's calm, unsurprised tone. In the back of his head, he heard the Trickster giggle. It was as if he saw something that had been in front of him all along, begging to be noticed. Of course Gavun had lied to him about Mage flower being involved in Veren's plot. Gavun saw profit and meant for Rhale Island to make it. "You used spiked Fire to provoke that riot. It's part of how you mean to turn people against Suryan."

Veren raised an eyebrow. "You disapprove?" he asked, a faint note of warning in his voice. "Gavun, you said he was with us."

"He is." Gavun's chair creaked when he shifted. "He swore on pain of banishment from the kinship."

So Fitch had, idiot that he was. He kept his gaze on Veren's face. "You smuggled the Mage flower in and put it in the Winter Fire you were legally importing."

"Hush, Fitch," Gavun said more loudly.

Veren's eyes darted from Gavun to Fitch. "I put it in the Winter Fire we imported, true, but your father supplied the flower."

The Trickster's giggle rose to a guffaw. Fitch spun toward Gavun, whose face went pale. "Is that true? Not only is there flower involved, but *you're* the supplier?"

Gavun patted the air between them. "Calm down."

"He brought it in last year, hoping to use it to drive his prices higher," Veren said. "I thought that's what he was doing even then, and this Festival, when I was ready to act on my plan, I knew where to go."

Still watching Gavun, Fitch choked on a laugh. "The Trickster let Nera fall the day she took up with Rhale Island men. You drugged her, and I sent her to her death."

"I swear I didn't know what would happen," Gavun said. "I was just trying out a new product. I wouldn't have hurt her on purpose. You were too lovesick for me even to consider it."

"But you took the chance," Fitch said. "And small gods curse you, you know this year."

"That's just business," Gavun said.

"We're all in this together, Gavun," Veren said. "If your boy won't cooperate, that's a problem."

A storm roared in Fitch's head. The cabin faded in and out. His chest was so tight, he couldn't breathe. There was a problem all right. His father had betrayed him, lied to him, poisoned Nera. Fitch had believed Gavun's protests of innocence because he wanted to. And now Gavun had sold the poison for Veren to use on everyone in Lac's Holding.

# Chapter 21

## Dilly

MY WRISTS BURNED in Cole's rope-rough grip as he shoved me up the *Storm King's* gangway. Hidden inside my still damp hood, I pushed my tongue against the snot crusted handkerchief he'd stuffed in my mouth as soon as he got me around a corner from the Blue Whale. The woman on watch looked quickly away from me before saying, "They're still meeting."

Cole flung me down the steep stairs to the cabins. I plummeted down, striking my shoulder on a step and finally landing on my knees and one elbow, sending pain jolting through them. I scrambled up again and threw my hood back, but before I could pry the kerchief out, Cole was on me. His weight slammed me against the wall. "Take it out. Go ahead. No one here will care if you scream." He pushed me into a cabin and yanked the door shut behind me. I hurled myself against it, but the lock clicked and Cole called, "I won't be long. The kinship heads will want to hear if you know anything useful about what's going on in the Fortress."

I yanked the cloth from my mouth and spat lint. I kept seeing Tuc flying across the alehouse and landing like a broken thing. Cole, Fitch, Suryan, Elenia, and for all I knew, even the stoning small gods had let me down. And before that, Mama. Only Tuc had stayed faithful. The cabin blurred, and I realized I was crying. Was he hurt badly? Was he in pain? I refused to believe he was dead. I had to get out of here and help him.

I needed a weapon. I dragged everything out of a cupboard onto the floor and opened a box that turned out to hold only leather-wrapped stones that were probably pricier than they looked. I helped myself to two, taking the leather square too so Cole wouldn't see they were missing. If stones were the only weapon I had, then stones were what I would use.

The latch rattled. I eased the box shut and faced the door, my fist curled around the stones. Busy hooking his key ring over his belt, Cole entered. I punched at him with the fist holding the stones, but he saw it coming and dodged so my knuckles only grazed his jaw. What's more, I'd thrown myself off balance. He pinned me with one arm with maddening ease and crushed me back against his chest.

"Calm down or I'll have to hurt you."

"I swear I'll kill you, Cole."

He laughed, making every muscle in my body tighten with the urge to smash him in the mouth. I managed to pocket the stones. *Later*, I promised myself. This vile piece of garbage kicked Tuc, and he was going to pay. Clutching my arm in a bruising grip, Cole escorted me into the next cabin, which turned out to be the mess where men sat around a table with Veren at its head. All but one of them turned toward us, and small gods help me, I realized the one who didn't was Fitch. How had he got away from the Watch? He stared at the man next to him with wild eyes. Maybe he'd been drinking the spiked Winter Fire he palmed off on me.

"You liar," I bit out. Fitch's head snapped toward me. "You railed against Mage flower and then sold it. You're as bad as him." I jerked my chin toward Cole. "The sack of muck kicked my dog! You're all involved, aren't you? You're greedy and don't care who you hurt."

"Watch your mouth." Cole twisted my arm up behind my back hard enough that I couldn't help crying out.

Fitch closed his eyes, his breath loud and uneven. The man next to him murmured, "Easy." I recognized his father.

Veren tapped the table. "Dilly, I hear my beloved threw you out. Did you tell her I was, perhaps, untrustworthy?"

"I tried. She didn't believe me." Bitterness fouled my tongue.

"And Suryan?"

"He doesn't like you," I said. "But you knew that."

Veren smiled. "I'm crushed. I hear he knows we're meeting. What's he planning to do about it?"

"I don't know."

"She probably doesn't," Cole said. "She's sly but remarkably stupid."

I hadn't thought I could hate him more than I already did, but it turned out I was wrong.

"Nonetheless, she can't run around loose." Veren glanced at the other men. "Lock her up again, Cole." He flicked his gaze over the other men, then back to me before smoothing adding, "Don't hurt her, of course."

"Of course," Cole said.

In a blur of movement, Fitch snatched the knife from Gavun's belt and dove across the table at Veren.

The small room exploded in shouts and moving men. Someone knocked Fitch aside, bumping Veren who fell toward me and Cole. Veren's elbow jabbed me hard in the ribs. Cole briefly lost his grip on me but blocked me from the doorway. When I could once again see the whole room, three men were on top of Fitch, including Gavun, who beat Fitch's wrist against the floor until he dropped the knife. Gavun wiped its bloody blade on his trousers and shoved it back in its sheath. "Fitch, you fool." He climbed to his feet and watched with his chest heaving as the other two dragged Fitch upright.

"I'm sorry, Dilly," Fitch said. "I swear that bag wasn't

mine." Blood oozed from his nose. He swiped the back of his hand across his face, smearing his cheek.

He'd drawn more blood than he lost, though. Veren pressed his hand over his shoulder where his shirt sleeve was turning red. "What's going on, Gavun?"

"Boy's got a bug up his butt about Mage flower," Gavun said. "He takes it personally. He'll calm down when he's had time to think."

Veren eyed him appraisingly, then said, "Lock them both up, Cole."

"He won't break his vow to me," Gavun said. "I can just take him home."

"Not until this is over," Veren said. "Excuse me while I change my shirt."

Cole dragged me back to the same cabin, and the two men holding Fitch shoved him in after me, hard enough that he fell.

He jumped to his feet, shook the latch, and then battered his shoulder against the door. When it held, he pressed his forehead against it. "Small gods strike me down as a fool," he murmured. "And curse you, Gavun." He went to look out the porthole. "Let's get out of here," he said. When I didn't answer right away, he glanced at me. "Unless you want to wait for one of them to decide what happens to us." I shook my head, and he leaned out the porthole. "Can you swim?"

I eyed him, trying to decide what to do. Something had broken between him and his father. That I understood. Something had broken between me and Elenia too, the way it had between me and Mama. But my sympathy went only so far. He'd been carrying spiked Fire. His smuggler's greed got me thrown out onto the streets. Still, at the moment, I was stuck with him as my only ally.

He drew his head in. "Can you swim?" he repeated impatiently.

"No, but you'd never get those shoulders through there. It doesn't matter. I don't plan for either one of us to go into that filthy water."

"You have a better idea?"

I held up the ring of keys I'd taken from Veren's belt when he stumbled into me.

"Healer bless you." He reached for the keys, but I tucked them behind me.

"You'll have to excuse me if I keep hold of these myself rather than trusting you."

He flinched. A bruise already darkened on his left cheek. He turned toward the door. "We'll have to get past the woman at the gangway. Maybe I can nudge her into letting us pass."

I shuddered. The less this boy messed with people's heads, the safer I'd feel. "She doesn't know Veren locked you up, right? Why don't you escort me off as if you mean to be cruel to me? You can fake something, I'm sure."

His mouth twisted. "You at least trust me not to *actually* be cruel?"

I puffed out a short laugh. "Bless your pointy ears, I

don't trust you at all. But you want out of here and so do I."

I unlocked the door, peered out, and then drew back quickly when I saw Veren returning to the mess, still buttoning his cuffs. I raised a hand to quiet Fitch, waited, and then checked again. All clear. When Fitch slipped out into the hallway after me, I relocked the cabin. "Let them wonder about that one," I whispered. As we climbed up to the deck, I could hear men arguing loudly inside the other cabin. Good. The longer they fought with one another, the longer it would take them to realize we'd escaped.

Fitch put his hand close enough to my back that I felt its warmth but not its touch. He jerked his chin toward the gangway. "Don't even think of giving me any trouble," he snarled, loudly enough to be heard.

I went where he pointed. "Please don't hurt me," I said as pathetically as I could without vomiting.

"What's up?" The woman on guard grinned at Fitch. "She the one who gave you that bloody nose?"

Fitch scowled. "Aren't you supposed to be watching for trouble?"

"Nothing's happening," the guard groused.

"Keep it that way," Fitch said.

When the woman turned to scan the dock, I dropped Veren's keys into the water, earning a surprised grunt from Fitch. We walked down the gangway and turned into Caravan Street. As soon as we were out of sight, Fitch sped up, so I had to pluck at his sleeve to get his attention. I hated to ask for his help, but again, he was my only resource. "I have to go to the Blue Whale alehouse," I panted.

He slowed slightly. "Forget the Blue Whale. You and I both have to get out of sight. Once Veren misses us, he'll send people to hunt us down so we can't spill his plans to Suryan. Not that I can go near him to spill as much as a cup of cocoa," he added. "Suryan's guards will be looking for me too, since they're supposed to be torturing me."

"So you've been busy making enemies everywhere, which is one thing that happens to liars. I can't leave Tuc."

He groaned. "Don't be so stubborn. My mother is leaving Lac's Holding tomorrow night and wants me to go with her, which has novelty value if nothing else. She'd probably take you too if you want to go. But we have to hide until then."

"You can hide if you want. I have to find my dog. That slime sucker Cole *kicked* him. He needs me."

Fitch looked at me from the corner of his eye. "After Cole kicked him, he didn't follow you? That would be… unusual, based on what I saw of him."

"Cole dragged me away pretty quickly. And don't you dare put that sympathetic face on! He just needs my help. Go. I can find him on my own."

He gnawed his lip. "Suryan really threw you out of the Fortress?"

"He thought I'd brought the spiked Fire into Elenia's quarters." I enjoyed watching Fitch cringe. He *should* feel guilty. He'd ruined my life with Elenia.

"The stuff in that bag? I once again swear to you it wasn't mine."

"Where did it come from then?"

"I think you picked up the wrong bag when we took Tira home."

"So it's my fault?"

"I didn't mean it that way!"

He sounded so convincing, I had to remind myself that he'd out-and-out told me he was a good liar. I found I was sorry over that. He'd been there when I needed him with Cole and then with Tira.

Ahead, two of the Watch appeared at the end of Caravan Street and stopped to talk to a juggler. Fitch shoved me into the shadow under a balcony, pressing close enough that once again, I felt his heat across the finger's width of space between us. A spot of blood smudged the cheek that wasn't bruised. My stomach fluttered. *Don't*, I told myself. *If you do, you are stupider than Mama.*

"They're gone." He backed away. He wasn't looking at me, but rather watching the end of the street.

I licked my fingers and wiped his cheek. *No more. That's it.* "Go if you need to. I can't leave Tuc. I lived on the streets of Rin for months after my mother died, and Tuc never let me get hurt."

Fitch's hand brushed the place I'd touched. He cleared his throat. "All right. If you're so determined to do a stupid thing, I'll go with you to look for him. We can take him with us when we hide out and leave."

"I'm not going anywhere with you, Mage boy. And watch who you're calling stupid." Cole's insult still burned in my mind.

He lifted his hands and let them drop. "I assume you'll go with me if I show you to the Blue Whale?" He sounded exasperated, like I was the one who'd tricked him instead of the other way around.

"Just go." We started walking. "So what did you do to make your own father knock you down?" I asked. "Oh, I know. You lied."

"He's the troublesome kin I've mentioned," Fitch said grimly.

"I don't get it. He also defended you."

"He needs me to nudge people's minds for him. I don't think he's even noticed how shaky it's made me the last couple of days. And healing seems beyond me." He frowned. "Something's changed," he murmured, softly enough that I barely heard.

"Kin is kin. At least you have some. You're not the one on the streets by yourself."

The pulse under his jaw jumped. "Don't sound so envious. The thought of being Gavun's boy makes me sick."

I looked down. There were salt stains on his trouser legs, as if his sea-bound island was clinging to him, or maybe he to it. I'd wager he'd find it harder than he expected to break with his father. I'd keep on being envious if I felt like it, thank you very much.

We walked on in silence while folks flowed around us, looking for a good Festival time. It must be nice to be them. Despite the crowd, when we entered the Blue Whale, the place was empty except for the counterwoman, who sat with her chin propped in her hand. "Fair afternoon, Fitch," she said. "Suryan's guards have been in here looking for you and Gavun. Drove all my other customers away with their Fortress stink." She glanced at me. "Is she all right?"

"Sort of," Fitch said.

I went straight to the back corner and looked around, but the only thing there was a ragged blanket.

"What happened to her dog, Evia?" Fitch asked the counterwoman.

"Gone." A tiny tremor rippled in her voice.

"Gone where?" I turned to find her face was pale.

"I don't know and that's the truth. Your mutt was hurt bad enough I figured he was dying and thought it might be merciful to end him myself." I clenched my fists, and she hastily put up her hands, palms out. "I couldn't bring myself to do it, so I snugged that blanket around him and figured the Trickster would decide. The place got busy then, and when I had time to check again, he was gone."

A moan fell out of my mouth. "He must have dragged himself away. Hurt like that, he can't have gone far."

"He couldn't have gone at all," the woman said. "He'd

have had to cross all the way from the back of the place to the front, and he was in no shape to do that." She hesitated before adding, "Not without help."

Fitch seemed to hear something in her voice. "Help? What help?"

"I don't know for sure. There was an old man. I didn't see him come in, but he was back there bending over the dog."

"A customer?" Fitch asked. "Did you know him?"

She shook her head. "He was… odd."

"Did he take Tuc?" I interrupted.

"I didn't see."

"You must know *something*," I cried.

"I'm sorry. I don't."

"This is useless. Have a good life, Fitch." I stomped out to the street, blinking. I didn't have time to waste crying.

# Chapter 22

## Fitch

FITCH HURRIED OUT after Dilly and found her scanning the nooks and crannies along the street's edge where a small, hurt animal might have hidden himself away. For a moment, he watched her, oblivious to early Festival goers strolling past behind her. Her repeated digs were starting to annoy him. He hadn't lied to her. Not about the spiked Fire anyway. It would take some effort to remember if he'd fiddled the truth at some other point. But he couldn't leave her alone and in trouble.

He approached her cautiously. "I'll help you look," he told her. "Then I'll take you wherever you want to go." He was relieved when she jerked a stiff nod.

He joined the search, still thinking about what Evia had said, or really about the tremor in her voice when she said it. Something spooked her, sure enough, and she was not a woman who spent time imagining things. He didn't know what to make of it.

Finally, Dilly stopped outside the small gods shrine on Sailmaker Street and turned back to look at territory they'd already covered. "We must have missed him." She cleared her throat, then pulled out a handkerchief and blew her nose.

Fitch turned too and glimpsed a figure in a blue and red uniform emerging from a side street. "Fortress guard."

He hustled Dilly down the steps into the shrine where he pulled her as far to one side as he could so they wouldn't be visible through the doorway. Her overwhelming fear for Tuc bubbled up in his head. He yanked his hand off her shoulder, and it eased. They waited in silence, his back pressed as close as he could get to a knobby-kneed god. He managed to resist the temptation to touch her again. There was something wrong with him, he thought unhappily. Nudging had done something to his hold on himself.

"He's gone," she said in a wobbly voice, then leaned against him and burst into tears. This soft-haired girl was apparently determined to test him. Despite his best efforts to block her out, he felt her pain, curling up through his gift. *Curse the thing.* Hidden truth often included pain. That's why it was hidden. He used to think he nearly always sensed pain in people because people in pain were the ones who went to a healer. Now he wasn't sure.

Dilly shuddered. He felt as if he were nosing into her

heart uninvited. Also, his body had decided it liked her pressing against him. He tried to distract himself by scanning the gods down near the floor until he spotted the bearded old man who was the god of healers. When he had first started training to be a Mage, he had thought of the healer god as his. When had he stopped doing that? When he started to use his gift to acquire things from his father? When Gavun set him to using it to help the kinship? As a kid, Fitch had liked the fact that he and his father shared a secret, that Gavun saw him as useful in a special way. Gavun was at sea much of the time, and when he was home, he wasn't a man who took much interest in a child, not even his own. Fitch had always believed his gift made his father see him differently.

Dilly straightened and blew her nose again.

"You had Tuc a long time?" Fitch felt torn between relief and the wish that she'd lean against him some more.

"Only a year and a bit, but some days, he was the only good thing in my life. He made me feel safe, and he *loved* me."

Fitch understood the power of that. "I'm sorry."

Dilly lifted her chin. "He'll find me as soon as he feels better. He can always find me."

"Sure he will. Are you ready to go to ground until we can leave with my mother?" he asked gently.

"With you? No."

He clenched his fists to keep from shaking her. "Can't you see I'm trying to help you?" The thought of her wandering alone made him frantic. Veren, Cole, any of the kinship heads could stumble across her. Veren's smooth "Don't hurt her, of course" hadn't fooled Fitch.

"Let me think." She went to stand by the god of lost women.

He stopped by the Healer, who reminded him uncomfortably of the old man who'd told him off the last time he was here, when he and Dilly first met, so he wandered over to nod at the Trickster. "Happy with yourself?" he asked.

Still scowling at the god, he heard Dilly murmuring and picked out Elenia's name. Small gods. Had she moved from saving Tuc to saving Elenia? The girl needed a little healthy fear for her own neck. And his neck too, he hoped. At least she hadn't called the Fortress guard in the street to arrest him. That beat what happened at the Fortress gates.

He felt movement at his shoulder, and Dilly stood there with smudged tears still on her cheeks. She pulled a satchel from behind the Trickster statue and fished in it for a clean handkerchief.

Fitch snapped his gaping mouth shut. "You keep clothes here?"

She put the satchel back. "Just temporarily." She smiled wanly at the Trickster. "I missed the small gods in Rin. They don't have shrines like this. But I always felt like the Trickster lived in Rin anyway. She was the one who taught me how to make a life with what I had." Dilly wriggled her fingers. "That was when I started picking pockets."

Fitch noted that Dilly called the Trickster *she*. He always saw the god as male, but it had both breasts and an erect male member. You found the god you needed, Fitch supposed. "The Trickster was never a god whose gaze I wanted on me. No smuggler does."

"I thought coming back to Lac's Holding would solve all my problems, especially if I lived in Elenia's household. I admired her. To me, it looked like she did what she liked and was independent."

Fitch snorted. "You're more independent than Elenia. You don't get to be strong by doing what you like. You survived a terrible situation that would break most people."

Dilly stilled her fingers by twisting them together. Her silence felt heavy. "It broke me a little. I've been putting myself back together ever since."

Without touching her skin, he prodded a red curl off her forehead. "Healers know that when a bone breaks, the place where it heals is stronger."

She jerked her head away and turned to face him. "I can't leave Lac's Holding yet. Elenia is about to do something foolish, and I have to stop her."

"She's romancing Veren, you mean. I know."

"It's more than that. She's agreed to marry him tomorrow night. After what we just saw on the *Storm King*, you know he'll be a bad husband."

For a moment, Fitch held back. He'd sworn to be part

of his kin's scheme with Veren. Betraying that would mark the end of something he found he still clung to. He closed his eyes, but when he opened them, reality was still there. "He'd be an even worse ruler. He intends to somehow push Suryan out and have Elenia take over, which really means *him* taking over."

Dilly's mouth opened and closed. "How?"

"I don't know, but I'm guessing that riot was an opening shot."

"We need to find out," Dilly said. "Veren's the one bringing in the Mage flower."

Fitch was strongly tempted to let her keep thinking that. How many truths was he supposed to cough up? He could have sworn the Trickster winked at him. "No. Gavun is."

She wrapped her arms around her waist and stepped back. "You knew that and let it happen?"

"I knew he was smuggling the Winter Fire. That's what he does. That's what we do." Fitch surprised himself by feeling defensive. "I didn't know about Mage flower until today when Veren told me." He swiped a hand down his face. "I wouldn't stand by and *let* it happen if I could stop it. Spiked Fire killed my girl last year, though I helped that along by nudging her, too." His gut twisted. It was the first time he'd ever confessed that he'd done more than merely suggest Nera do something exciting. He'd pushed her into it. Pushed her toward her death as sure as if he'd pushed her off that wall.

"The girl the charm belonged to," Dilly said.

He nodded.

She pursed her lips. "From the way you handle that charm, you couldn't have meant to hurt her."

"No, but I did." Outside the shrine, a woman laughed. A man called a greeting whose echo was lost in the rumble of a passing cart. Normal life went on for normal people who hadn't sent someone they loved to their death. Dilly held still, waiting. He felt as if he were on trial, only he didn't know if he or Dilly was the judge. "Her name was Nera." He cleared his throat. "She was keeping me company while I healed people on the first night of Festival last year. She'd brought a jug of Winter Fire. I didn't have much because strong drink interferes with my healing."

"I take it the Fire was spiked."

"I swear I didn't know."

She lifted an eyebrow.

"I didn't! Anyway, she started to fidget. She was bored, which I should have figured. She was always one to like adventure."

"So she went off after it?"

"She claimed she'd rather stay with me, but then Gavun showed up."

"Why?" She frowned.

"He wanted me to lend a hand with a big delivery. I didn't like the way he'd talked about her before I left home. He... he said I should nudge her into bed so I could move on and get over her."

Dilly's eyes narrowed. "Fine fatherly advice."

Fitch tamped down the fury he felt even remembering the scene. "I wanted Nera out of his sight, so I hugged her, and when I did, I nudged her to leave. 'Have a good time,' I said. 'Do something exciting.'" The pain in Fitch's chest felt like it might stop his heart. When he'd kissed the place below Nera's ear, body heat had funneled up her collar. "I never saw her alive again. She tried to walk along the top of the break wall and fell onto the rocks."

For a moment, the shrine was silent.

"I'm so sorry," Dilly said.

"I left Lac's Holding the next day. I couldn't stand to be around where she'd been. It felt as if she'd left me." For an instant, he was struck by the notion he might be talking about his mother as well as Nera. He crammed the thought into a hidey hole in his head. "I told Gavun her death was my fault, and he tried to talk me out of thinking that, but he never said anything about the Mage flower. Even this year, he convinced me he had nothing to do with it."

"You must have known. Can't you read his mind?"

"It doesn't work that way. I'd have had to nudge him around to thinking about it, and he's too aware of what I can do to even touch me."

"Your father doesn't touch you?" She tipped her head.

"No." For the first time in a long time, it occurred to him that that was odd.

She scanned his face as if looking for truth. "So," she said slowly, "you know what will happen with a bad man in charge. I can't let Elenia marry Veren."

With dwindling hope, Fitch groped for an excuse to hide until they could run. "You don't have to be the one who stops her. And didn't she let her father throw you out?"

"She made a mistake, just like Mama. Anyone can make a mistake. And it *has* to be me. I'm the one who knows the truth."

"Truth is a pain. Take it from one who knows."

"It's still truth. I can't let Elenia fall into Veren's hands. I can't let that happen to Lac's Holding either."

Small gods help him. What Dilly was arguing for sounded like the right thing to do. How had Gavun's boy, Fitch of Rhale Island, smuggler from toddlerhood, come to feel responsible for the fate of Suryan and his daughter? "Maybe you could tell someone else," he tried. "They could take it from there."

"There's no one else who'd believe me. It has to be me. You don't have to be part of it though. You can go."

For a moment, he was tempted. The impulse floated away at the sight of her tear-streaked face. "I told my mother I couldn't leave until tomorrow night anyway. And smugglers have practice at moving around while staying out of sight. I'll help."

It seemed to him her shoulders relaxed. "I appreciate that." She raised a hand, palm out. "That doesn't mean I trust you, Mage boy.”

He swallowed his annoyance. She had reasons for being untrusting, not all of them to do with him. “Where do you want to start?”

“We have to go to the Fortress to warn Elenia.”

Fitch nearly choked. Dilly was already moving, but she stopped as something snagged her gaze. The statue of the Guardian Dog, Fitch saw. Dilly drew a deep breath. Fitch followed her out of the shrine, pausing only to look back and give the Trickster the finger.

# Chapter 23

## Dilly

I STOPPED WHEN Fitch quietly called my name. The crowd eddied around us with the Fortress looming ahead. "I'll be right over there." Fitch nodded toward an apartment building doorway. "As long as you stay by the gates," Fitch went on, "I'll be able to see you. I'll come if there's trouble."

I wiped my sweaty hands on my skirt. "If there's trouble, don't come near me. The guards are after you. I don't need that kind of help."

"Those two don't know me." He faded into the shadows under the apartment doorway. I wasn't sure how truly he meant to help Elenia, but he was sticking by my side like a bur.

The two guards watched me come, their eyes as sharp as the points of their pikes. My legs felt heavy. I wasn't afraid they'd hurt me, but the scathing things Suryan had said echoed in my head. In Suryan's mind, I was still a street kid. Maybe the guards thought that way too.

Not that there was anything wrong with being a street kid. Well, there was plenty *wrong*. You starved and slept in a gutter and were prey for every robber and rapist who came along. But that wasn't your fault, and Fitch was right that it had toughened me up. I could do this.

I slid my gaze between the two guards and picked the woman. "Excuse me, but I need to speak to Lady Elenia."

"I'm sorry, miss, but we've orders not to admit you." Her polite tone made me feel better.

I had my next step ready. I hadn't started with it only because Fitch said it was better not to put things in writing, wisdom he'd apparently learned from his troublesome kin. I fished in my pocket for the note I'd written, finally finding it under one of the stones I'd taken from the *Storm King*. I held it out. "Will you see that Lady Elenia gets this as soon as possible?"

The guard shook her head. "Lord Suryan also told us not to take any package you might bring."

"It's not a package. It's just a note. A note can't hurt anything."

One corner of the guard's mouth lifted. "It's been my experience that a note can do a lot of damage. I'm sorry, but you have to move along."

Now what? I crumpled the paper and shoved it back in my pocket, my fingers brushing the stone. The covering was loose, and the stone felt faintly warm.

When I reached the apartment doorway, Fitch stepped out. "Well, you tried," he said, annoyingly cheerful.

I pushed him back into the shadows. "Let's hear your helpful smuggler's idea for how to get in."

He groaned. "We've done our best. Now we have to go."

"You said you'd help warn Elenia. Was that a lie?"

He flapped his arms. "I'm here, aren't I?"

"You are, though I'm not sure why. Guilt for sticking me with that spiked Fire maybe?"

He spoke through gritted teeth. "For the last time, that wasn't mine."

He sounded truthful, but then he always did. "So can you get me in or not?"

He scrubbed his hand over his hair. "I don't know. Maybe."

I leaned against the apartment door and waited.

He drew a long breath. "Sometimes Gavun buys off guards and smuggles goods up from the river."

My shoulders relaxed. He was going to help me after all. This time at some risk to himself. Maybe he wasn't all bad. "How?" I tried to picture it. "There's a cliff there, and a wall around the Fortress yard."

"There's a door above the cliff. They use it to lift in legitimate freight from ships with ropes and pulleys. Gavun sends a single climber up the rocks carrying goods on his back."

"Surely someone spots a climber."

His hand sketched out a roof-like shape. "The path runs behind rocks and under overhangs."

"You can find this path? You've been on it?"

"Just once. Gavun never sends the same person twice if he can help it. But I know generally where it is."

"Elenia's quarters are on that side of the Fortress. And there's a gate from the yard to her garden. Let's go." I darted out of the doorway.

"Don't run." He hustled to my side. "Walk. Act innocent."

"I know. I'm a pickpocket, remember?"

Still I had to force myself to keep pace with him, strolling next to me as if we were a young couple looking for amusement rather than trouble. He faked it well, smiling and pointing out flowers on the balconies. I was impressed. *Remember he can put that mask on*, I told myself. *Don't go soft headed.* Then I thought about his kindness in the shrine. Surely that was worth remembering too.

He led me along the street that ran past the Fortress and then curved out between the back of a building and the cliff down to the river. Fifty yards or so along, he halted and sat on the low stone wall meant to keep drunks or wobbly carts from going over the edge. Far below, the river slipped lazily along, brown with mud and muck.

"Why are we stopping?" I asked. "We have to get all the way down to the river."

He gave the wall next to him a firm pat, and I got the message and sat. Over my shoulder, I could see up and down the river. To my right, guard towers marked the place where it entered the Center Sea. And to my left loomed the Fortress.

Still smiling pleasantly, Fitch leaned close and said, "I think we can pick up the path from here. Look down. See the ledge?"

I turned to look. A gull floated past at eye level. I looked down, then quickly up again to find him watching me, brows pinched together.

"If you tell me where you want your message left, I'll take it by myself." Fitch held out his hand.

"No." I drew a breath, looked down, and spotted a ledge not much wider than the length of my shoe. Small gods help me. I stood. "If anyone goes alone, it will be me. Just show me the way."

He curled his fingers back. "Just what is it you think I'm going to do?"

I could read nothing in his dark eyes. "I don't know. And that's the problem."

"All right, then," he said, voice hard. "We'll both go. You need me to nudge whoever's on gate duty anyway." He scanned the road. Few people had passed us on this backstreet where nothing was happening except us. He waited until no one was in sight. "Now," he said, and swung over the wall.

I scrambled after him and jolted to a stop with my

head below the top of the wall. He caught my elbow, then dropped his grip. Feet turned sideways and fingers dug into the cracks, we stood on what was probably some buried edge of the roadbed. I pressed my cheek to sun-warmed stones and swallowed the urge to vomit.

He glanced down at rocks rising from the edge of the river fifty feet below, chewing on one corner of his lips. "I can still go alone."

I sucked in air. "Just go."

He crept toward the Fortress, moving carefully from one rock and handhold to the next. I stepped in the same places he did, heart beating so hard, it threatened to choke me. I kept straining my ears for someone shouting there were invaders on the cliff. I thought he was ignoring me, but when my foot shot off a boulder, he grabbed my arm again. "Sorry. I didn't realize it would be this risky." He sounded grim, and I remembered that his girl had fallen from a break wall onto rocks.

"This is a terrible path," I forced out.

He prodded a stony outcrop with his foot, then drew back hastily as it crumbled and bounced down the cliff. He raised a shoulder to wipe sweat from the side of his face. "I haven't found the path yet."

I dug my skinned fingertips into a gap. "You said you knew where it was."

"I said I knew generally. Not being fools, the guards sometimes find it, and Gavun has to make a new one. He's good at hiding what he's doing."

"Like you?"

"Give it a rest," he cried. "I'm concentrating." A moment later, he blew out a relieved breath. "Here." He slid off a boulder and onto a ledge. It was less than a yard wide, but compared to what we'd been on, it felt like Corsair Street. He ducked behind one rock and under another. "Watch your head."

This was better. We were more or less concealed much of the time, and I didn't feel as if I was about to make a long, unplanned dive into the river. We inched upward until I could see the Fortress wall. And there, as Fitch had promised, was a wide double-door, both sides firmly shut. Over its top jutted a long wooden arm with a pulley at the end.

"Stand there while I take care of the guard." Fitch pointed to a hollow next to the door, waited until I'd squeezed in, and pounded his fist against the weathered wooden panel. I rubbed my arms, trying to wipe away my nerves. I was sneaking into Lord Suryan's Fortress after he threw me out. If I was caught and dragged before him, he'd feel the need to show what happened when someone disobeyed him. I'd never seen his cells, but I knew I didn't want to end up in one.

The door creaked open, and a guard stuck his head out. He was young, with rooster red hair sticking out from under his helmet. He flinched back when he saw Fitch. "What are you doing out there?"

"Why is this closed?" Fitch demanded as if he ran the

place. "My master has a shipment just clearing customs."

"I wasn't told." The guard's eyes widened. "Someone should have told me."

"I'm telling you now," Fitch blustered.

"I need orders," the guard said, doubtfully.

Fitch's foot slipped, and he tilted backward, arms windmilling. My heart stopped, but before I could move, Fitch grabbed the guard's shoulder. The guard gripped him and dragged him through the gate. I was left clutching at empty air.

*Wait.* Small gods. What a faker. I couldn't see the two of them, but I could hear Fitch's soothing voice. "You don't want to get in trouble," he said. "Go see whoever's supposed to give orders. I'll wait." A moment later, he leaned out the door and beckoned.

At that moment, a voice far below shouted, "Hey, who's up there? Fortress, someone's there!"

Fitch grabbed my arm, hustled me inside, and slammed the gate. He pushed me behind a cart. "Shh," he hissed.

"Someone saw me," I choked out, making him flinch. "He'll get the guards' attention eventually. We have to hurry."

He nodded toward the other side of the cart. "Not with them there."

Twenty yards away, several dozen guards in blue and red uniforms stood in rows with their backs to us and two officers striding along the lines. "What are they doing?

Will they leave?"

"I don't know. I'm never in this part of the yard." What if they stayed? Whoever saw us would have people searching for us.

But when the officers reached the end of the lines, one of them nodded at the other, and the second man shouted, "Move out." They marched away toward the front gate.

As soon as they were around a corner, Fitch snapped, "Which way?"

I spun toward where I knew Elenia's quarters had to be, hidden behind barracks and other buildings. When I stood on tiptoe, I glimpsed the garden's treetops. "That way."

We slipped along, ducking under cover if we heard anyone coming. I kept one ear cocked for the sound of an alarm, knowing time and safety were flying past. Finally, we darted across a last open space to the garden gate. I'd never seen it locked, but I was still relieved when the latch gave under my hand. I peeked through to find no one seated on the benches by the fountain or strolling the paths between flower beds. I lunged inside, with Fitch right behind me.

At the bottom of the spiral stairway, I stopped and looked up. The ornate iron steps wound up to the closed door to the Glass Chamber. Did I dare go up there and find Elenia? Once she heard what I had to say, surely she'd protect Fitch and me.

"Don't even think about it," Fitch murmured in my

ear. "There's too much risk of meeting guards or the other women."

Reluctantly, I moved away from the stairs to run across the grass and between bright flower beds to the benches. I pulled the note out of my pocket and set it on the bench. It slid sideways when a breeze caught it, so I weighed it down with one of my stones. "The other women will find it if Elenia doesn't."

"Her name is on it?" Fitch asked.

I nodded. "Mine too, so she'll know who it came from."

His mouth opened and shut. "You signed it? Wonderful idea. That way the guards won't have any trouble figuring out who snuck in."

A whistle shrilled on the other side of the building. "They know we're here." I whirled toward the garden gate.

The door to the Glass Chamber whooshed open, and at the top of the stairs, Captain Jaf said, "You can't go down there, miss. That's the signal for intruders."

I'd reached the gate before Jaf finished the sentence. Fitch shoved it open.

"I just want to pick some flowers," Jessa said.

At that moment, I heard a faint *pop*. I looked back at the bench in time to see the stone blow up. Bits landed on the grass, and a dozen tiny fires flickered to life from the fragments. The bench rocked, fell over, and burst into flame. Someone squeaked. I realized it was me.

Fitch pushed me through the gate and closed it. "Small

gods," he breathed. "What did you do?"

"Nothing!" I cried. "It was just a stone." I showed him the second one I'd taken.

He stared at it for an instant before he tried to slap it from my hand. "Leave it. Let's go."

I curled my hand around its warmth. In the garden, Jaf shouted, "Fire! Fire!"

I ran at Fitch's side.

# Chapter 24

## Fitch

FITCH FLED ALONG the back of an outbuilding with Dilly at his heels, some Gavun-trained part of him sorting coolly through escape routes. The cliff was out. A trip as slow as the one they just took was an invitation for guards to pick them off with crossbow bolts. A fast trip along the same route was a way to splatter their brains on the riverbank.

The whistle still sounded. The guard's shouts of fire hadn't been widely heard yet, but they would be, he thought. Their only chance to get out of the Fortress was to wait until everyone else was focused on the fire as their first priority. He tried to map the yard in his mind, but the Fortress scared him silly, so he'd never spent much time there. "Which way to the front gates?" he asked.

Dilly pointed in the direction the guards had marched.

He noted with approval that though her face was pale, that pointing finger was steady. The girl had guts.

"Stay close." He craned his neck around the corner, saw no one, and sprinted for the next building. He edged to the far corner of it, ready to run again.

In the distance, he heard a shout, and an alarm bell began to clang.

"Run for the gates, *now!*"

Dilly took off, and he let her lead. Other people appeared from every side and ran in the opposite direction toward the bell, any concern about intruders lost in the more immediate danger of fire. The hair of the back of Fitch's neck rose at being surrounded by so many guard uniforms, but thank the small gods, no one had attention to spare for him and Dilly.

Dilly led him around a corner, and the front gates appeared.

Fitch grabbed her dress between her shoulder blades and drew close. "Walk." She slowed and settled at his side. He heard her rapid breathing. A crowd of people swelled outside the gates, drawn by the clanging bell, and both gate guards faced outward, pikes crosswise, ready to fend folks off if someone got too excited. Fitch ducked around Dilly so that he was between her and the woman guard she'd talked to earlier, then held his breath and walked briskly between the guards. At the last moment, the woman guard's head flicked in their direction, and Fitch glimpsed her frown. He slithered into the crowd, drawing

Dilly with him. When he looked back, the guards were lost among the growing sea of people. In silent agreement, he and Dilly slipped around a corner. He let out his breath. His thudding heart slowed. "That was close."

"Elenia won't get my note." Dilly bit her lip.

Fitch restrained himself from rolling his eyes. "I hope not, given that it came wrapped around a fire bomb." He tried to think of a place they could go. As soon as the fire was out, the Fortress guards would be trying to figure out what happened, and the guard at the river gate would be shouting Fitch's description until someone listened.

"We'll have to wait for her near the *Storm King* as it grows dark tomorrow," Dilly said. "That's when she agreed to be there."

Fitch skirted around a trio of musicians just claiming a spot and setting up for the coming evening. Their heads were turned toward the Fortress and the faint but still audible clang of the bell. "Wait for who?"

"Elenia, of course." Dilly frowned at him. "We agreed to warn her away from Veren, right? The note's not going to work now."

Fitch flung up his hands. "What we *have* to do is hide until we can get out of Lac's Holding tomorrow night with my mother." If things didn't work out for that plan, he could jump ship at the first port and be free of every relative he ever had. He could take Dilly with him, assuming she'd go. He couldn't very well leave her on the streets here.

"We had this argument already," Dilly said. "You don't have to stay with me if it's too dangerous, but I'm not abandoning Elenia."

"They're going to think we attacked the Fortress." He heard his voice rise, sucked in air, and spoke more quietly. "After last night's riot, they'll think we're part of some sort of actual rebellion. Which I, at least, am, since I signed on with Gavun. That will not end well for me."

She edged closer to him, and he caught a tang of her fear sweat, though it was possible that it came from him. "Fitch, your father's done some foolish things."

Fitch snorted. "That's one word for it."

"Would you abandon him?"

After the scene in the *Storm King*, Fitch found the idea of leaving Gavun much easier to swallow. Gavun deserved to lose him. "Absolutely."

"I don't believe it," Dilly said. "As you islanders say, he's blood of your blood. Lac's Holders value family too, and Suryan values Elenia. If we keep her away from Veren, Suryan might forgive us for an accidental explosion."

"Or he might torture us to find out who we're working with." He thought of Erald and Royce Half-Moon but hastily blotted the image out. Maybe Owun shook them loose.

Dilly set her jaw. "I have to be here tomorrow when Elenia goes to the *Storm King*. It doesn't matter that she let Suryan dismiss me. Letting her make the same mistake Mama did is different."

Something in Fitch's chest twisted in unreasoned panic. "I'm not going to leave you all alone in the dark with spiked Winter Fire all over the place. I'm not making that mistake again."

"Well, I'm not leaving. So are you staying?" Her voice was tight. "Whose side are you on?"

He found himself stopped dead in the street with a scowling footman elbowing him out of the way. This was Dilly, not Nera. Still, the painful lesson held. He might abandon Gavun. Gavun had failed him even more than Dilly's mother failed her. But he would not leave this girl on her own while she was in danger. Danger she was foolish enough to court, of course, but that seemed to be the kind of girl he kept finding. "Your side. So I guess I'm staying."

Slowly, she smiled. He felt as if he'd passed some sort of test.

"I still say we need to get out of sight until tomorrow," he said. "Let's fetch your satchel. The shrine is on the way."

"Where are we going?"

"The only place I can think of. Rhale Island."

"Your father's place? I thought—"

"No, elsewhere on the island." As if Fitch would ever rely on Gavun again. He might be a fool, but not that gigantic a one. Alert for Watch members and Fortress guards, he led her through the streets and retrieved her bag. The muscles in his back didn't ease until they slogged out into the marshes where sunlight filtered thinly through the trees.

She kept close to him. "I've never been out here. It's very… not city." Something splashed into a pond to their right, and she jumped.

"Just a frog," Fitch said, which might or might not be true. He'd seen alligators out here and given them a wide berth. He turned into the last path leading to where he'd docked the *Sea Wind*. "Rhale Island has hiding places Suryan's guards will never find even if they turn up." He steadied the boat as Dilly climbed in, then untied the line, stepped in, and took the oars. When they came out into the bay, the sail filled, the wind brisk in the rain's aftermath. He moved to the rail, clutching the line tied to the tiller.

When the boat heeled, Dilly grabbed the gunnels but made no sound. After a few moments, she loosened her grip enough to look back at the city spread along the shore. "Tuc liked it here," she said, voice thick. "It was like he was home too." She swallowed hard enough for Fitch to see her throat convulse. "It's funny how strong that instinct is. I felt it all the time I was in Rin."

"What instinct?"

"You know. The one to go home." She waved vaguely in the direction of the islands.

"Rhale Island can't be home for me anymore."

She cocked her head. "And yet, that's where you're going."

Fitch could swear he heard the Trickster laugh.

They were nearing Rhale, and Dilly twisted to examine it. "I've never been out here before either."

"The kinships tend to discourage visitors."

"Are they all as rugged as Rhale?"

He eyed the steep rise. He was so used to it that he noticed it himself only when carting things up and down the steps. "More or less. Once again, it's useful."

"Will your family be here?"

"Small gods save us, no," Fitch said. "Gavun's with Veren. Everyone else is on leave or stuck on the *Shark's Teeth*. Our schooner," he added, when she raised an eyebrow.

"Are there children?"

"The ones too young to be useful will all be with my great uncle on the other end of the island. Get ready to duck." He moved the tiller, steering the boat toward the island's west end. The sail swung over her head. "We'll beach away from Gavun's dock in case he turns up," he said.

Dilly watched the island swing by, a crease between her brows. "I don't understand what happened. Something must have been wrong with the stone."

"I'd say so," Fitch said. "Where did you get it?" He caught sight of the gap that led to a hidden beach and headed toward it.

"On the *Storm King*. There was a box of them. They were all wrapped in individual leather squares as if they were jewels, but they just looked like rough red stones."

Something tickled in Fitch's memory, something he'd been trying to retrieve since she showed him the second stone lying on her palm at the garden gate. It had felt dangerous, but in the chaos of the moment, he couldn't pin the danger down. Now his mind popped the memory into the light. "Small gods. I saw stones like that in Janda. They're weapons. Rebels used them to blow up a jail. Veren has a whole box? How big? How many stones?"

She made a space with her hands, maybe two feet wide and a foot and a half deep. "I can't guess how many. Lots."

The boat scraped sand, and he jumped out to pull it ashore, his mind busy with what the presence of a box of those stones meant for Veren's plans.

"How do they work?" Dilly scrambled out of the boat.

"They're harmless until they're exposed to air. Then they gradually heat up until they explode."

Dilly's brown eyes grew huge. "Elenia can't get on that ship with all those stones."

"It's what happens when those stones come off the ship that I'm worried about." Maybe Dilly's love and loyalty to the city and Elenia had begun to rub off on him, but to his astonishment, he felt alarm for the people of Lac's Holding.

This time, the Trickster guffawed so loudly in his head that he was astonished the gulls on the beach didn't take flight.

# Chapter 25

## Dilly

FITCH PULLED THE *Sea Wind* farther ashore, picked up my satchel, and led me up the steps zigzagging on the cliff face, high enough that my thighs burned. The path at the top ran through rustling waves of tall grass that sounded and looked like a dusty green version of the sea we'd just been on. "I have to get my stuff," Fitch said, "but obviously we can't stay at Gavun's, or even one of my kin's. They'd send word to him."

"Your kin all live on the island?"

"Most of them, when they're not at sea."

"And every house here belongs to someone you're related to?"

"Every single one." He bit out each word.

I felt something akin to awe. Mama was the only family I'd ever had. "It must be comforting to be surrounded by family. Who lives there?" I looked over my shoulder at the cottage we were giving a wide berth.

"My cousin Loni and Aunt Senay."

"No uncle?"

"He was killed by pirates eight years ago."

"Does that happen often?"

"No, but even apart from storms and customs officers, smuggling is not a gentle way to earn a living. Not everyone is happy here." He kept his eyes straight ahead.

I thought about his mother leaving and shut up.

We approached a bigger house from the back, and Fitch had me wait while he scouted. It wasn't long before he waved for me to join him at the front. I peered over a cliff where steps ran down to an empty dock.

"Gavun's place," Fitch said briefly. He took a key from a hollow log and let me in.

I stood just inside the door, scanning the square room. It looked cozy, with a padded bench near the fireplace and upright chairs on either side of a small table. *Gavun's place*, Fitch had said. Not his. It made me sad. I'd lived with Mama in places that threatened to fall down around our ears, but I'd always thought of them as *ours*. "It's tidy for a place where two men live."

"Not for two men who go to sea. You've heard the word 'shipshape'? That's what it is." Fitch shut and locked the door. "Are you hungry?" He closed the shutters and lowered the latch, dimming the room. "There's bread and cheese. Not much else, I'm afraid. We should probably take some with us too."

"Bread and cheese would be fine."

Fitch threw open a cupboard and brought out food, knives, and two cups of small beer before he vanished down a hallway leading toward the back of the house.

I wandered around the room, fingering and conscientiously dropping a handful of unfamiliar coins heaped in a basket. Before a small statue of a woman with a baby at her feet, I paused. Someone else's god maybe? What was it like where it came from? For a moment, I envied Fitch his adventures. I'd uncorked a jar and sniffed at the contents when Fitch returned with a carry bag.

"Would you prefer that to small beer?" he asked. "It's tea from the South Coast."

I replaced the cork. "Small beer is fine." I sat down.

Fitch collapsed into a chair and started talking as if we'd been in the middle of a conversation. "Of course it was Gavun who smuggled the Mage flower. That's why there was so much money to collect the other night." His mouth twisted. "Me and Mage flower. To Gavun, we're both just ways to soften up buyers."

I let go of any last notion he'd deliberately given me a bag of spiked Fire. Hard as I tried, I hadn't really believed it since he snuck us into the Fortress and got me safely out again. Instead, I saw a boy who'd had refused to abandon me at Festival, or while I tried to save Elenia. Refused to leave me even when I told him to. He'd stuck by me as fiercely as Tuc, as faithfully as my street friends in Rin

City. A little flicker of warmth came to life in my chest.

I spoke carefully because I knew I was getting near a sore spot. "On the *Storm King*, you attacked Veren, not your father."

Fitch ran a finger around the rim of his cup, making it sing softly. "Veren is one of those people who ruin lives for their own gain. Gavun is only following his instinct to make a coin out of anything he can."

*Including your heart*, I thought. We sat for a moment in surrounding silence except for the rush of waves and blowing grass. I sliced bread and cheese and ate. I wasn't exactly a street kid again, not yet. But I was close enough to eat every time food turned up.

"I used to like helping Gavun." Fitch looked into his cup, not at me. "Then my gift got stronger, maybe because I was getting older or maybe because I was learning to use it better. I started sensing not just the feelings I was looking for, not just how much the mark would pay in a pinch, but other emotions too. Worries, fears, unhappiness, joy. And I started to see they were people with their own lives. It made me cringe to push them around."

I didn't need Fitch's gift to feel his guilt. "It's hard to know what to do when our kin want something from us." I considered telling him how I'd got rid of Cole, even though I knew Mama wanted him to stay, but I decided now was not the time. I clinked my cup of beer against his, making him look up. "How unlucky for your father that your gift made you useful but at the same time gave you insights so you didn't want to use it. If that's not the Trickster at work, I don't know what is."

He drank. "Why are you so hot to help Elenia anyway? She hasn't done anything to earn your risking yourself like this."

I crumbled a bit of cheese while I thought, then looked up to find him watching me intently. I touched the tip of my finger to his hand. "Elenia is the closest thing I have to kin now, even if she is *troublesome*. When it comes to family, you're a rich boy, Fitch of Rhale Island, and I'm dirt poor."

He let his hand lie still, but the pulse throbbed in his throat. "I told you when we met, kin make problems."

"You wouldn't really leave them all, would you?"

Outside, a man's voice spoke. That was our only warning before someone banged on the door and bawled, "Open up in the name of Lord Suryan."

"Small gods." Fitch jumped to his feet and shepherded me into the cupboard, closing the door quietly behind us. It was dark enough that I barely saw a jug of small beer teetering. Heart in my throat, I caught it and steadied it back into place.

"They'll look in here," I whispered. I heard a crash that sounded like large Fortress guards battering a door into submission.

Fitch slid his fingers along the back wall, found what he was looking for and pushed. A two-foot wide space opened. He didn't need to tell me what to do. I slid in, and he came after me. The space was so tight he had to press close to me before he jammed the false panel shut. We were utterly in the dark.

"Useful for a family of smugglers?" I whispered.

"Shh." Fitch had his head tilted to listen. He shifted his weight, and I became aware that he was touching me. The Trickster help me but I found myself wondering what it would be like to kiss a Mage.

Fitch shifted again, as if trying to fade into the false panel. I remembered too late he might be able to sense what I was feeling. My face got hot.

Boots stomped through the front room and faded down the hall before returning. "Now what?" the voice asked.

"Someone's eaten here recently. We'll have to search the island. I'm not going back to Suryan empty handed. He's already breathing fire because this boy gave us the slip. We better not let him get away again."

I didn't recognize the voice of either man, which meant they weren't the type who guarded the Fortress's living quarters. My throat went dry.

A new voice came from what sounded like outside the house. "Fitch, I saw the *Sea Wind* in—" The guards in the front room must have reacted quickly. "Wait!" the new voice cried. "What's going on?"

Fitch shut his eyes. "My cousin Loni," he whispered. "Curse the Trickster with every curse there is."

"Where's Gavun's boy?" the voice demanded.

"I don't know." Loni squeaked as if someone twisted his arm. "I was looking for Gavun. I haven't seen Fitch in days."

"Liar. You called his name. You thought he was here."

"Let's take him in and see what he tells Suryan," the second guard said.

"Muck it," Fitch said. "Stay here. Slide the panel shut behind me." He lunged through the hidden door and burst out of the cupboard.

So she had been right. He wasn't ready to abandon all his kin after all.

# Chapter 26

## Fitch

IN THE MIDDLE of the room loomed two Fortress guards, one of them holding Loni. They all spun toward Fitch. The one with his hands free reached for his sword, but Fitch tackled him, sending him crashing full length to the floor. Fitch crawled up the man's body and punched him in the jaw. From the corner of his eye, he glimpsed Dilly running straight toward the guard holding Loni. Of course, she hadn't stayed hidden. He hadn't even really expected her to. She smashed the back of the guard's head with a jug from the cupboard. Fragrant beer splashed in a wide arc.

The man under Fitch flung him off. He skidded across the floor on his back until his head collided with the fireplace. The house around him faded in and out.

"Stop where you are."

Fitch's vision settled to show him the guard he'd been grappling with holding his sword tip pressed lightly into Loni's gut. Loni sucked it in until his spine curved. Dripping beer from his hair and whiskers, the other guard pinned Dilly back against him. Dilly wrestled in his grip and he yanked her back hard enough to make her head snap. Before Fitch could react, she reached behind her as if to grab the guard in a tender place, but her hand slid off his hip.

"It's me you're after." Fitch staggered to his feet, pain stabbing the spot where his head had rammed the fireplace. The room wobbled. For a moment, he feared he might fall. "Let the others go."

"Not until I know how they connect to you and Gavun. The boy looks enough like you that he has to be part of the kinship. The girl, on the other hand, was just tossed out of the Fortress, which doesn't speak well for her either." The guard with the sword wore a sergeant's sash. "Suryan's tired of dealing with you islanders. You're all criminals, and today he's bringing you to heel. Let her go," he added, speaking to the other man. He backed an inch away from Loni. "Be ready to stab this one if Gavun's boy gives us any trouble."

The other man released Dilly, who whirled away from him. The guard drew his sword and shoved the end into the dent in Loni's shirt.

"Careful with that!" Loni cried. The guard twitched. Loni yelped, and a spot of blood appeared.

Fitch clenched his fists. Maybe he could grab the sergeant's sword and turn this into a standoff.

"Don't even think about it." The sergeant pulled a leather tie from the bundle on his belt. "You do something stupid, and he gets skewered like a chunk of goat meat. Understand?" Fitch looked at Loni's sweaty face and nodded. The sergeant moved behind him and began tying his wrists. "Where's Gavun?"

"He's on his way." Fitch felt the man's fingers brushing against him. His heart sped up. He backed closer, slipped into the sergeant's mind, and found excitement over some reward he'd been promised. Fitch spent a moment or two convincing the sergeant that his wrists were tightly tied, then began to nudge. *Don't take them in yet. Gavun's on his way. You can please Suryan if you wait and the reward will be even bigger. Put them in the room that's farthest from here. That way they can't warn him.*

The thought was close to one of the sergeant's own anyway. It was a tiny nudge. "We'll tie the others up too and put them in the back." The guard stepped away from Fitch to tie Dilly's and Loni's wrists. Fitch's heart still raced, but he forced his mind to go cold and calm. He needed to find a way out.

The guards herded the three of them down the hall, shoved them into Fitch's room, pushed them to sit on the floor against the foot of the bed, and tied their ankles. "Sit tight," the sergeant said. "We'll be back." The two of them left the room, banging the door shut.

Fitch began working his wrists loose.

"They've seized the *Shark's Teeth*, Fitch," Loni said.

"Who has?"

"Suryan's men. And they're on Half-Moon Island. From the Heights you can see three Fortress boats there."

"Curse them all." Fitch twisted his wrists faster. "There's no smuggled stuff on the *Shark's Teeth*, is there?"

"Of course not. We took the last of it ashore this morning. Something tells me Suryan won't care." Loni eyed Dilly sideways. "Fitch has very bad manners, so he's neglected to introduce us. I'm Loni."

"I'm Dilly." She cocked her head toward the door.

Loni looked as if he wanted to continue the conversation, but she didn't so much as glance at him. He turned back to Fitch. "Why did you tell him Gavun is coming? They'll never leave now."

"I made that up. The last I saw Gavun, he was plotting with Veren. You lied to me about the Mage flower, coz," Fitch added sharply.

There was a moment's silence. "I'm sorry." Loni's voice was small. "Gavun told me not to tell you. He said you'd be upset, and it was too late to stop this year's shipment anyway."

Fitch's gaze caught on the model ship he and Loni had built the winter they were nine, not long after Loni's father was killed. The death had left Gavun more silent than usual, suffering from the loss of his brother. Fitch had kept the ship model partly because, to his thrilled surprise,

Gavun had helped them build it. "You two are brothers now," he'd told them. "Brothers look out for one another."

"I *trusted* you," Fitch forced out through gritted teeth. He flung the ties off his wrists, leaned over to undo Dilly's wrists, and then bent to free his ankles. He leapt to his feet and raced to the window as Dilly untied Loni's hands. "You ready to run, Dilly?"

"I don't think we need to," she said.

"Well I'm ready," Loni said.

A loud boom came from the front of the house accompanied by a cry of pain. Into Fitch's mind flashed the image of Dilly sliding her hand over the hip of the Fortress guard holding her. Fitch yanked the hall door open to confused shouts, then ran after Dilly to the front room where the man who'd hurt her lay with blood gushing from a butt cheek and the sergeant sprawled flat out, looking stunned. Fires flickered around the room. Pushing Dilly ahead of him, Fitch scrambled over the flattened front door and pelted along the path to the back with Loni at his heels. When they were deep in the elf grass, he stopped and looked back. Smoke drifted lazily up.

"What happened?" Loni sounded awestruck. A trickle of blood seeped between the fingers he had pressed over his belly.

"An explosion and fire, that's what." Fitch glanced at Dilly. "You planted a stone on him, didn't you?"

The corners of her mouth curled.

"Was it the stone I told you to leave?"

"I thought we might need it," Dilly said.

Fitch considered all the places he'd been with her while she had that stone. "You could have warned me when we were on the *Sea Wind*."

She showed him a leather wrap. "It was covered until I put it in his pocket."

"Surprisingly enough, I don't find that comforting."

Loni licked his lips. "You set Gavun of Rhale Island's house on fire." He sounded as if he were trying out the words to see whether they sounded right.

"Only as a side effect," Dilly said.

"Small gods," Loni said. "My Guardian Dog preserve me."

Fitch had to laugh. He hadn't heard Loni call on his Guardian Dog since the time they stole his mother's boat and managed to sink it. Aunt Senay had come after them with a switch, making Loni claim he'd lost his faith.

Loni looked at him hopefully. "I'm sorry, Fitch. Gavun just... I don't know. I guess I liked partnering up with him."

Fitch rubbed the back of his neck. "Stone Gavun anyway." He let his hand fall to his side. Dilly reached as if to pat his shoulder, stopped, and then lightly touched his arm. Fitch cleared his throat.

Loni cocked his head, watching them. He gave a knowing smile that made heat rise to Fitch's face. "We need to get out of sight," Loni said. "The Fortress guards on the *Shark's Teeth* will come running."

"Let me see what I can do with that cut first."

Loni lifted his shirt, and Fitch bent to frown over the wound. "It's only skin deep. The guards know their business."

"Good for them. Get on with it. Deep or not, it hurts."

Fitch took the hand Loni offered and tried to focus on his cousin's body, but he sensed only Loni's worry. "Relax. You're getting in my way."

Loni looked down at the cut. "I'm not doing anything different than usual."

"You are."

Loni frowned at Fitch. "Maybe something happened to your healing gift while you were away. Maybe it comes from the island or something."

"Don't be ridiculous. I healed people while I traveled. That's how I earned my bread and cheese. My gift worked fine."

Dilly leaned close to watch. "Did your nudging work while you were away?"

Loni glanced at her. "What nudging? What do you mean?"

Fitch stared at the waving elf grass. In the back of his head, he heard a quavery, old man's voice. *You have a gift. You abuse it. Learn anything yet?* "I didn't try. Not until I came home again. That night I met you in the shrine was the first time in a year." He flexed his fingers, a terrible fear blossoming in his head.

A shout came from the direction of Gavun's house. Loni jerked his shirt down over the still bleeding cut. "Time's up. We have to get moving. You think Suryan will come after Mama?"

Fitch shook his head. "They'll search her cottage though, and if you've been working with Gavun, you're in trouble. They'll ask her about you."

Loni grimaced. "She's been questioned before. I'll tell her not to look for me for a while, and we can take off for the marshes. Don't tell her I'm hurt." Loni draped his hand casually over his middle.

"Of course not," Fitch said. "You think I'm crazy?" He started after Loni on his way to Aunt Senay's cottage.

"Fitch and I need to be at the town docks at darkfall tomorrow," Dilly said.

Groaning, Fitch jammed to a halt. Of course Dilly hadn't given up. She was the kind of girl who carried a fire bomb around.

"That's not a good idea." Loni's eyes were wide. He looked back and forth between them.

Dilly shrugged. "You sound like Fitch as well as look like him."

"I told her I'd help her," Fitch confessed. "I can't disappear yet."

"If you don't, maybe you really are crazy." Loni unexpectedly grinned, and Fitch felt sudden gratitude for his obvious affection. "But crazy for a girl can be good." They had come in sight of his cottage. "Dilly, I'm relying on you to look after him for me." He banged his fist against Fitch's shoulder and trotted toward the cottage. Fitch could see only the top of his head over the waves of grass as he pulled ahead.

Fitch set his worry about the failed healing aside. The smoke over Gavun's house was thickening. "We're going to have to cut our losses on our bags. Loni's right that guards will come running. If the two who were in the house say they saw me, they'll search all the houses on the island. Are you willing to camp out?"

"I don't think we have any choice. And I think our bags are a lost cause."

From the corner of his eye, Fitch glimpsed movement near Loni's cottage. A second head leapt into view. Fitch was running even before he heard the faint cry. He veered off the path to cut through the grass, stumbled over a hidden root, and bounced up to run on. When he burst into the clearing in front of Loni's cottage, he had to stop to make sense of what he saw. Aunt Senay knelt next to Loni, who had a knife sticking out of his back. Her hands were pressed to the wound as if they could stop the flow of blood.

She lifted dazed eyes to Fitch. "He thought Loni was you. He called Loni by your name."

Fitch dropped to his knees. "Oh gods. Loni. Oh gods." He pressed his hands next to hers. She shifted and made to pull out the knife. "Leave it until I'm ready," he managed, struggling for air. She held her hands hovering, ready.

Dilly bent over him, her breath stirring his hair.

Fitch closed his eyes, tried to still his mind to let the Healer slip into him and flow out through his touch into Loni. It should have been easy. Loni was blood of his blood. Fitch's head filled with his cousin's damaged body. He should have felt heat as the god's grace knit the failing organs into some semblance of what they'd been. He waited, waited.

Nothing happened.

He felt pain and loss and wonder. He felt the life slip out of his cousin. He let his hands fall away.

Aunt Senay jammed her fist against her mouth, smothering a moan.

"Oh no," Dilly murmured.

Fitch rose, choking on grief and guilt. "Who did this?"

"I only saw him for a moment," Senay said, "but I think it was the man who came to see Gavun the other morning."

"Cole." Fitch looked wildly around to where the grass was trampled. Dodging Dilly's attempt to grab his arm, he ran after the man who had killed Loni because Loni had the bad luck to look like Fitch and be where Fitch might be, and because Fitch had squandered a gift. He was too late to stop death and, as it turned out, too late to catch Cole.

# Chapter 27

## Dilly

I PULLED BACK into the hollow, listening to the guards sweep past. They weren't grousing or even talking, which told me how serious they were about finding us. My heart kicked against my ribs. Next to me, Fitch must have been holding his breath because six inches away, I couldn't hear it. I pressed my face flatter against the earth, ignoring the small stone digging into my cheek.

The guards tramped on. Breath eased out of Fitch, but he didn't move. Just as I thought I might jump out of my skin, he raised his head and took a good look. "They're gone. For now, anyway. At least they put the fire out."

We scooted back through the tall grass, dragging along the blankets his aunt had given us. She'd wanted us to stay with her, but Fitch was afraid the guards would find us there and add to her troubles. Fitch rose, scooped up his blanket, and led me on a crouched run toward a huge tree whose roots spread out like fingers to anchor it atop a bluff overlooking the sea. We climbed over roots and into the shelter of a flat space among them.

Still breathing hard, I spread my blanket and flopped onto my back. We'd already moved three times, but Fitch had a seemingly bottomless barrel of hiding places. I looked out over the water, where stars pierced the darkness all the way down to the sea. Fitch lay next to me, and flung a blanket over us both. I huddled under it. I'd slept outside in Rin City, but never in a place so wild. The sound of waves was constant, like a heartbeat for the island. Surely the guards would soon quit for the night. My whole body jangled with tension.

"Loni and I used to camp here." Fitch hadn't spoken in a while, and his voice was rough.

"I'm sorry," I said.

"Cole was after me, not Loni."

We'd been through this already. "That doesn't make it your fault," I said again.

"It's my fault I destroyed my healer gift by nudging."

I glanced over to see him staring at the sky, stars reflected in his glittering eyes. The pointed tip of his ear poked through his hair. Something spasmed in my chest. He'd scared me when he tore after Cole, and I didn't think his fury was done. "Your cousin was right, you know. It's a bad idea for you to hang around Lac's Holding. Cole is still out there. So is anyone else Veren or Suryan might send.

You should leave with your mother."

He drew a shaky breath. "I sure can't stay with a father who'd join up with Veren."

"I'll bet your father didn't know Veren sent Cole to kill you."

"To kill you and me both, probably."

I pulled the blanket higher around my shoulders. It smelled comfortingly of soap and the herbs his aunt had hanging to dry in her house.

"I can't leave yet, though," Fitch said. "Not until I make both Cole and Veren pay for Loni."

I hesitated. "You mean kill them?"

"That would be justice. What else am I supposed to do? Go to the Watch? To Suryan?"

I studied the line of his forehead, his nose, his chin. I wished I had his gift and could sense what he was feeling. "Have you ever killed anyone?"

He stirred and drew his own half of the blanket up. "No."

"I was in a fight in Rin, defending my friends. I didn't kill anyone, but someone else did. Afterwards, I had nightmares, and that was in a fight which is different than killing someone for vengeance. And it's not like I'd be sorry to see Cole or Veren pay. Cole once came after me in Rin City, and I had to drive him away."

"Came after you?"

"You know what I mean. His going away left us badly off and Mama... well, she did what she had to. So I want to see Cole suffer. But if you mean kill them, I'd be sorry you were the one to do it."

"Yes, well, *sorry* is the story of my life."

"That's a bad story," I said. "Sometimes at the Fortress, I tell stories to pass the time. Shall I tell you one?"

"Why not?"

"In the time of times, on a wild island, a Healer child was born. The child played and learned and grew. And after a while, the child, now reaching for adulthood, began to feel pinched by the wild island—"

"Maybe a Trickster girl was born in a beautiful city," Fitch interrupted.

"Hush. I'm telling this story. People who the child loved left him, betrayed his trust, or died."

Fitch hovered his hand an inch over my mouth to hush me. His palm smelled of long grass and salt water. "People she loved failed her or died. Even her dog disappeared. And the people around her didn't value her as she deserved."

Under his palm, my chin quivered. "The child was a healer and could have left and healed people elsewhere, but that was hard to do because—" I drew a shaky breath. "—because the healer still felt like a child who wanted love, and if he left his kin, troublesome as they were, he was afraid no one else would have him, and he'd be alone forever."

Fitch swallowed hard. Slowly, I stretched my arm toward him. My hand brushed across his chest, light as a butterfly. I held my breath, waiting for him to duck away from my touch. A long moment trembled by before he made a strangled sound and turned toward me. We buried our faces in each other's shoulders and wept, with only the sea to shush us.

# Chapter 28

## Fitch

FITCH FOLLOWED DILLY out of Aunt Senay's cottage, trying to put his grief for Loni out of his mind. Behind him, Aunt Senay was stowing the blankets they'd returned, moving stiffly, stunned by her loss. The kinship would care for her, he told himself, assuming any of them were left after Suryan did whatever he meant to do. Today, Fitch had to help Dilly head Elenia off from marrying Veren, stop whatever Gavun and Veren were plotting, and then wreak vengeance on Veren and Cole for robbing Fitch of someone who'd been as close as a brother. *Blood of my blood*, he thought. In his head, it turned into a grim vow.

In the night, something he'd forgotten had popped back into the front of his mind. He caught up to Dilly. "I've been wondering something. If Veren means to use

Mage flower to influence people into preferring Elenia to Suryan, why does he need explosives?"

Her steps slowed. "He used spiked Winter Fire to set off that riot. Maybe he plans to push another mob to blow up the Fortress, though how that would help him put Elenia in power, I don't know."

"It might convince King Thien that Suryan didn't have control of his own province," Fitch said. "Maybe that's how Veren means to show Thien that Elenia would be a better ruler."

"Would folks blow up the Fortress?" Dilly asked. "Could they even get past the Watch and Fortress guards so they're close enough to do it?"

"They might if the Watch were standing aside."

"Why would they do that?"

They'd reached the top of the stairs leading down to the *Sea Wind*. "Because some fool messed with their minds." Fitch resisted the urge to take Dilly's hand. After they'd cried in each other's arms last night, he'd vowed to let her begin any touching. He wanted her to be sure, to be sure himself, that he wasn't nudging her. He longed for her to trust him enough to do it, but he'd just learned again that his longing didn't change anything in a cold world. There'd be time to mourn. Right now, it felt like mourning would last forever.

FITCH ROUNDED THE corner onto Corsair Street and spotted a pair of Fortress guards no more than five yards away. In front of a fish monger's stall, one of them gripped the arm of a terrified looking woman. "You were in that mob the night before last," he shouted. People faded away from the scene, eyes averted. The smell of fear mingled with the odor of fish that had sat on the counter since early morning.

Fitch drew back, raising his hand to silence the question Dilly looked ready to ask. If the guards dragged the woman to the Fortress, they'd head straight to where he and Dilly stood. He scanned the crowd frantically. Almost lost in the adults around him, a small, red-haired boy wrestled a cart loaded with heavy round cheeses. Fitch hustled to his side and grabbed the cart handles. "Let me help you, boy."

"Let go." The boy tried to pry Fitch's fingers loose. "That's mine."

Dilly darted to the boy's other side and put her arm around him. "Of course it is. Let my friend push it a little way to give you a rest." She bent over him, her face in his hair. "It's all right."

The boy frowned at her and tried to shrug free, but she kept hold and trotted after Fitch, shepherding him along.

Fitch turned his head away from the Fortress guards as they plowed past the end of Corsair into the crowd on the other side. The guard's raised voice boomed as they passed, loud enough to feel as if it slapped Fitch on the back. "You're under arrest in Lord Suryan's name."

Twenty yards along, Fitch looked back over his shoulder and stopped. The guards and their prisoner were nowhere in sight. He drew his first breath in far too long. "Here you go." He released the cart and pointed Dilly toward Corsair.

"Thank you?" the boy said. Fitch looked back to find him smoothing the hair Dilly had disturbed.

When he turned, he found Dilly grinning, but she sobered when she focused on his face. He forced the corners of his mouth up. "I have to say it feels odd to be seeking out the Watch. Usually I'm dodging them and the Fortress guards both." At that moment, he glimpsed a uniform and recognized one of the Watch he'd nudged to prefer Elenia to Suryan as a ruler. Fitch had done it on Gavun's behalf, but no matter how many excuses he thought of, the responsibility lay on him. Add it to the list of damage he'd done, he thought. "That's one," he murmured to Dilly. "You're still all right with it?"

She grimaced. "Not really, but I don't know what else to do. The question is whether you're all right if you think this is what wiped out your healing gift."

"I have to be all right with it. I have to try to undo what I've done even if it does cost me."

"Maybe taking a nudge back undoes whatever harm you did yourself."

"I like a girl who's an optimist." He caught himself stumbling over *like*. What terrible timing. There was no space for *liking* in this day and it felt reckless to assume he'd have another.

Dilly skipped up to the Watchman with Fitch right behind her. "Sir, could you tell me where Flatfish Street is?"

Fitch offered the man a map he'd sketched with several streets missing. When the Watchman took it, Fitch kept hold with his finger brushing the man's. The man didn't seem to notice. Instead, his Watch-y frown softened when he took a good look at Dilly. He began giving directions while she dithered and looked confused. He was concentrating on her so completely that Fitch had no trouble slipping into his mind and finding the thought he'd planted. *Suryan is greedy. Elenia would make life better.* Fitch tried to tease it loose, just to correct the trouble he'd made, but it seemed firmly lodged.

Dilly glanced at him and read his frustrated expression correctly. "So do I go right or left? Tell me again."

Fitch felt the beginning of exasperation in the Watchman. He shared it. He'd done Gavun's bidding well. The thought he'd planted would be in this man's mind until the day he died. Fitch was going to have to settle for another nudge. *Suryan is greedy but he's getting better.* He nodded at Dilly.

"Thank you," she gushed. "I believe I understand. You've been so helpful." Fitch yanked his map from the man's grip, and the two of them strolled away around a corner. "Did it work?" she asked.

"Maybe," he said. "I can't be sure." They'd approached a dozen Watch members with more or less the same results.

"Surely if you can do it, you can undo it."

He thought of Nera and Loni. "Some things can't be undone ever."

Her brows drew down. "True enough."

He skirted a crowd waiting for a puppet show to start, still scanning for the Watch. He and Dilly had found good hunting in the few blocks near Lac's Square where the Festival platform stood. The Watch was thick on the ground there. Suryan would close the Festival in the same square tonight, just as Elenia had opened it three nights earlier. The Watch undoubtedly wanted to be sure a second riot didn't mob Suryan.

Dilly must have been thinking of Suryan too. "You don't mind helping Suryan stay in power? He means to destroy the kinships. And he meant to have you tortured."

"Fortress guards didn't kill Loni. If I have to choose between Suryan and Veren as a ruler for Lac's Holding, I choose Suryan."

"Even if that means you can't go back to Rhale Island? Means your kinship is broken up? You'll never have your old life back."

Fitch's heart felt as if a knife was slicing into his chest. He closed his eyes, shutting out the busy street around him and seeing the stark, rocky beauty of his home. He inhaled as much air as he could force around the lump in his throat. "Even then."

She sighed. "Fitch of Rhale Island, for a boy with kin everywhere you look, you're the most alone person I've ever met." Before he could speak, she pressed on. "It's getting late. We have to go to the *Storm King*."

Fitch's mood darkened with the oncoming loss of light. Going to the *Storm King* meant going toward Cole and Veren and finding a way to make them pay for Loni. "All right. We've done what we can. Let's go."

# Chapter 29

## Dilly

I COULDN'T STOP jigging from foot to foot in the chilly evening shadow of Veren's warehouse. The alehouses and brothels were doing a brisk business, but only a single man stood watch on the *Storm King's* deck, silhouetted against a lantern. Elenia had planned to come alone. If Fitch and I caught her before she went aboard, I was sure I could get her to believe Veren meant to use her to get rid of her father. From what I'd seen, Elenia loved and respected Suryan. She wouldn't toss him out of power even for Veren. I leaned out and looked up the street, willing Elenia to appear. Seeing only the gathering dark, I drew back and returned to being acutely conscious of Fitch close behind me.

"If you don't want to be seen, you have to stand still," Fitch murmured, his warm breath sliding down my neck.

"A watcher sees you best when you move."

I waited for the buzz the breath had sent through me to subside. "She's late."

"Dilly," he started, then stopped.

"What?"

"Yesterday, you said Cole went after you. Why didn't you just tell your mother?"

Old pain clogged my throat. I swallowed. "I did."

"And?"

"She didn't believe me." My chest was so tight I had to shove the words out. I'd never told anyone that secret, not even my friends in Rin City. Mama's disbelief had felt like the ground dropping out from under me.

Silence gaped in the night. "I'm sorry," he said.

I blinked against the sting in my eyes. Then movement at the corner made me come alert. For a moment, I was disappointed because it was a couple who solidified in the dusk. Then the little swing in the woman's walk made it clear she was Elenia. Behind me, Fitch swore, and I realized the man was his father.

Fitch and I arrived at the foot of the *Storm King's* gangway just as Elenia and Gavun did. Elenia wore a lace trimmed red gown with pearls sewn along the sleeves: a wedding gown. She'd been looking eagerly at the *Storm King*, but at our approach, she twisted to face us. Her eyes narrowed when she saw me.

"Get out of here, Fitch." Gavun stepped between Elenia and us. "Run. Right now."

"Done making money off me?" Fitch curled his lip.

"Don't go aboard, lady," I said. "It was Veren who spiked the Winter Fire and sent people to attack the Fortress."

"Don't be ridiculous." Gavun elbowed me farther away. "You can't believe that, lady. For one thing, Veren would never risk your being hurt."

"You weren't there, lady." I spoke too quickly, my words tripping over one another. "Remember? Veren kept you inside his warehouse. He wants you safe all right. He plans to shove your father out of the way and make you ruler of Lac's Holding."

"What?" Elenia took a step back as if dodging my avalanche of words.

Gavun called to the man on watch. "Get the captain." He looked over his shoulder at Fitch. "For you own good, go."

Fitch licked his lips. "I won't leave Dilly to come to harm, and I can tell you now, she won't give up."

Gavun groaned. "Stupid boy. Think with what's in your head, not in your trousers."

Men raced along the *Storm King's* deck and down the gangway with Veren in the lead. "Elenia," he cried, "you're late. Is something the matter?" He swept Elenia into his arms with his gaze nailed on Fitch and me. The other men slid to all sides, surrounding us. I recognized them as the men I'd seen around the table in the ship's mess. A man coming out of an alehouse took one look at us, turned around, and went back in, shutting the door behind him.

Fitch scanned the men, and I knew who he was looking for, but Cole wasn't there. Someone who'd been coming with the rest had drawn back into the shadows on the *Storm King's* deck. Fitch leveled blazing eyes on his father. "Loni's dead."

"What?" Gavun's mouth sagged.

"Cole killed him," Fitch said.

"Nonsense." Veren snugged his arm tighter around Elenia's shoulders. "I've been with Cole non-stop for the last twenty-four hours. He didn't kill anyone."

Gavun frowned at him.

"Lady, don't trust any of them," I said. "They're going to use you to seize control of the city."

Elenia pushed free of Veren's embrace. "Is that true?" The threats to her father and Lac's Holding seemed to pierce through whatever else she was feeling.

"Of course not," Veren said. "She's lying, though she may not know it. The boy is more than just a Hedge Mage. His father says he can shape thoughts, and he's done it to Dilly."

For one painful moment, I doubted. I'd seen Mama. I knew how feelings for a man could leave a girl too stupid to see reality. Fitch glanced at me, face flushing. Guilt? No. Hurt. He deserved better, I thought. He'd earned it. "Fitch is risking arrest to help you, lady," I said firmly.

Veren reached for Elenia again, but she put up a hand palm out and he halted. "Swear it," she said, sounding remarkably like Suryan.

"I swear it," Veren said easily. "Come aboard, and we'll sort this out." As he put his arm back around Elenia and guided her up the ramp, he glanced over his shoulder. "Bring them," he ordered.

I shook off the hand of a man I didn't know. I didn't need pushing to start up the gangway. I wasn't about to let Veren lie Elenia into something she'd regret forever. To me, she still looked worried.

Behind me, a man shouted, "Hold him!" I spun in alarm to see Fitch with a man gripping him from behind. He twisted and heaved against him. A second man ripped a knife from his belt. He charged at Fitch, the point of the knife searching for an opening. My heart froze.

"Stop it!" Gavun shouldered between Fitch and the man with the knife. "Let him go. And put the knife away. I know how to handle him." After a moment's hesitation, the other men obeyed. To my enormous relief, the knife disappeared.

I tried to see what happened next, but the man at my side shoved me off the gangway, along the *Storm King's* deck and into the lantern-lit stairwell. Ahead of me, Veren escorted Elenia. Waiting in the hallway was Cole.

"Have you washed your hands?" I asked. "Or are they still sticky with the blood of Fitch's cousin?"

"Shut up," Cole said.

"You thought he was Fitch. You must have been shocked to see a supposedly dead man on the dock."

At the top of the steep steps, the two men who'd been wrestling with Fitch came through the door from the deck.

"Where's Fitch?" I asked. When no one answered, my chest tightened. He was probably with Gavun, but how safe did that make him?

"Veren, it's late," Cole said, voice tense.

Veren drew his hand down his face, then kissed the side of Elenia's head. "Fortunately, the ceremony is short. Are you ready, Owun?"

"Of course," an island man said. He must be presiding over the marriage, I realized, despite this being Veren's ship. A captain could stand witness that a couple had pledged themselves to one another on a ship, but Veren couldn't swear to his own actions in court. He must have asked this other captain, this Owun, to do it.

Veren opened the door to the mess. "Cole," he said, "there's no room for an extra person. Put Dilly in your cabin."

I'd been locked in that cabin once and once was enough. I planted my feet. "Lady, you know me. You know I've served you. And Veren told me himself he likes having power over people."

Brow crinkling, Elenia's gaze flitted from me to Veren. For an instant, I thought I'd won. Then she turned her back on me and walked into the room.

"Lady, please," I begged.

The other men herded in after Elenia and Veren. The door closed.

# Chapter 30

## Fitch

FITCH WRESTLED IN his father's grip, his eyes on Dilly being shoved along the *Storm King's* deck until she vanished, like a boat disappearing into the dark. The other kinship heads slid out of sight too. The man on watch shifted and light from the open stairway door fell on his face. Fitch recognized the man who'd been with Dilly's friend when she passed out the night of the riot, the man with the bag of spiked Fire whom Fitch had chased from the Blue Whale. Of course it was. Of *course*.

"Fitch!"

He snapped his gaze to Gavun, and fury rose. Gavun had sold the Mage flower that led to Nera's death. Instead of taking that as a warning, he'd smuggled in more of the poison. Even now, he was helping Veren, who'd sent Cole to kill Fitch and wound up killing Loni. With a twist of his body, he broke Gavun's grip and charged at him, driving his shoulder his father's gut. Arms windmilling, Gavun slammed against the wall of the Eastway warehouse. Fitch swung at him, catching Gavun on the jaw and bouncing the side of his head off the wall. Fitch's vision narrowed to Gavun's exposed throat. He thrust his hands toward it.

Gavun seized Fitch's wrists and pushed, hooking his foot behind Fitch's ankles. Fitch went down, Gavun on top of him.

"Stop it," Gavun hissed. "Look at me, you fool."

Fitch was startled enough to obey. Chest heaving, he stared at his father. "What?"

"You're a Mage with some sort of further gift. I'm touching you. Read me."

Gavun had avoided touching him for years. Fitch had almost forgotten what his father's too clever mind felt like, but Gavun was blood of Fitch's blood, and among islanders, blood told. Without effort, he slipped into Gavun's head among all the twists and turns and schemes. There was greed, plain as the darkening sky above. And there was pleasure in ignoring any rule someone else laid out, a bent that Fitch recognized because he shared it. But over all of it, he felt Gavun urging him to run as far and fast as he could.

"Let go of me," Fitch breathed. "I need to know my own mind."

Carefully, Gavun released him and rolled off. He struggled to sit up as Fitch pushed to his feet. "Go, you idiot," Gavun wheezed, draping an arm over his drawn up knees.

Fitch turned away and back. "Gavun, what are you doing with these scum? Cole killed Loni!"

"This is about the kinship's survival. You were the one who said Suryan had decided to destroy us. Fortress Guards are on Westway Island's ship, and Owun Half-Moon told me one of his nephews spotted fire on Rhale Island!"

Fitch decided now was not the time to tell Gavun about his house burning. "You think you're going to get past the guards to blow up the Fortress? It won't happen."

"It's too late for me to back out now." Gavun's eyes shifted away.

Fitch felt an instant of despair. "You don't believe you'll succeed either, or you wouldn't be after me to leave."

"Cole killed Loni," Gavun repeated, "but he had to be after you." He struggled to his feet and put his hand on Fitch's arm again. "I didn't know about that. You're my boy. I won't let harm come to you."

Again, Fitch sensed his father's fear for him. It wiped away all Fitch's doubts. He pulled his arm away, and at the last instant, glimpsed an image: a ragged, stuffed Guardian Dog being held out to a small boy with pointed ears.

"Go," Gavun said again. He ran up the gangway and vanished on the *Storm King*.

# Chapter 31

## Dilly

COLE'S HAND CLAMPED on my arm. I swung around, grabbed a handful of his hair and yanked as if I could pull off a chunk of his scalp. He yelped and drove his fist into the side of my head. Pain exploded. He dragged me toward his cabin, my shoes scraping the wooden floor. When he fumbled for the latch, I got my feet under me enough to kick his leg.

He slammed me against the wall. The back of my head hit hard wood and lights flashed behind my eyes. "You slippery little trickster." Cole's breath was hot on my face.

"You don't scare me, Cole," I forced out. In truth, this was the most frightened I'd ever been of him. His eyes were wild. He had reached some desperate point I didn't understand, maybe having to do with whatever he had in the works with Veren. But I'd been afraid long enough.

"If you're planning to rely on Gavun's useless boy, he's probably dead," Cole said.

My heart tripped. "His father would never kill him. Not his own blood." Was I convincing Cole or myself? "And Elenia will come to her senses."

"Veren is taking care of her. Think again, Dilly. She let Suryan throw you out, didn't she?"

"She thought I'd brought spiked Fire into her quarters. What do you think she'll do when she finds out Veren is feeding it to her people?"

"It won't matter because it will be too late."

The door at the top of the stairs opened, and Fitch's father started down. A bruise was already showing on his temple, and his mouth was bleeding. Where was Fitch? What had this man done with his son?

When he saw us, he halted. "What's going on?"

"Nothing," Cole said. "Go on in. You're missing the ceremony. The more witnesses, the better."

Gavun looked from Cole to me, pinned against the wall. For a moment, he hesitated. Then he came the rest of the way down the steps. The hallway was narrow enough that Cole had to turn sideways to let him pass. The instant the weight of his hands on my shoulders lessened, I twisted, slipped free, and ran for the mess. I yanked the door open, nearly whacking Gavun in the face.

Inside, the family heads pressed back against the wall watching Elenia and Veren standing by the central table. Veren was just lifting the ceremonial cup. He prodded

Elenia's lips with the rim and tilted it. As the liquid trickled, I smelled the unmistakable odor of Mage flower.

Cole grabbed me from behind. I twisted around to face him. In a lie worthy of Fitch himself, I said, "You told me Veren already has a wife. This is an offense to the laws of Lac's Holding and the gods."

Elenia drew her mouth back, letting spiked Fire spill onto the table.

"Don't listen to her." Veren jerked his head toward the door, and Cole yanked on my arm. I grabbed the back of a chair so hard my knuckles went white.

"It's true," I said. Cole pulled at me until the chair crashed backward, and my hands slipped off. He dragged me out into the hallway. Someone – Gavun? – closed the door.

I kicked and bit as Cole bundled me toward his cabin.

The door to the mess opened, and Elenia stumbled out with Veren right behind her. She braced her hand against the opposite wall and vomited.

"Shatter every small god," Veren swore. The other men crowded into the doorway. "Go back inside," Veren said. "We'll be there in a moment." Noses wrinkled, they backed out of sight. Veren closed the door and turned to Cole. "There's no time to waste. Lock Dilly up so we can get on with the marriage." Cole wrestled me toward his cabin.

"Lady," I coaxed, "please come with me. You're sick. I'll take care of you."

Elenia wiped her mouth on the sleeve of her fancy wedding dress. "I want to go with Dilly."

Veren scrubbed his hand through his hair so it stood on end. "We don't have time for this."

"Why not?" Elenia asked, head thrown back.

He closed his eyes, and when he opened them, he smoothed out his face. "I'm impatient, love. But I have business tonight that can't wait, so if you're ill, we'll have to finish the marriage afterwards, because now Cole and I have to go." He flicked a finger toward Cole's cabin. Cole shoved me inside, and Veren escorted Elenia in and seated her on the bunk. He kissed her forehead. "Trust me, love. I'll come for you at the Fortress later." He closed the door. I heard the lock click but tried it anyway. No good, of course. I felt as if I might be sick along with Elenia.

I turned to her. "Don't trust him, lady."

Elenia's eyes were unfocused, but she managed a smile. "I'm forced to admit I've been a fool, but I'm not a complete one. I smelled the Mage flower. Why do you think I made myself throw up?"

For a moment, I was speechless. Then my legs softened under me, and I collapsed next to her. "Thank the small gods."

"So he *was* using me," Elenia said bitterly. "I should have known. It's not like a ruler's heir is approached by many people who want nothing."

"I'm sorry," I said. "You deserve better."

She grimaced. "Lac's Holding deserves better from

me." Seated as she was, she swayed. "Give me a few moments, Dilly. I still feel sick. I hate throwing up."

"Of course." I jumped to my feet, and Elenia toppled sideways to lie full length. I didn't know how she could lie still like that. I felt as if I were bursting out of my skin. What was Veren doing that time was such a factor? If it was a factor to him, I knew it had to be one for me. I paced the small room.

Judging by the soft tone in which the cockroach called Elenia "love" and said he'd come back for her, he didn't know she'd caught on to his lies. I stopped pacing. What was it Veren had said exactly? "Why did Veren say he'd come for you at the Fortress rather than here even though he's locked us in? How did he think you'd get there? Now that I think of it, why lock you up at all? Me, I can see, but you?"

Elenia frowned as if trying to concentrate. "I don't know."

We needed to get out of there. The box of stones was gone, or I might have tried to blast the cabin door open, though that would have obvious dangers for me and Elenia. I could have pocketed a handful for emergency use though. And what had happened to Fitch? His disappearance made my mouth go dry. Surely his father hadn't done as Cole said and killed him.

I became aware that the rumble of voices in the mess had grown louder to be replaced by a sound like fists banging on the door.

"Veren!" a man shouted. "Open up."

Elenia stirred and sat up, brushing her hair from her eyes. "Are the islanders locked in too?"

I heard new voices, moving closer, and then the sound of feet scrambling down the stairs and tramping along the hall.

"Veren?" the man in the mess called.

I waited for him to answer. Whatever he had planned, I needed to be ready. But instead of Veren, a vaguely familiar woman's voice murmured something in the hall. A door opened so suddenly that it crashed against the wall, jarring the door my ear was pressed to. The woman said, "You are all under arrest in the name of Lord Suryan."

A chorus of cries arose from the mess. "What for?" asked a man who sounded like Fitch's father.

"Plotting the overthrow of your lawful ruler," the woman said.

Elenia's mouth tightened. "The weasel," she murmured. She rose and slammed the palm of her hand against the door. "Sergeant Anni, let us out. It's Elenia."

Shouts and scuffling broke out in the mess. It lasted only a short time before dying down. "Take them to the Fortress," Sergeant Anni said, and I heard people stamping past. "Where are those keys?" A moment later, the door opened and a Watch sergeant stood there with ring of keys in her hand.

"Lady, are you hurt?" Sergeant Anni asked.

"No. What's going on?" Elenia said.

"We got a tip that the kinship heads were all here plotting treason," Anni said. "How did you come to be here?"

"It's a long story." Elenia smoothed the wrinkles out of her bridal finery and swept out of the cabin. "I would like to go home now."

"Of course."

"Dilly comes too," Elenia said.

"Lady, I can't," I said.

Elenia turned to face me. "You are one of my attendants, Dilly. I don't care what my father said. You've earned the right."

I felt a flush of gratitude. "Thank you, lady."

"Then come home."

I'd wanted to call Elenia's household home for so long that I caught my body swaying toward her. But sometimes a girl finds *home* isn't enough. "I can't. I have to find Fitch and make sure he's not locked up or hurt." Now that Elenia was safe, every muscle in my body twitched to go after him.

Elenia raised an eyebrow. "The boy you say gave you the spiked Fire?"

"It wasn't his," I interrupted.

She pursed her lips. "Are you sure? You trust him?"

"I do," I said with some surprise.

"Very well. It's your choice after all." Elenia started toward the stairs with Anni behind her.

"Sergeant," I said, and Anni turned. "Where did you

get the keys?"

"They were in the lock of the mess, right where our tipster told us they'd be." She climbed the steps after Elenia, her boots thumping alongside the soft whisper of Elenia's slippers.

I slowly followed. Could Fitch have tipped the Fortress guards off about the islanders' meeting? Despite his anger at his father and the two Eastways, I didn't think he'd do that. I didn't even think he *could* have in the time since I left him on the dock. And if he did, where would he have gotten the keys left in the mess door? Something wasn't right. I'd done what I meant to. I'd kept Elenia from marrying Veren. I felt lighter than I had since I drove Cole away from Mama, not realizing it would shatter her. I hadn't always believed it was possible to make up for that and break the iron chain of guilt wrapped around my heart. But I'd done it, yet Lac's Holding felt in as much danger as ever.

I needed to find Fitch, and I needed to do it quickly. He was somewhere waiting for me, and he was fine. He had to be.

# Chapter 32

## Fitch

FITCH STUMBLED INTO a walk, then broke into a run, shoving past two men entering an alehouse. The tide was starting to turn, but surely his mother would have waited. His body still thrummed with Gavun's fear for him. On some level, he marveled at it. His father valued Fitch enough to pry him loose from Veren's grip. Even if it was because he saw Fitch as belonging to him, it was still a kind of love. He tore along the line of visitors' boats until, near the end, he spotted the *Escape*. His mother stood on the deck, scanning the dark.

At the sight of her, his mind flashed onto Dilly scrambling after Elenia on the deck of the *Storm King*. His steps slowed. He pictured glimpses he'd had of Dilly's memories of Rin City, gathered from the times he pushed or fell into her feelings. In Rin she'd tied herself to other street kids and taken their struggles as her own. Now she'd done the same thing with Elenia. All he could conclude was that Dilly wanted something to fill the void left by not having a family. In Fitch's opinion, Elenia didn't deserve Dilly, and Dilly was putting herself in danger. She needed help, and Fitch was the only person at hand to provide it. What had he been thinking when he gave into Gavun's urgent need for him to run?

"Fitch, hurry!" his mother called. Brend trotted down the gangway to the dock and started untying the *Escape*. "Brend, wait!" she cried. Brend tugged at a knot.

Fitch stopped. If he went back, he argued with himself, he was jumping into a hopeless fight. His shoulders sagged. He was a fool. Gavun would have mocked him mercilessly. Curse the Trickster anyway. He pivoted and started back for the *Storm King*.

"Fitch!" his mother called. "Don't leave me!"

*I'm not the one who left, Mama. But I'm sorry. I'm so sorry.*

He arrived out of breath, in time to see two men hurrying down the *Storm King's* gangway. In the dark, they were little more than denser shadows. He lingered in the same place he'd waited earlier with Dilly, trying to make out who the men were. They turned into Caravan Street, and by the light from an alehouse window, he recognized Veren and Cole. He smothered the urge to break Cole's head and fling his body into the harbor. One against two, he cautioned himself, and really one against all of Veren's crew. Those odds had caused Gavun's panic on Fitch's behalf. No, this fight called for a smuggler's guile. First though, he needed to make sure Dilly was safe.

With almost physical pain, he watched Veren and Cole go. Then he scanned the *Storm King*. The deck was empty, without even someone on watch. If Veren and Cole were gone, was anyone else still aboard? Veren didn't strike Fitch as the type to leave his ship or anything else he owned unguarded. And surely Elenia was too important to his plans for him to leave her anywhere alone, so she likely wasn't aboard. Did that mean Dilly was gone too?

He'd decided to sneak aboard and check when he heard tramping feet. A squad of Fortress guards swept from a side street and boarded the *Storm King*. He shifted from foot to foot. Talk about being in the Trickster's hands. He felt as if he were watching a confusing play. If Dilly was still on board, he needed to be ready to act his part in it, whatever the Trickster decided that would be. He slipped closer.

*Guile*, he thought with gritted teeth, and forced himself to wait. Not for long though. He had just started toward the gangway when Fortress guards emerged from below with prisoners in tow. He ducked back into the shadows to watch. With a start, he recognized Gavun's familiar silhouette and then realized all the island kinship heads were being arrested. He felt an unexpected pang. Gavun wasn't a good father. He wasn't even a particularly good man. But a child's love didn't depend on a parent being faultless. Dilly's love for her mother hadn't. And to his dismay, neither did Fitch's for his father.

*Later*, he silently promised Gavun as the guards hustled him away. *I'll see what I can do later.*

A final guard came down the gangway with Elenia at her side. Fitch's heart leapt because even in the dark, he knew the person trotting behind them was Dilly. He stepped nearer, not so close that the guard might feel the need to draw her weapon but close enough to call. "Dilly." He heard the tremor in his voice and cleared his throat as if that would fix it.

She spun to face him, flung two words at Elenia, and ran toward him while Elenia walked away with the guard. Fitch was about to ask what happened when she threw her arms around him. "I knew Gavun wouldn't kill you!"

Fitch choked on a laugh. "He'd be grateful for your faith in him, I'm sure." He held his hands out away from her, but her body was warm against his. "Dilly, I can't—"

She rose onto her toes and kissed him.

How much was a man supposed to resist? He wrapped his arms around her and kissed her back. The world shrank to this small space where he stood kissing Dilly.

Then she backed a few inches away. "I've been worried about you, Mage boy."

He touched his forehead to hers and tried to catch his breath. At last, he managed, "I've been worried about you too, butterfly girl." Farther along the wharf, a door slammed, and a couple came out of an alehouse, reminding Fitch that time sailed on. Reluctantly, he lifted his head. "I saw Veren and Cole leave just before the guards arrived. What happened?"

"I'm not sure, but I think Veren betrayed the rest of them. The sergeant said they had a tip, and I think the tipster was Veren. He told them where he left the keys."

So the confusing play was still underway. Fitch ran his gaze over the docks and ships and warehouses as if one of them would yield an explanation.

"Maybe he decided to ally with Suryan rather than shove him out of the way," Dilly said. "Maybe he thought that would please Elenia."

Fitch marveled at the streak of optimism that had somehow survived the life she'd lived. "Do you believe that?"

She sighed. "Not really. He threatened to let Cole loose on me, which tells you how twisted he is. I was trying out the idea."

Fitch's muscles tightened. If anyone ever needed killing, it was Veren. "So he still intends to unseat Suryan," Fitch said, keeping his voice even. "Maybe he decided he didn't want the other islanders around to cut into his power any more than Suryan does."

Dilly twisted her fingers together, considering. "That fits. But can he stir enough people up on his own? What's he planning?"

"He has those fire rocks stowed somewhere. If he could blow up the Fortress gates or punch a hole in the wall, he could get in, but Suryan would be well guarded, and a mob is a chancy tool with a mind of its own once it gets started."

"Maybe he means to kill Suryan," Dilly said. "But how could he expect Elenia to forgive that?"

"He'd have to do it in a way that didn't come back on him." An image of Lac's Square as he'd seen it a few hours ago formed in Fitch's mind. He'd been thinking he was watching a play, and, small gods, there was a stage in the square. "Suryan won't be at the Fortress until late. He'll be blessing the Winter Fire for the final night of Festival."

They stared at one another. "Veren means to blow Suryan up," she said.

"Let's go." The two of them took off for Lac's Square.

FITCH PICKED HIS way through a crowd that thickened as he and Dilly drew closer to the platform in Lac's Square. Torches flared everywhere, but shadows still lay thick. A man stumbled against him, breathing Mage flower fumes and sharing a ripple of confusion with Fitch. He shoved the man off. He had to figure out how to damp down the wash of other people's feelings, he thought. If he couldn't, he'd never be able think straight for himself.

Dilly kept close to him. "Folks must be trying to finish up last night's Winter Fire before it goes bad."

"If you mean they're looking for an excuse to get

falling-down drunk, you're right. Let's hope they don't let the Mage flower drive them to stupidity." Clutching a fold of Dilly's skirt, he slipped them both into a pocket of space between two men, a yard closer to the stage. Barrels of that night's Fire were already lined up, waiting for Suryan.

"I saw those at the warehouse." Dilly nodded toward the barrels. "They were fussing with the stoppers. My bet is they were adding the Mage Flower."

Fitch nodded to show he'd understood. *Curse you, Gavun*, he thought. *You had to make an extra gull.* Fitch would spring his father loose if he could, but then he *had* to get away.

Dilly rose to tiptoe. "Do you see Veren or Cole?"

"No." He chewed his lip, then bent and spoke in her ear. "If I wanted to blow up Suryan, I'd put the stones under the stage. That's the only place I could be sure Suryan will stop and stay for a while. It's possible they already did that."

"Would they have had time?"

"I don't know."

"If they did, a lot of other people are likely to get hurt," Dilly said. "If not by the explosion, then surely by the crowd panicking." She looked at the people penning them in and shuddered.

Fitch knew how she felt. "We have to get closer."

At the sound of a trumpet, folks cheered and pressed closer to the stage. "Make way," a voice bawled.

Fitch spotted a squad of guards shoving through the

crowd. There were more of them than he'd seen in previous years, enough to form a double line with men sheltered between them. Important visitors maybe, he guessed, before his father's figure once again caught his eye. "Healer help me," he breathed.

"What?" Dilly jumped up and down trying to see.

His throat too tight to speak, Fitch gestured toward the steps leading to the stage. The heads of all the island families except Veren were being marched onto the platform, their hands bound behind their back. Fitch couldn't look away from his father's face. He knew he'd left bruises, but not that purple one on Gavun's left cheek or that black eye swelling shut. A guard shoved Gavun into a line and forced him onto his knees with all the others. Fitch spotted a battered Royce Half-Moon and realized all the kinship heirs were being dragged onstage too. Except for him, of course. He'd come to the square of his own free will. Somewhere, the Trickster was laughing.

A herald stood in front of them. "All bow to Suryan, Lord of Lac's Holding," he cried. Suryan walked up the steps and into the blaze of torchlight.

"Fitch, what does it mean?" Dilly asked. "What's going to happen?"

Fitch's heart pounded. "We have to find those stones." The crowd shifted for a better look at the captives, and Fitch moved smoothly into a space that opened, Dilly squeezing in behind him. The guards who'd escorted Suryan arranged themselves around the stage, facing the crowd.

On the stage, Suryan began to speak. "My people. Shortly, I will bless the Winter Fire, and together, we will celebrate the last night of Festival. Tomorrow, we will welcome the return of the light and the start of a new year. But before I do that, I fear I must deal with those who have defied our laws for decades and planned to seize control of the city this very night."

The crowd erupted in cat calls. "Long live, Suryan," shouted a Watchwoman Fitch recognized as one he'd tried to un-nudge, apparently successfully in her case. He took grim satisfaction from seeing the Mage flower-addled crowd stirred up for Suryan rather than against him.

"You know them," Suryan said. "They're smugglers, robbing the Lac's Holding treasury of coins needed to maintain the docks and keep the streets safe."

Fitch was islander enough to feel the urge to spit. He'd wager most of those cheering would soon be grumbling over the absence of cheaper silk and wine.

"They're nothing more than thieves," Suryan said.

"Thieves," someone shouted.

"Thieves! Thieves!" The chant spread through the crowd, sounding far too much for Fitch's comfort like they had during the riot. People pressed against Fitch's back. He struggled to shut out the wave of hatred. Away to his right, someone was knocked down. A woman screamed.

The guards around the stage turned to assess the disturbance, and Fitch let himself be pushed into a rolling fall. Dilly too must have seen their chance because she tumbled under the stage at his side. He lay still, eyes on the gap they'd come through. Feet scrambled and stumbled in the square and people were still shouting, but no one crouched to look under. He rose to his knees, neck bent to avoid hitting his head. The space was a dark maze of wooden frames with fingers of torchlight leaking between the boards.

"There." Dilly pointed behind him, and he twisted to see a small, glowing stone stuck into a crook of the stage support. A square of cloth had been laid loosely over it but had slipped aside. He grabbed it, then tossed it from hand to hand, finally smothering it in the cloth and shoving it in his pocket. It made a warm spot against his hip that felt like a warning.

"We need more coverings," he said. "What do you have?"

She fished her handkerchief out and handed it to him. "Wait." She scuttled out from under the stage.

"Careful," he called to her disappearing foot. Cursing, he moved left to search but still be where Dilly would find him. He should have thought of bringing a bag or something.

"Fitch," Dilly whispered.

"Here."

She crawled toward him and thrust out a scarf and a pair of leather gloves that looked like they'd come from a guard's belt. She dumped out a purse. A shaft of light glittered off four coins. She tucked the purse in her pocket, hesitated, then stowed the coins too. "I might need them," she said without looking at him.

"I'm not in a position to judge anyone's honesty," Fitch said.

A corner of her mouth bent upward. "Use your pockets or shoes or shirt when the gloves are full. I don't have time to go back." She pointed right. "I'll go that way." She crawled away until she was a dim ghost in the dark.

Fitch crept only a yard before he found two more stones. He crammed them in a glove. From directly overhead, he heard Suryan. "Peace! Peace! I will deal with them. I show them to you only to promise you that justice in Lac's Holding is sure, if not always swift."

*To scare you a little*, Fitch translated. He tried not to think of what Suryan would do to *deal with* Gavun and the others. Except that, of course, Suryan wouldn't. Not if Veren had his way. Suryan would be gone, and no one would have to deal with the island kinships because in one explosive moment, their heads and heirs would all be dead. Assuming the crowd didn't tear them apart in a riot – which the noise suggested was still possible. He couldn't help being awed by how sweeping Veren's victory would be.

He crawled on, filling and discarding both gloves. He hoped the gloves smothered the stones because he wouldn't have time to come back for them. He unbuttoned his shirt, ready to shed it. He'd just realized that he'd lost track of Dilly when he heard a noise behind him. "How many—?"

A weight hit his back, flattening him. A fist pounded into the side of his head. "Where are they?" Cole's voice was a hysterical shriek. "Put them back."

The scent of hair oil clogged Fitch's nose. He tried to heave the man off, but there wasn't enough room between Cole's back and the bottom of the stage. Cole flattened his body over Fitch's and a tumble of Cole's emotions and fantasies swept through Fitch's brain. Himself a bloody mess. Dilly naked and struggling. Flames shooting into the night sky. His gut twisted. He struggled not to vomit.

When the crowd roared again, Cole put his mouth close to Fitch's ear. "You hear that? You saw the gift Suryan gave Veren and me? We figured we'd be rid of him, but we never could have hoped to take out the other kinships with him. Are you happy? Your old man will die with the rest of them."

Cole's vision of Gavun blown to pieces and screaming in pain forced its way into Fitch's head.

"Where are the stones?" Cole asked again. He knotted his hand in Fitch's hair, pulled his head back, and banged it into the cobbles of Lac's Square. The world began to fade.

# Chapter 33

## Dilly

I THRUST ANOTHER stone into the stocking I'd stripped off and skittered to the next crosspiece, cursing the way my skirt caught beneath my knees. Each stone I found was warmer than the one before. Even under their loose coverings, I could spot their glow now. From the corner of my eye, I saw something move. *Fitch*, I thought. But the voice that came wasn't his.

"Where are the stones?" Cole screamed over the sound of the crowd.

I froze. My whole body cringed with the urge to run away. But there was only one person Cole could be screaming at. Heart clogging my throat, I crawled toward where Cole had just let go of Fitch's hair and was now crouched staring down at him.

"Where are they?" Cole demanded.

Fitch lay as still as his cousin had.

My fingers closed over a chunk of wood probably left over from building the stage. I clawed my way up behind Cole, trying to quiet my breath. Whether warned by my panting or some animal survival instinct, he jerked his head toward me as I raised the wood to swing, awkward in the cramped space. My blow glanced off the top of his head.

With a cry, he lunged for me. He grabbed my wrist and twisted until the crunch of pain forced me to drop the wood. Then he was on me, pinning me down. He shoved his flushed face close so I smelled the fish on his breath. "You with him?" Cole jerked his head toward Fitch's motionless body. "Maybe you're the one who has the stones." He shifted to pin me with his weight and run his hands down my body. I took the chance to jab my thumbs at his eyes. He dodged and grabbed my hands again.

"I don't have them," I said. "And Fitch doesn't either. Elenia told the guards what you planned, and they cleaned this place out."

"Right." Cole laughed. "You claiming she knows anything? She's a fool. And the guards haven't been under here. They're too busy restraining the good people of Lac's Holding. Veren!" he shouted.

Small gods help us if Veren came scrambling out of the darkness. I struggled to shove Cole off.

"As soon as I get you out of here, I'll show you the difference between a boy and a man, you little thief," Cole said.

"If you're still alive tomorrow, I'll see you in jail forever." I gathered up the scarce moisture in my mouth and spat in his face.

Cole reared back, then jerked as something landed on him. I heard a familiar growl. *No. It couldn't be.* But Tuc dug his claws into Cole's shirt and sank his teeth into the stoning man's right ear. He screamed and slapped at the dog, then rolled, trying to knock Tuc off.

I wrenched myself out from under him, groping for the hunk of wood and breathing in tiny gasps. Where was it? Panic choked me. Behind Cole, Fitch rose to his knees, the wood clasped in both hands. He swung. There was a sickening thud, and Cole collapsed with Tuc still attached to his ear.

"Tuc," I cried. "Let go."

Tuc shook Cole one more time, dropped him, and trotted to me with a piece of Cole's ear in his mouth. I hugged him anyway. "Where did you come from? What happened to you?"

"Is Cole dead?" Fitch's eyes focused only vaguely. He dropped the wood and braced his hands on his thighs.

"Yes. No. I don't know."

Fitch stared at Cole, chewing his lip. "Loni," he said as if to himself.

"You avenged him. The back of Cole's head is crushed." I truly didn't know if Cole still lived, but Fitch had never killed someone, and I found I wanted that to stay the same. He'd lost enough of himself already. "Move, Fitch! We need to find the other stones."

Fitch drew a deep breath and shook himself the way Tuc did when he moved on to something new. "Small gods drag him to darkness. Did you see Veren?"

"No. Surely we would have if he's under here."

"It would be just like Veren to abandon Cole with the explosives." He crab-walked away.

As I looked at Cole lying helpless, my eyes caught on the knife at his belt. I pulled it loose and weighed it in my hand. I'd seen him flat out like this in Rin City when he was drunk and hadn't had the nerve to do anything. Afterwards, I'd wondered if things might have turned out differently if I hadn't been so soft. Maybe I should finish this. Beyond the payback I owed Cole, it would remove temptation from Fitch's path. I tightened my grip on the knife.

Tuc whined. I looked across Cole to see him watching me with his head cocked, looking for all the world like the Guardian Dog image in the temple. "You ripped his ear off," I said.

Tuc spat out what looked like a hunk of Cole meat.

"Dilly," Fitch called in a hushed voice. "Come on. The last stone I found was close to blowing up. People are way too close to the stage."

Tuc jumped across Cole and licked my face, which to tell the truth was disgusting.

"Oh all right." I shoved the knife through my belt and

crawled after Fitch, not minding at all when my scrambling foot kicked Cole on the ripped side of his head.

Tuc raced in front of us and sniffed an upright where a stone glowed. Fitch pulled off his shirt and wrapped it around the stone. I dragged myself after Tuc who pattered ahead, but I couldn't help noticing that I'd been right about Fitch having muscles in his shoulder, chest, and back.

*All those island boys do*, I told myself. *It's not special.* I smiled despite myself and the situation.

"Small gods," Fitch said. He lunged toward a stone near the platform's edge, sparking in the darkness. Beyond it, I saw a sea of legs. I was closer than Fitch, so I dove to grab it. Pain seared my palm. I yanked my hand back and looked around for the covering that had undoubtedly been there.

Fitch grunted. To my surprise, rather than seizing the stone, he'd grabbed a pair of booted legs and was yanking the man wearing them under the stage. I recognized Veren only as Fitch rolled him over the stone to smother it. Veren shrieked, his face contorting. He rolled to one side and scooped the stone out from under him. It slid to within a foot of me. Fitch flung himself across Veren, pinning his arms. Tuc raced in and sank his teeth into Veren's calf.

"Dilly, the stone!" Fitch cried.

A spark burned a hole in my skirt. I reached for the stone, bracing myself for the pain. At the last instant, I spotted the covering, half hidden behind an upright. I snatched it up, wrapped it over the stone, and grabbed the glowing bundle. Right through the cover, I felt my fingers blistering. It was too late. The covering wasn't enough. The stone was about to explode.

"Here." Fitch grabbed for my wrist and shoved my hand under Veren. I let the stone go and yanked my seared hand loose. Veren struggled under Fitch's weight. His voice rose in a scream.

I pressed my unburned hand to Veren's shoulder and leaned with all my strength until he stopped moving.

My heart tripped. *Defending people I love*, I thought desperately. *Not vengeance.*

"Come on, Fitch!" Even with the stone gone, my hand felt like it was on fire. I scanned as far as I could see under the stage but spotted no sparks. Still, I didn't think we'd found them all. There were parts of the space we hadn't had time to search. I rolled out into the crowd, ready to jump to my feet. People scrambled backward. "Get away," I shouted. "The stage is… about to collapse." I didn't want them trampling one another. I just wanted them away.

Fortress guards sidestepped toward me from left and right, still fending off the crowd. I cradled my burned hand. "Get them away," I begged one I vaguely recognized through the tears blurring the world. "There's a fire under the stage."

At my feet, Fitch crawled out, looking toward the stage where Suryan and the kinship heads gaped at him. He clambered to his feet. Guards hustled toward Suryan, ready to get him away from any trouble – which they *thought* meant me and Fitch. Fitch and his father locked eyes. "Run, Gavun," he cried. "Veren booby trapped the stage."

"What?" A man right behind us drew back, then spun. "Get out of the way!" He shoved. The crowd swayed, then began to move, slowly at first, then faster and faster. Trickster help us, it was going to be a mess.

A loud *pop* came from under the stage. An instant later, a flame licked up through the cracks between the floor boards. Screams echoed off the buildings around the square.

I should run. I knew it, but the pain in my hand made my head swirl. Nausea threatened to choke me. I dropped to my knees, cradling my hand. Tuc yipped and darted to my side as Fitch dragged me to my feet. "Get us out of here," he said to the two guards closing in on us.

The guards on the stage had bundled Suryan out of sight, leaving only one to deal with the kinship heads. With flames spreading, the heads broke ranks and, even with their hands still tied behind their back, they swept over the remaining guard. Gavun had already vanished into the dark.

Guards dragged Fitch and me toward the Fortress, with Tuc bounding ahead. I found I was shaking. Fitch wrapped his arm around my waist. He was still shirtless, but his skin was warm.

From behind us came a series of pops and then a loud *boom*. I glanced back. The stage had blown up. Fire licked at the night sky.

"If Veren wasn't dead before, he is now." I heard my own voice shake. "Cole too, given that we left him under there. We killed them."

"They planted those stones, not us. And we had to leave them. Don't think about it."

"I know. Stopping them was the right thing to do." And it was. If only I hadn't wanted to hurt them so much. If only it hadn't felt like payback. Curse the Trickster with every curse there was.

# Chapter 34

## Fitch

BUTTONING THE SHIRT the guard had handed him, Fitch leaned against the stone wall of the same guard chamber he'd been brought to before. The room hadn't improved any since Suryan questioned Fitch and the Half-Moon boys in it. It still stank of sweat, leather, and fear. The lantern light left shadows in the corners.

He watched the Fortress doctor bandage Dilly's hand. *I should be doing that.* A wave of hatred shuddered through him. *Veren's, not mine.* But he wasn't sure. The emotions he'd felt from Veren seemed to linger. He felt damaged, soiled. And the worst part was he'd done it to himself, not just today but over the years when he'd drifted away from using his gift to heal. Now, of course, he couldn't be the one to treat Dilly's hand. He hadn't been able to help Loni. He might never be able to heal anyone again.

*We killed them.* Dilly's voice echoed in his head. Small gods only knew what that had done to both of them.

He felt again the heave of Veren's body as he pinned it over the glowing stone. It shut the man's lying mouth, he told himself. He got what he deserved. The nasty voice in his head said *Was it the lies you objected to? Or the truth he told about Gavun that you didn't want to hear?*

He turned away from the thought, back to Dilly.

The doctor tied off the bandage and laid the hand gently in Dilly's lap. "That's a bad burn. If it scars, you may lose some flexibility in your fingers."

Fitch pushed himself erect. "Is that how you encourage your patients?"

Tuc had been lying at Dilly's feet, but he stood when Fitch did, thrust his muzzle toward the doctor, and growled.

"You and the dog can both stop growling." The doctor scowled. "I'm not some fraud of a Hedge Mage who encourages people to cling to lies. She deserves the truth."

Shame throbbed through Fitch's veins. He rubbed his eyes. "Doctor, if you know a clean truth, I'd appreciate you telling me how you got there."

"Books, young man, and listening to my teachers." The doctor picked up his bag and left the room.

*What a crock*, Fitch thought.

He crouched next to Dilly, who was staring at her burned hand and stroking Tuc with her good one. He hesitated, unable to think of anything to say. She raised her eyes to his, and he was struck by how vulnerable she looked. A man didn't need to be a Hedge Mage to see her weariness. He let his hand hover above hers on Tuc's head. "I'm afraid I can't do anything about the scarring or even the pain."

"It's all right." She smiled, but her lips trembled. She drew in her breath, turned her good hand over, and clasped his.

Sweet joy lifted in his chest. It was his, but maybe it was hers too. "Dilly," he said slowly, "I don't know what's going to happen now, but if Suryan sets me free, I mean to leave Lac's Holding."

"With your mother?"

He shook his head. "Too late. She's gone." He felt a throb of pain that he set aside to think about later. "I meant on my own."

"Why?" she cried.

"When I'm here, I'm Fitch of Rhale Island. I'm Gavun's boy, a smuggler from birth. Even if the kinships are broken up, I can never be anything else."

"Not everybody sees you that way." Dilly squeezed his hand, and Tuc pressed a cold nose against it.

"I see *myself* that way," Fitch said. "Another year or two on the road and maybe it would be different, but not now."

"Gavun might not even be here anymore," Dilly said.

Fitch tried to smile. "I must be a hard man to please

because it turns out that doesn't make me happy."

She caught her lower lip in her teeth. "Where would you go? Some of the places you went before seem more interesting than others." She sounded genuinely curious.

"I'm not sure. Anyway, if you like, I thought that maybe—"

The door opened, and he jumped to his feet as Lady Elenia swept into the room trailed by two women Fitch recognized as the attendants who'd come with her to the shrine on the first night of Festival. Dilly struggled out of her chair and made a wobbly curtsy. Fitch caught her elbow to steady her, then conscientiously dropped it.

One of the attendants spoke even before Elenia. "You left that stone in the garden, didn't you, Dilly? I knew it would be you. Did you plant more under that stage?" She prodded Tuc away with her foot as he sniffed at her skirt.

"Hush, Jessa," Elenia said. "If you can't be pleasant, then be silent. Dilly, what happened after I left you?" She frowned at Fitch. "This is the boy you were worried about. Someone tried to blow up my father. Was that him?"

"No, lady," Fitch said. "I'm afraid that was Veren. He tried to blow up *my* father, too." Fitch didn't say it, but he was relieved that Gavun was still intact, wherever he was. *Blood of my blood.* "I don't know if anyone told you, but Veren is almost certainly dead."

Elenia paced as far away as she could in the small room. She stood for a moment with her back to them. When she turned, her face was composed. Fitch recognized the effort. He'd read too many people who wore masks year-round, not just for Festival.

"I'm sorry, lady," Dilly said.

Elenia held Dilly's gaze. "Luckily for me, I have friends who keep trying to help me even when I don't listen."

"Lady," Dilly said, "how is Tira?"

Elenia grimaced. "Her family came and took her home. She's still unconscious from the Mage flower."

"Oh no!"

A stir in the hall announced the arrival of Suryan, accompanied by guards. He stopped in the doorway when he saw Elenia. With a flick of one finger, he motioned his guards and the other women out of the room.

Seizing Dilly's elbow, Fitch took a single step toward the door. "Not you two," Suryan said. Fitch froze. Next to him, Dilly swallowed audibly.

Suryan drew himself up in a move that seemed to suck all the air from the room, as if it all belonged to him and the rest of them needed his permission to use some. The eyes he turned on his daughter were hooded. Fitch pressed himself and Dilly back out of the dangerous space between them. Even Tuc scrambled out of the way and pinned himself to Dilly's leg.

"The islanders tried to overthrow my rule tonight, daughter," Suryan said. "They tried to assassinate me. The leader of the plot was Veren, the man you've been defying me to see and, I'm told, agreed to marry this very night."

Elenia sank gracefully to her knees. "My lord, I swear

to you I knew nothing of this plot. I'm guilty of disobedience and an imprudent romance, but not of treason. For the offenses I've committed, I beg your pardon." Her face was pale, but her voice held steady.

Dilly's lips parted. Fitch supposed she'd never imagined Elenia humbled like this. It was hard to watch.

Suryan considered Elenia for a moment longer, then motioned her to rise. "Sit there." He pointed to the chair from which Dilly had risen. Eyes straight ahead, Elenia obeyed.

Fitch braced himself as Suryan looked from Dilly to him and settled back on Dilly. Fitch thought the man had misjudged if he believed her to be the easier mark. "Tell me what you know about what happened tonight," Suryan said.

Dilly launched into the tale, occasionally looking at Fitch to confirm or supply a bit of information she didn't have. Her voice faltered when she got to shoving the stone under Veren. She glanced at Elenia, who flinched, but then drew a deep breath and said, "Lac's Holding was in danger. As my father's heir, I understand."

Fitch wasn't sure she really did. Small gods help him, he wasn't sure he himself understood what Dilly and he had done. That would take time. Suryan gave an almost imperceptible nod though, so Fitch figured Elenia was doing herself some good. Truth telling served her well, he thought cynically. He'd watched Gavun long enough to know that a person in power like Elenia acted quickly when the power threatened to slip away.

When Dilly finished her story, Suryan thought for a moment, then looked at Fitch. "You're Gavun's boy?"

Fitch heard Dilly let out a small puff of air. "I am."

"How do I know you weren't plotting with him?" Suryan asked.

"Why don't you ask Gavun, sir?" Dilly asked.

Suryan cut his eyes toward her. "I would but he's missing."

Dilly's eyes widened in an astonishment that left Fitch in no doubt that, like him, she'd seen Gavun go.

"My lord," Elenia said, "you heard Dilly's story. She and Fitch helped me. They defended you."

Suryan rubbed his jaw, then dropped his hands to his sides. "Fitch of Rhale Island," he said formally, "I banish you from Lac's Holding for a span of three years. Be gone by morning."

Fitch felt a stab of dismay that surprised him given that he'd meant to leave anyway. Tuc licked the hand hanging at his side.

Suryan turned to Dilly, but before he could speak, Elenia stood. "Dilly stays with me," she said, "assuming that's what she wants, of course."

Suryan raised an eyebrow. "You're asking me to trust your judgment after what happened tonight?"

"I am," Elenia said steadily. The air between them once again quivered with tension, tight as a cocked crossbow.

"I hold you responsible for her behavior," Suryan said.

"I accept the charge," Elenia answered.

"Very well. The guards will see you home." Suryan strode from the room.

The muscles in Fitch's back relaxed. He blew out his breath.

As soon as Suryan was gone, Elenia said, "Thank you, Fitch. I'm sorry my father felt he had to do that. Come, Dilly."

"Lady, a moment with Fitch?" Dilly said.

Elenia looked back and forth between them. "Take care, Dilly," she said mildly. She left, and Fitch could see guards and the other women flock around her before the door shut.

Fitch turned to Dilly and found her rocking from foot to foot. Hope sparked in his chest. For an instant, Nera rose before him, but she'd been nothing if not generous. She blew him a kiss and let him go. "So, staying with Elenia is good, Dilly? It's what you want?"

"Can you tell what I'm thinking?"

"If you mean, am I in your head, no. But maybe you seem uncertain?"

"Maybe. The thing is, I dreamed of living in Elenia's household for so long that it's hard for me to admit it's not what I expected."

Fitch raised an eyebrow and waited, ready for her to spill more if she wanted to but unwilling to push in where he didn't belong. He wasn't even tempted to touch her and read her. He recognized yet another feeling that had leapt out of the depths when he wasn't looking.

Dilly bit her lip. "I didn't know I'd feel squashed in, like I was always hiding who I was. Only, it's hard to think of what else to do now."

He opened and closed hands that turned out to be sweaty. "Before everyone came in, I meant to ask if you might want to go with me. As I said, I'm not sure where to go. I was thinking of roaming the Center Sea looking for work as a healer if I can still heal, or as anything I can get if I can't." He held his breath.

She took one step and stopped. "We'd just be traveling together, right? Because I can't be yours, Fitch. I'm still learning to be mine."

"I'm not asking or promising anything, Dilly," he said. "We can choose where to go from here. We could even head for the Dolyan Islands, which is where my mother is going, if having a woman around would make you feel better."

She pursed her lips. "I don't want you to go looking for her for my sake, but it seems to me you might want to spend some time with her and see what's there. It might be more than you think. I'm getting to see how complicated things can be between kin."

"I could do that," he said cautiously. He'd worry about living with Brend if he ever had to do it. "So what do you think? It would be a harder life than what you'd have with Elenia."

She frowned down at a muddy dog paw print on her skirt. "There are worse things." The corner of her mouth curled. Then with a laugh, she came close enough to lay her hands on his chest. "It turns out a girl likes a bit of adventure now and then."

To Fitch's regret, Tuc wriggled between them, and Dilly stepped back. If a dog could glare, Tuc glared at Fitch. Dilly didn't seem to notice.

"So, we're hopeful?" she said.

He found he was smiling. "That sounds about right. Hopeful."

# Chapter 35

## The Guardian Dog

TUC SAT DOWN to wait while The Girl climbed the steps with the boy. They were doing some incomprehensible people thing that involved visiting the boy's aunt. Tuc preferred to stay near the stone cairn tucked into a hollow. It was a good, high one. He'd already peed on it to show his approval. He was warming to the boy, mostly because The Girl smelled less of sadness when he was around.

The breeze brought a smell of sweets that might be traps and surprises that could go either way. Tuc tilted his head and sniffed. The god was a woman today, he decided. The Trickster's tall shadow fell across the rocky beach before she sat down with a grunt. "They're leaving," the Trickster said in a voice that hinted at disapproval. "We sent you to bring her safely home."

Tuc scratched his ear.

The Trickster sighed. "I know. A dog can do only so much. And her mother was a wanderer at heart. You'll have to guard her for a while longer. The elf boy too, though he's quite rude. He seems to have ignored his own Guardian Dog for so long that the poor mutt wandered off hunting rabbits and decided that was more useful."

*Silly god*, Tuc thought in fuzzy dog thoughts. *What else would I do?* The Trickster was right about the boy though. Now that she mentioned it, he did reek of elf. Tuc approved of a good reek.

"They're damaged, you know. Stealing, smuggling, nudging, leaving two gravely injured men to die. People don't do those things with no cost to what's inside them. You'll have your work cut out for you." The Trickster stroked Tuc's head. "You be careful. Don't get so broken the healer god can't fix you again."

The Healer had drifted past Tuc's bed in the night and lightly touched the back of the elf boy's neck, reclaiming the boy as his. He'd patted Tuc before he left.

Tuc heard The Girl saying, "I'd forgotten it was New Year's Day."

The Trickster vanished as The Girl and the elf boy appeared, coming down the steps. Tuc shook himself. The boy was absentmindedly rubbing the back of his neck where the Healer touched him, like he wondered what went on back there where he couldn't see. He looked at his fingers and shrugged.

"While we're traveling, I think I'll write our story down," The Girl said. "You can tell me your parts, and I'll write them down too."

"That will be interesting. You're a good storyteller." The boy did people things with the boat, and The Girl climbed in.

Tuc hopped in and put his paws on the edge to keep watch. They were sailing east toward the sunrise and one pale star, into a new year and things that had never before been.

# Dear Reader

Thank you for reading *The Trickster*. If you enjoyed this book (or even if you didn't) please consider leaving a star rating or brief online review on the platform of your choice. Your feedback is important to both me and my publisher, and it will help other readers decide whether to read the book, too.

# Acknowledgements

Writers don't do their best work alone. At least, this writer doesn't. So it's not surprising that as *The Trickster* came into being, it benefited from numerous people's feedback.

The members of the Barrington Writers Workshop stuck with me and Dilly (or perhaps were stuck with us) week after week for over a year. Their perceptive advice made the story better, and their continued support helped me to keep writing.

I workshopped the book's first two chapters at the 2019 WisCon, where Lauren Moody, Nino Cipri, and Amy Sather gave me some much needed perspective on how the book looked to readers coming to it fresh.

After I had a complete draft that I thought was nearly ready, Amanda Yates took a run at it and pointed out all the places where I'd taken the easy way out. In particular, she helped me think more truthfully about Elenia's romance.

Kel Andrews read the book for me and gave me much needed encouragement.

And finally, Sara-Jayne Slack, my editor at Inspired Quill, went through the manuscript with care and was particularly insightful in helping me think through the ending.

Many thanks to all.

# About the Author

At one time, Winsor taught technical writing at Iowa State University and GMI Engineering & Management Institute (now Kettering). She then discovered that writing fiction is much more fun and has never looked back. If you visit Winsor's blog and sign up for her newsletter, she'll send you a free short story.

Dorothy A. Winsor writes young adult and middle grade fantasy. Her novels include Finders Keepers (Zharmae, 2015), Deep as a Tomb (Loose Leave Publishing, 2016), and The Wind Reader (Inspired Quill, 2018) and The Wysman (Inspired Quill, 2019).

Find the author via her website:

www.dawinsor.com

Or tweet at her: @dorothywinsor

# More From This Author

## The Wind Reader

Stuck in a city far from home, street kid Doniver fakes telling fortunes so he can earn a few coins to feed himself and his friends. Then the divine Powers smile on him when he accidentally delivers a true prediction for the prince.

Concerned about rumors of treason, the prince demands that Doniver use his "magic" to prevent harm from coming to the king, and so Doniver is taken—dragged?—into the castle to be the royal fortune teller.

Now Doniver must decide where the boundaries of honor lie, as he struggles to work convincing magic, fend off whoever is trying to shut him up, and stop an assassin, assuming he can even figure out who the would-be assassin *is*. All he wants is to survive long enough to go home to the Uplands, but it's starting to look as if that might be too much to ask.

## The Wysman

"The Grabber is just a fright tale."

Former street kid Jarka was born with a crooked foot and uses a crutch, but that no longer matters now that he's an apprentice Wysman, training to advise the king. When poor kids start to go missing from the city's streets, though, Jarka suspects that whatever's causing the disappearances comes from the castle.

Now he needs to watch his step or risk losing the position he fought so hard to win… but when someone close to him becomes the latest victim, Jarka knows he's running out of time.

His search takes him from diving into ancient history, to standing up to those who want to beat or bleed the magic out of him.

Will Jarka succeed in uncovering an evil long-hidden, or will he see friends and family vanish into the darkness?

Available from all major online and offline outlets.